Druid's Enchantment

Druid's Enchantment

MILLIE J. RAGOSTA

DOUBLEDAY & COMPANY, INC.

GARDEN CITY, NEW YORK

1985

Library of Congress Cataloging in Publication Data

Ragosta, Millie J.
Druid's enchantment.

I. Title.
PS3568.A413D75   1985   813'.54   84-28748
ISBN 0-385-19700-4

for my *Marda, Keagh and Benen*

CHAPTER 1

On an early spring morning between the lambing time and Beltane, Marda, foster daughter of King Laeghaire, ardri of Ireland, knelt in the kitchen garden below the hill of Tara, just outside the outer ramparts, planting the last of the onions, parsnips and carrots.

Colmagh, the plowman, had turned over the plot for her last month, and she herself had broken the clods with the heavy farcha. The peas and beans had been planted then as Colmagh planted oats and barley in the greater fields. Laeghaire's wife, the Ardrigan Angas, had objected to her gardening when she'd first started it years ago as a little lass of seven.

" 'Tis not seemly, child," she'd laughed, hugging Marda and brushing at the dirt on the little hands. "Although your father was but a charioteer, still he was the ardri's! And when he died defending Laeghaire, my good lord vowed that you, his orphan daughter, would be reared as though your rank were equal to his other foster daughter's. And you well know Daneen is the king of Connaught's daughter."

Marda had wanted to behave in a "seemly" manner. She knew that no king or members of his household ever tilled the soil. Yet, so yearning for the open fields and woods did she become that the queen had had her druid liaig, Lochru, prepare her a potion against the yearning sickness. Even that had not proved efficacious and, at last, the kind ardrigan had allowed her to return to her gardening.

Marda rinsed her hands in the leather pail of water from which she'd been lightly watering the newly covered seeds. She flicked her hands to dry them, then straightened up, stretching to ease her back. She sat down on the grassy bank beneath the ramparts and gazed in deep contentment at the garden plot where the first shoots of the peas and beans were nosing through the dark soil.

Beyond the garden lay Colmagh's fields and beyond that, the beginnings of the forest where a woodcutter was bearing home to the ardri's dun a great brosna, or bundle of firewood. The sun drew ever westward, toward the magical Isle of the Blessed, and wood doves cooed a homing song. She loved this time of day when the winds hushed as if listening for the fairy folk's secrets, and the light over the green, green world seemed molten gold even though it was also the solemn, yearning hour too.

She supposed it was because she was already sixteen, two years past the usual limit of fosterage for girls, and not yet promised, let alone married. Her father had dared ask this boon of Laeghaire as he lay dying after the battle in which he'd thrown himself in front of the spear directed at the ardri. And so, according to his wishes, she must not be married until she was seventeen—not until after Samain, when summer ended and the winter came again.

A shadow fell across her and she looked up quickly. She'd heard none approach in the lush grass. Keagh, the ardri's new liaig, or physician, was standing above her smiling slightly. He'd discarded his white druidical robe and wore only his toga. Somehow, divested of the robe's dignity, he looked like a mischievous boy with his sturdy, wide-legged stance. His hair, around the druidical tonsure, was chestnut-colored and curly and his eyes were wide-spaced and russet beneath heavy dark brows. As she met his eyes, the humor which he seemed never quite to master, despite his lofty position in the ardri's dun, spread his full lips into a wider smile that showed even, strong teeth.

Marda found herself answering his smile, although there was that in his eyes that made her feel shy.

"You look like the goddess Dana sitting there, little one," said Keagh. "Admiring the fields that will feed your children."

She laughed. "Aye, I admire them. There are few sights sweeter to my eye than a well-tended garden patch."

Without thinking she lifted her hand to straighten the braids twisted across the top of her head, for they were no doubt disordered from her hours of laboring in the garden. Then, realizing it was likely a matter of indifference to Keagh whether or not her appearance was neat, she lowered her hand to her lap.

He sat down beside her on the grass. "There are few sights sweeter to *my* eye than a slender maiden with slanted eyes the color of Samain-tide leaves floating in amber water, and braids as thick and molten as the golden balls that hold them," he said.

Marda felt the warm blood flood her face at that, although she was not in the least displeased by the young physician's admiration. He'd been at court only a short time, having come from the druid school of medicine in the south the previous Imbolic-tide, when the first of the lambs had been born. She'd watched him covertly, thinking him comely and gentle, not like most of the druids who were imperious and often very cruel in their judgments, they being the law-givers as well as wizards, physicians and poets among the king's household. Yet she'd not talked privately with him for she was, despite her position in fosterage, only a charioteer's daughter.

"I have wondered, Marda, why you are not yet married," Keagh said, plucking a long strand of grass and, putting it between his teeth, whistling along its length, all the while watching her curiously.

In a few words, she explained her dying father's wishes and why the high king had chosen to honor them.

He nodded and rolled over onto his stomach.

"And when will you be seventeen?"

"Eight days after Samain, at the beginning of the winter."

"Has anyone spoken to Laeghaire for you, Marda?"

She caught her breath sharply. The handsome young druid hadn't even one wife, although Lochru had three and many of the other druids two. For a wild moment she thought he was thinking of asking Laeghaire for her, but as she darted a quick glance at him, she saw that the question was merely an idle one and the quick, bright happiness faded. She shook her head.

He propped his head on one hand and grinned at her, closing one twinkling brown eye whimsically.

"Perhaps . . ."

But he was interrupted by a sharp call from the ramparts.

"Marda, daughter of Killa-dubh, the ardri and ardrigan bid you leave off the plowing and delving and bathe, for the evening meal is almost ready and they would have you attend them privately immediately after," a deep voice shouted.

Marda whipped around to behold Lucat-mael, the ardri's chief druid, standing arms akimbo, his forehead creased in a frown.

He was a tall man, almost as tall as King Laeghaire himself, with a dark and solemn visage. He no longer had need to be tonsured, for his head was completely bald and his powerful arms protruded from the long white robe, giving him the appearance of a king's champion or strong man. His eyes seemed to pin her to the bank and she shivered involuntarily. Just so did he always seem to look at her as if nothing under her clothing or in her thoughts was hidden from him. She folded her four fingers around her thumb instinctively in the gesture her old nurse had taught her as a charm against evil.

"I come, reverend Lucat-mael," she said, scrambling to her feet.

Keagh followed her more slowly.

"Are you frightened of him, Marda?" he asked gently.

"Aye. They say he still sacrifices babies though Ardri Laeghaire says the gods have blessed his four-year reign and there's no need."

Keagh laughed at that.

"There have been no children missing from Tara," he scoffed.

"There were two last Samain," she whispered, clambering up the bank to the gate.

"Do not be afraid, maiden—you are the king's own fosterling," Keagh said, giving her arm a reassuring pat. "I go now to the sweating house, for I've been feeling a muscle spasm and the steam is efficacious against such maladies."

She nodded and watched as he turned toward the woods where the sweating house and pool of cold water for immersion afterward lay. She hurried past Lucat-mael who stood near the gate, staring at her earth-soiled gown and bare feet disapprovingly.

"Farming is for the celes," he said contemptuously. "Angas has spoiled you shockingly by allowing you to pursue such low things. 'Tis a woman grown you are now and should stop such low pursuits."

Marda squared her shoulders pridefully.

"My father was a cele, reverend Lucat-mael," she said, hurrying past him. "And, for all my fosterage, so am I."

In the cubicle of Laeghaire's dun which she shared with Daneen, the other female fosterling, Marda stripped off the soiled clothing and bathed herself quickly in the water the gilla, Lugdh, had brought earlier, while Daneen dressed her hair at the brass mirror.

Daneen was two years younger than Marda but towered a full head over her already. She was magnificently beautiful with shoulders wide as any man's in the court, yet softly feminine too. Her hair was fine and fair as the soft feathers of the little yellow birds and she was adept at dressing it herself, braiding the front part in becoming coronets or loops and letting the back part cascade in sunny ringlets to her waist. Her eyes were blue-green and arched with wheaten brows, while the pink-tinted cheeks had deep dimples when she laughed.

Which she did often. She and Marda had grown as close as sisters over the years they'd shared fosterage. Marda, soft-spoken and quiet herself, drew a deep enjoyment from Daneen's chattery and kindly ways.

"Where have you been, Marda?" the younger girl said as she gave a last pat to her shining curls. "At your garden again?"

Marda nodded. "Propitious is the moon for planting, Daneen. I got all but the kale in."

"Why do you like caring for the garden so much, Marda?" Daneen said, watching as Marda drew a clean linen shift over her head.

" 'Tis a glory to me, watching the good food the gods provide growing bigger each day—a full edible plant from a seed smaller than a wee bird's eye. And to know my careful husbandry—nourishing the soil with the dovecote's offerings and lime, riddling the chaff from the corn—increases the yield. It's as satisfying as weaving cloth from flax or wool or embroidering it when it's been made into garments."

"You're a funny girl," Daneen said with an affectionate hug. "Imagine thinking of all that. I've enough to do just brushing the ardrigan's hair. Glad I am that my betrothed, Fiacc, will provide plenty of gillas to do my work. But come, little one, kneel here and I'll rebraid your hair. Ye've chaff from the riddling in it."

Marda was glad of the offer, for she had no skill with hairdressing or patience to sit long under a professional's hands. She closed her eyes and gave herself up to Daneen's gentle brushing and braiding, thinking dreamily of her short encounter with Keagh. He was kind as well as handsome, she thought, remembering how he'd reassured her when she'd showed fear of Lucat-mael.

Thinking of the druid, she wondered what Laeghaire and Angas wanted to see her about. Seldom was she summoned specifically, for Laeghaire's entire household ate together three times a day and the ardrigan spent part of most days teaching her and Daneen skill with distaff, loom and needle. No doubt she'd find out soon enough.

When the household had finished eating, Laeghaire and Angas withdrew to their own wicker-partitioned cubicle, motioning Marda to follow. She was aware of the other courtiers watching as she washed her hands in the wooden basin held by a gilla and followed them.

Angas pulled the sliding partition across the opening, enclosing the three of them. She sank down on the edge of the sleeping shelf and smoothed her yellow linen gown across her knees. Marda thought the ardrigan wondrously lovely with her brown hair dressed and held by a gold circlet and her pearly flesh just stained like the foxglove's bloom. She was lushly pregnant and Keagh had proved she would bear a son by offering her an early lily and a rose. She chose the lily, sovereign proof that her child would be a boy. She carried him high and proud, too.

Laeghaire was the tallest man at Tara. His piercing eyes were light blue with golden flecks, and his hair and beard fiery golden red. He had a long, autocratic nose and a deep voice that used to frighten Marda. He was every inch a king and well worthy of having been chosen ardri by the entire cinel, or membership of the clan, when his cousin Nathi had died. Laeghaire's father, too, had been ardri and called Niall of the Nine Hostages, so that the family was coming to be called Hui Niall.

Laeghaire lounged against the wall and, for all he was ardri, looked toward Angas to broach the matter for which Marda had been summoned. Angas smiled gently at him and patted the spot beside her on the sleeping couch for Marda to sit.

"I know you're wondering why we've asked you to attend us, child," Angas said in her curiously sweet voice.

"Yes, my lady, I am," she said softly.

"I—I hope the news we have for you will be pleasing to you," the ardrigan said, not meeting Marda's gaze. "Indeed, 'tis a bit of good fortune I never would have expected to come your way."

Marda waited politely. The ardrigan reached out and took one of her small, brown hands, squeezing it fondly.

"You have attracted the attention of one of the flaith, the nobility, Marda. He has asked for your hand in marriage and Laeghaire has accepted on your behalf."

"And this man is?"

"Lucat-mael, Marda."

Marda jumped up, withdrawing her hand from Angas's and clapping it to her heart.

"No. Oh, no, my lady, not Lucat-mael!"

"You aren't pleased, child?"

"He—I am afraid of him. He already has a wife."

"Of course he has. Gaida will always be his cetmuinter . . . first wife," Angas said kindly, "but you will have most of her rank and privilege. Unheard of for a freeman's daughter."

Marda dropped to her knees at the ardrigan's feet, her hands clasped tightly. "Please don't make me, my lady!"

Angas looked deeply distressed and reached out to touch Marda's cheek gently. But Laeghaire made an impatient sound and pulled the girl to her feet.

"What nonsense is this?" he snapped. "Do you think suitors are standing in line for you, Marda? Your father would never have dared dream such honor for you."

"The age of fostering is long since over, my child," Angas added. "What would you have us do?"

"Could I not be a servant in your house?" Marda pleaded. "I can keep the vegetable gardens for your dun. Or the weaving. You said yourself my weaving is as fine as any you've seen—"

"You'd shame me, then," Laeghaire said harshly. "For what kind of man would put the daughter of him who saved his life to such labor?"

"I do it now from my own choice."

"You will not do it from mine, Marda, and there's the end of it," the ardri shouted. "You will marry Lucat-mael as soon as you've completed your seventeenth year. For your father's sake, I allowed you to go so long a maid; I've done enough and more than enough."

Marda lowered her head, stifling the sobs that threatened to engulf her. The king was generally affable but when he was angry, when he'd once declared himself in such stubborn anger, there was no gainsaying him. Indeed, in her heart she knew that he dare not refuse Lucat-mael. The druid was the power behind the throne. He could call up the dread ceo druidechta—the magic fog that was so thick enemies could not see their hand before them, or cause demna aeir, demons of the air, to so confound men in battle that they'd rush, frenzied, to impale themselves on their enemies' spears. How could even mighty Laeghaire, mortal that he was, defy a druid with such intimate connections to the terrible fairy folk?

"I am distressed that you feel so, Marda," Angas said unhappily, shifting on her couch to ease her babe-filled body. "What my husband says is true enough. Lucat-mael is a far better match for you than you would have had in the normal course of things."

"Be comforted, child," said Laeghaire, more moderately. "There are worse things than to be an old man's darling."

"Why does Lucat-mael lower himself to me?" Marda said bitterly.

"He finds you wondrous fair, child," said Angas. "And, in truth, who would not? He will be kind to you."

"He is not kind to Gaida." Marda thought of the druid's pale wife. Some said she'd been touched by a banshee, a fairy woman, for her senses were not always right.

"There is nothing I can do about it, Marda," Laeghaire said. His eyes seemed to plead with her for understanding, even though his tone and posture were imperious as befitted his position.

She sighed deeply and sat back on her heels.

"Have I your leave to withdraw, my lord?" she said softly, not meeting either pair of anxiously watching eyes.

Laeghaire nodded shortly. Marda stood up and, bowing, backed from the cubicle, drawing the partition into place behind her. She was sorry the kindly ardrigan was distressed, but her own heart was too troubled, now, to find words of reassurance for her.

In the main hall all but a few servants, clearing the dinner leavings, remained. Firelight flickered against the various cubicles along the walls where the members of the household had withdrawn to their own sleeping couches or pallets. Marda steadied herself for a moment with a shaky hand against a roof post.

"I could not be more sad if it were one of our own daughters," she heard Angas say behind her. "Oh, Laeghaire, is there nothing you can do?"

Marda closed her eyes, waiting for Laeghaire's answer. It was as disappointing as she'd known it would be.

"I would gladly fight ten giant Britons for the girl, wife," he said in the impatient way he had when he was confounded, "but I can't gainsay my druid."

She slipped quietly off to the cubicle she shared with Daneen. The younger girl was sitting up on her pallet, already dressed in her bed shift, her golden hair undone and brushed. The only light was from the fire without when she opened the partition; when she'd closed it she could scarcely see her friend in the small illumination that filtered through the wickerwork.

"What did they want, Marda?" Daneen whispered excitedly.

Marda unfastened the brooch that held her cloak in place and groped her way along the wall to hang it in place. Quickly she undressed in the dark, pulling the golden balls from her braids and laying them on the shelf beside her pallet. She stretched out beside Daneen before she answered.

"They have found me a husband, Daneen," she said bitterly.

"But that should give your heart joy," Daneen said brightly. "Glad I was when Fiacc spoke for me."

" 'Tis Lucat-mael," Marda cried softly, her voice breaking in spite of herself.

The younger girl gasped and threw her arms around her friend.

"Oh, Marda, well do I remember the day the gilla, Aird, dropped a sack of grain on his foot. Lucat-mael fixed him with that malign gaze and roared a terrible malediction. 'May your manhood wither when you enter into your wife and may your lungs burst with water!' he yelled and, Marda, you know from that day Aird grew thin and sad until he drowned himself in the sea. And his young wife said he—he couldn't . . ."

"I know, Daneen," Marda said miserably. She drew her bedcover around her shoulders and sat up, trying in vain to stop the awful trembling that had started when the ardrigan had told her Lucat-mael wanted her for his wife. "I can't marry him—I just can't."

"They say he sacrifices babies to Cromm Cruach," Daneen continued, her voice filled with horror. "How can the ardri do this to you? Your father saved his life!"

"He's afraid of Lucat-mael's maledictions too," she said bleakly. "Yet I would rather be sacrificed to Cromm Cruach myself than to wed with him. I will not."

"Will you run away, then?"

"What good would that do? For where could I run? If I went south, east, north or west, there'd be other kings' lands and wild men who cared not that I was fostered with Laeghaire. They'd not believe me. No, I must use my wits, Daneen. If all fear Lucat-mael, then I must find one who also has druidical powers to help me."

Daneen's eyes were round as shields. "Keagh? Oh, I saw you stealing looks at him this night at dinner. Indeed, you've looked often since he's come to court."

Marda flushed and shook her head. "Nay, for no kindness would I do him to earn him Lucat-mael's wrath. 'Tis old Breeca I had in mind."

"The druidess?" Daneen's voice had risen almost to a squeak.

Marda frowned and made hushing motions and the girl resumed in a softer voice.

"You mean the old crone Lucat-mael drove from the court four years ago when word came that Ardri Nathi had been struck dead by lightning in Gaul?"

"Aye. And 'twas wrong of him to drive her away. She'd served both Niall and Nathi and was growing old and feeble."

"They say she lives near a holy well in the forest. You would go there?"

Marda didn't see any reason to tell Daneen that she'd been going there, alone, every week for four years, stealing silently through the forest to leave a joint she'd begged from the cook or a length of cloth she'd woven. Vegetables in season. Anything, in short, that she thought might make the old woman's life easier, for she had pitied her greatly when she'd been driven from court, Lucat-mael declaring contemptuously that she'd lost her powers. Marda knew that she had not, for often in the old days the druidess had filled her with awe when she'd drawn a plover's egg from Marda's own braids. She'd once given her a magic spell for the wart on her knuckle, too, and when she'd faithfully said it for a week, the wart had miraculously disappeared. She'd never dared confront the druidess, fearing the old woman's anger against Laeghaire's druid might extend to the rest of the king's household. Always she'd had the pity feeling, especially for the aged ones of the clan.

"Aye, I *am* going there, Daneen. Though I am afraid, I must have help against Lucat-mael."

"I fear you choose between two evils. And Lucat-mael is all-powerful. Maybe being married to him wouldn't be so bad, Marda. He already has one wife and many concubines. Perhaps he'd leave you to yourself. He would have to provide you with your own timber house here at Tara. And if he had so many other women to visit, his time with you would not be too great."

Marda pulled the cover about her and lay down, sighing deeply.

"Even if he were kind, Daneen, I could not bear it. Never will I marry a man with another wife or a concubine. *I* would not split the gifts of my heart, so I won't stand for it either. Nor would Lucat-mael allow me to garden as the ardri and ardrigan have done. I should have to sit in my timber house and have no friends —nay, not even lift my eyes to speak to a neighbor, as poor Gaida is forced to live. Nay, I would go right now to Breeca for a charm but I fear the Morrigan, the queen of night demons. She might change herself into a large raven and attack me as I walked through the dark woods. But at first light, before the household stirs, I am off."

"I will go with you, Marda," Daneen said suddenly. Her water-hued eyes sparkled in the near-dark with her excitement.

"Are you not afraid, my friend?"

"Aye, a little. But you're willing and so am I. 'Twill be a great adventure. And besides, I like not Lucat-mael. 'Twould please me much to thwart him. You are right, Marda. Were you to marry him, like as not he'd never let you even speak to me again. I couldn't stand for you to grow like Gaida, fairy-touched and wan."

"Then go to sleep now, Daneen," Marda said kindly. "We must leave the rath before daybreak."

She turned on her pallet and closed her eyes. Presently she heard Daneen's soft, even breathing and knew she slept. But it was long before she herself dropped off. And when she did, the Morrigan sent nightmares, each with Lucat-mael's sardonic face.

She rose quietly at dawn and dressed, binding her hair under a linen scarf rather than taking time with the braiding. She knelt and shook Daneen gently to wake her, laying a soft finger against the girl's lips so she'd not yawn mightily as she usually did upon waking.

"Come, Daneen, I hear the larks far off in the meadows nearer the eastern sea. We must slip over the ramparts before they awaken, else someone might stop us."

Daneen dressed as quickly as Marda had and they slipped out into the great banqueting hall, nearly eight hundred feet long, with cubicles set all along the walls, some large enough to accommodate whole families with their own dining areas, others mere sleeping closets as was the one assigned to her and Daneen. They left the hall through the great double oak doors and only then stooped to tie their sandal laces. They crossed the vast courtyard, climbed a ladder to the inner rampart and dropped down to the bank of the water ditch below. Here they crossed on a plank kept lying on the dun side, climbed the outer rampart and, dropping off, ran pell-mell toward the path into the wood.

Once there, they paused and leaned against a large tree, still only faintly visible in the scant light, to draw breath.

"We made it. No one saw us go, I'm sure. And the morning comes. The night demons will have faded back to their sidhes in the hills," Marda said, heaving a sigh of relief. "Are you rested now, Daneen? Then follow me. I'm sure I can find my way, dark as it is."

It was not only dark, but foggy.

"Think you Lucat-mael summoned the ceo druidechta to confound us?" Daneen whispered hoarsely.

"Nay, 'tis but a spring fog," Marda reassured her. "Watch, I am about to release a branch. Have a care it strikes you not."

Slowly they felt their way along the narrow path into the forest. Breeca lived some three miles from Laeghaire's great rath, or fortress, but distances were hard to gauge in the misty dark. Marda was only partially aware of where they were. Fog billowed in silent, menacing forms; she could almost fancy she saw the Morrigan in her various shapes—now a fearsome, screeching old crone, now a gorgeous temptress, now a huge, blood-feasting raven. A late-prowling owl sounded his mysterious call deep within the wood.

"Are you frightened, Marda?" Daneen said softly.

"Nay, I'm not frightened now, Daneen," she replied, not quite truthfully.

"Neither am I," Daneen murmured, but nevertheless Marda heard her friend murmuring a charm against evil as she groped along.

> "Spirit of Lug, the sun protect us.
> Spirit of the moon, save us.
> Stars, bright as water, surround us.
> Dagda, guard us well."

The journey through the fog-enshrouded forest seemed to take forever. Marda thought perhaps she'd missed the short turnoff to Breeca's hut in the dense mist, and twice she backtracked a little way to be sure she hadn't. But gradually the trees and rocks that served as landmarks for her became a bit more clear as the sun rose east of the dense forest, thrusting long, bright fingers through the fog.

"Now I know where we are," she cried softly. " 'Tis only a little way now."

And shortly Breeca's tiny stone hut, looking for all the world like a beehive and nearly hidden by a vast outcropping of rock above the stream that flowed beside it, appeared on her left.

" 'Tis a mean and lonely spot," Daneen said, shivering and clutching Marda's hand.

Marda nodded and led the way to the hut. There were no

windows at all and the only entrance was a small opening, hung with the hide of some animal, which was so low even small Marda would have needed to crouch to enter. Hesitantly she knocked at the stone wall beside the entrance. There was no stirring within the hut, so at length Marda drew herself to her full height and called loudly.

"Oh, Breeca, wisest of women, we come to you in supplication."

At this they heard a faint movement from within, and at once a thin, dirty-nailed hand appeared at the edge of the animal hide and drew it aside. The old woman's face soon appeared beside the hand. It seemed to be one great mass of down-drawing lines underneath a lofty ridge of forehead edged by shaggy white eyebrows. Her iron-gray hair, coarse as the strings on Feldhaigh, the harper's harp, was drawn into a bunch at the crown of her head and braided, the resultant long rope encircling her thin shoulders and lying across her breast like a serpent. Her neck supported so many great laps of flesh that it was easy to see she'd once been a much fatter woman than the starving creature in the aperture. Her woven garments were so dirty that their original color was quite obscure. Marda knew, however, that they'd once been white, for druids wore no other color.

"Who calls Breeca?" the old woman called in a sibilant voice.

" 'Tis only Marda, foster daughter of Laeghaire, ardri of Ireland," Marda replied.

The druidess peered at Marda from beneath the obscuring white eyebrows. It was unnerving but Marda stood still, unflinching, even when the old woman moved out of the hut and touched the brooch that held her cloak in place.

"I know that brooch," Breeca rasped. "I've seen it often when its owner brought offerings to Breeca. Oh yes, I saw more than you thought, child. Yet never before did you ask anything of me."

"You need feel no obligation," Marda said hurriedly. "I didn't mean for you to know about the things I brought nor would want you to feel I now seek payment from you, good Breeca."

The old woman stared at her thoughtfully, cast a quick glance at Daneen, and returned to studying Marda's face.

"No, I think you gave freely, girl. There is a generosity in you that one need not have the gift of prophecy to see. Come within, then."

She turned and led the way into her hut, standing back and holding the animal hide door out of the way to allow them to enter. They looked at each other fearfully but crouched over and followed.

Breeca let the door fall behind them while she poked at a fire in the center of the small room, causing it to flare a little. She threw some brushwood onto it and warmth and light sprang up. The smoke drifted around the ceiling, barely able to escape through the inadequate hole in the center of the roof.

Marda looked around in wonder. Somehow Breeca had contrived to jam sticks into cracks between the stones and lay flat, thin rocks thereon to form shelves all around the walls. There were earthenware pots and jars, pictures scratched on each, to identify the roots and worts within she supposed, for she saw rude drawings of wild strawberry and betony and of almost every plant she'd ever seen grow in Ireland. There was one iron cauldron at the edge of the firepit, and the dirty fleece of a large sheep was thrown into a corner—Breeca's only bed, she supposed. Beyond that, only a rough, low table furnished the squalid hut. The smell was at once fetid and earthy but well overlaid with woodsmoke. She looked quickly at Daneen in unspoken pity.

"What come you to seek of me, then, girl, speak!" the old woman cried gruffly. "I've no love for Laeghaire, for he suffered Lucat-mael to drive me away from Tara though I was a valued member of Nathi's household, aye and Niall's before him," she continued bitterly. "Yet you have done me many a kindness. These old bones would have been picked by ravens ere this had you not. So speak!"

Marda twisted her hands nervously as the two girls sank to sit cross-legged on the hard-packed floor, for the stooping made their backs ache. "I need a spell, oh Breeca, to turn Lucat-mael's desire for me to abhorrence."

"Lucat-mael! I will give thee a death potion for him," the druidess cried in a fury. "May Dagda cause his rotten heart to swell and burst, corrupting his whole body with its vile stench! May ravens peck a hole in his skull and feast on his brains."

Marda's apprehension returned at the fierce malediction and

at the two human skulls she'd just caught sight of on the topmost shelf. For although she was used to seeing human skulls on the walls of the ardri's dun—it was the custom to display one's slain enemies' heads—she'd hardly expected them in this old woman's hut. She began to shiver despite the warmth of the fire.

"I would not have you poison him, Breeca," she said hurriedly.

"Couldn't you just make a spell for her that would make her appear loathsome to Lucat-mael?" Daneen said, speaking for the first time. "Though not to others."

"To turn his desire to wed me into distaste, even loathing," Marda added.

The old woman took her chin in her thin hand and turned her so the firelight fell full on her face. "You ask a powerful charm of me, girl, for you've a strange, frail beauty, yet the frailty, I think, is somehow strength. You're nigh as beautiful as I was in my youth."

"You were once beautiful?" Daneen said, her voice clearly incredulous.

"Thou *bathais un naire!* Cease thy insolent tongue," cried Breeca angrily.

"Breeca, I would gladly be ugly," Marda interjected hastily to draw the druidess's wrath from her friend, "if there were no other way to save myself from Lucat-mael. Even if—if no other looked at me either."

The old woman turned to her, giving Daneen her disdainful back.

"Tell me, girl—and don't lie for I can read all the secrets of your heart. Is there no one it would grieve you to have think you ugly?"

Marda felt the warm pink flush upward across her neck and face. Although he'd spoken to her alone but once, that only yesterday, she *had* been deeply aware of the young physician for all of the two months since he'd come to Laeghaire's court.

"I see that there is," Breeca croaked triumphantly. "Well, then, let us cast a spell that will make you abhorrent in Lucat-mael's eyes, yet just so much as you are abhorrent to him, you will be beautiful and desirable to the other."

"Oh, no, I would not have him in that way," Marda cried.

"Besides, he is far above me, the king's physician, whereas I'm but a freeman's daughter."

"I know your history, girl," Breeca said dryly. "I think you foolish, though. If you're good enough for Lucat-mael, why not for him you fancy? Never mind; because you have shown me kindness, your will in the matter prevails."

She turned and hobbled toward the shelf above her squalid bed. Peering closely at the primitive scratched pictures on the jars, she selected one and brought it back, taking the lid off carefully.

"My best charm will I give you," she said, her old face splitting in a ghastly grin that showed several places where her teeth had worn down to blackened stumps.

"Two things must you do and the first of these is attend my words, for there is a charm you must learn by heart. This you will say at the holy well as you anoint yourself with this salve and then scrub it off. Attend, girl:

'Hear me, oh water sprite,
    Black as the burned offal of the hedgehog
        will I be to Lucat-mael,
    My smell will be to him like rotted fish.
    His gorge shall rise at the thought of touching my skin.
    Even to look upon me will pain his eyes.
    Hear me, oh water sprite, and so do with me
        unto Lucat-mael.' "

The old woman made her repeat the charm three times.

"To the sprite, you will say it three times—three times," Breeca said, sniffing the salve and, putting the lid back on, handing it to Marda. "Then you must give the sprite an offering. Your cloak, perhaps."

Marda nodded and unfastened the brooch that held the cloak at her shoulder. "Then I will have no further use for this brooch, good Breeca," she said diffidently, handing it to the druidess. " 'Tis unjeweled, but of gold and will buy your necessities for some time."

The druidess accepted the brooch eagerly, handing Marda the salve jar in return. "Lucat-mael will not be able to bear the sight

of you when you return to court, I promise you," she cried gleefully. "But I would sooner have given him a death potion."

"Thank you, Breeca. If ever you have a need, send word to me
for great gratitude do I have to you."

"Hurry, now; the charm is most efficacious on just such a morning before the sun burns off the mist."

The girls nodded and got up, crouching their way out of the
smoky little hut. The sun was well above the forest now and the
fog was beginning to dissipate except along the quickly running
stream.

"Yonder is the holy well, child," Breeca called from the doorway of the hut, "at the foot of that old oak. See? It rushes forth
from the roots of the oak itself."

Marda nodded and made her way along the narrow forest
path.

When they reached the well, which was really a small pond in
the stream formed by a gushing spring above it, Marda began to
remove her clothing, handing the garments to Daneen as she did
so.

"Keep watch, Daneen, that my nakedness be not exposed to
some wayfarer," she said, kicking free of her sandals. She opened
the jar and sniffed at the thick ointment within. It was not un-
pleasant, though at least one of its ingredients was rancid animal
fat, from the smell. There had been flowers smashed in it, too,
along with the magical herbs that would complete the spell.
Slowly she began spreading the ointment on her face, in her hair,
and over her entire body, solemnly reciting the charm Breeca
had given her. Daneen watched her, enthralled by the magic
incantation. When every smidgen of the salve had been rubbed
onto her body and hair, she set the jar on a rock and stepped into
the pool.

The water stung her flesh like icy needles and mist swirled
around her head, for the sun hadn't yet penetrated the heavy
foliage above her. She scrubbed vigorously at her hair and body,
immersing herself again and again, even holding her head under
the rushing torrent of the spring itself. And she repeated her
charm steadily, counting as she did so. To her surprise, the mixture washed away fairly easily, leaving her skin shining and pink,
her hair smelling pleasantly clean. Finally, as she finished the

saying for the ninth time, she climbed out of the pool, twisting her hair to remove most of the water. She switched it around in the sunlit air, trying to separate the strands with her fingers.

"Bring my shift, Daneen; 'tis cold as the inside of a fairy mound," she cried, teeth chattering.

"You'd best let the sun dry you, Marda," Daneen said, "else you'll be making your shift wet and so will be cold for the walk back."

Marda nodded and smoothed as much water from her body as she could. The sun did feel good.

Suddenly a voice from the path above the holy well cracked through the forest.

" 'Twas easy to follow your trail on the damp path, Marda. What means this coil?"

Marda whipped around, trying to cover her body with her hands. It was Lucat-mael.

"My cloak—nay, 'tis an offering to the sprite—quick, my shift," she cried.

Daneen bounded toward her, throwing her clothes toward her, then turning and spreading her own cloak wide to shield her friend from Lucat-mael's gaze.

The druid stared at her contemptuously, then strode down the bank and thrust Daneen roughly aside as Marda struggled to get the shift over her head.

"You're even more beautiful than I expected," he said exultantly. "And a grave ill it is to cover such glory. I have chosen wisely indeed. Come, Marda, a kiss, foretaste of what's to come."

He reached out to take her wrist, but Daneen, too angry to be afraid, slapped his hand away and pulled the shift down over Marda's head.

"No right, yet, have you to touch her," she shouted in fury. "Now go away—we need not such an escort as you back to Tara."

Lucat-mael smiled and drew back as Marda gasped.

"Don't defy him, Daneen," she whispered. "Remember what he did to the gilla, Aird."

Daneen's face turned white as she realized what she'd done. She kept her back to the druid, helping her friend get decently covered.

"Nevertheless, when you two were found to be gone this

morning I demanded the right to go in pursuit, for you are mine, Marda. 'Tis best you get used to the idea. I'll teach you to burn for me as I do for you. In only half a year, now, though why Laeghaire agreed to your father's foolish ban I don't know."

"If you'll but retire, reverend Lucat-mael, we'll join you," Daneen said with as much dignity as she could command. "Until she is seventeen, Marda is not yours but still her own."

He laughed in triumph. "From the look of her, I'm glad 'tis no longer. A rare beauty, indeed. All right, play what little games you will, then, Marda; I will remember them well when you are in my bed."

Marda shuddered at the sinister words. But for now the druid turned away and let Daneen help her finish dressing. The younger girl suddenly gasped and looked up from the sandal she was tying.

"He says you are a rare beauty, Marda; the spell didn't work!"

Marda's heart turned over in despair.

CHAPTER 2

To Marda's intense relief, Lucat-mael retreated back up the path a short distance as she finished dressing. She tied the scarf around her head as she followed Daneen to join him. He made her feel like a naughty child who had to be pursued and harried homeward, she thought resentfully.

But as they reached the path, a flurry of white against the greenwood announced the arrival of others—all druids, it seemed.

"It's Keagh and Fiacc," Daneen said joyfully. "And Fiacc's teacher, Dubhtach Maccu-Lugair." She hurried forward to salute her betrothed with an exuberant kiss.

Lucat-mael cursed.

Fiacc smiled and hugged Daneen. "What coil is this, Daneen? I can see you'll lead me a merry dance when we're married if you go off into the forest without so much as a hello-goodbye!"

"We're not children, Fiacc," Daneen said with an air of injured dignity and a glance at Lucat-mael. "We'd have been home for breakfast."

Keagh, who'd been looking intently at Marda, laughed shortly. "Laeghaire has sent searchers in all directions to find you. Said you never know if the Ulstermen are looking for a fight again and had kidnapped you both."

Marda shivered, from the chilling bath she'd just had and, perhaps a little, from the tender look in Keagh's dark eyes.

"I'm sorry to have caused anyone trouble," she said. "We should have told someone where we were going, I guess."

"If you felt the need of an early bath, there are springs nearer Tara, Marda," Dubhtach said, glancing at her damp hair. "Both Laegh well and Tober Finn have curative powers."

Embarrassed, Marda returned his glance. He was a solemn, almost cadaverous man with eyes like pools of indigo in a startlingly handsome face. She didn't remember her father but had often daydreamed that he'd been like Dubhtach, who was unfailingly kind to her. Fiacc, his pupil in poetry, was blond and big and merry, enough like his betrothed to be her twin.

"I . . . I wanted to make an offering to the sprite of *this* well, reverend Dubhtach," she faltered.

Lucat-mael made a derogatory sound. "The silly girl objects to our ardri's command that she marry me," he said. "She sought a charm to dampen my ardor from the old enchantress, Breeca— oh yes, lass, easy to learn of your ridiculous notion it was. I had only to split the old harridan's lip . . ."

"You've hurt Breeca?" Marda cried furiously. She started toward the old woman's hut but Lucat-mael grasped her wrist in an iron grip.

"You're going back to Tara," he snapped.

Keagh had been watching silently. Now he reached out and loosened Lucat-mael's hand.

"I will escort Marda back to Tara," he said calmly, narrowing his eyes as he stared at the druid who was at least six inches taller than he. "I will need her help in treating the old woman you injured."

"And what will Laeghaire say to his liaig, his own physician, treating the likes of that old pythoness?" hissed Lucat-mael.

"I serve the ardri well," Keagh said imperturbably, "and he well knows, for I told him when I came here, that I would never turn my back on anyone who needs medical care should they fall into my way. So return to Tara yourself, Lucat-mael. Tell Laeghaire we'll be there soon and that Marda is well." He turned to Daneen, ignoring the chief druid. "Make sure the ardrigan, too, knows all is well, Daneen. She loves Marda."

He smiled and nodded to Marda, indicating that she was to precede him into the hut. Lucat-mael stood on the path, clenching and unclenching his fists in a fury as Daneen and the two poets started back to Tara. As Marda went into Breeca's hut, he finally turned and followed the others.

Keagh grinned and patted her arm.

"When did this betrothal take place, then?" he asked.

"Only last night. But I will never marry him," she said tightly.

Breeca was sitting against the wall, vainly trying to staunch the blood from a cut on her lip. She looked up fearfully as they entered. Marda stared down at the tiny old woman pityingly.

"Breeca, helping me has brought you grief," she said contritely.

She pulled the scarf from her hair and moved to help Breeca.

"Wait, Marda," Keagh said gently, kneeling beside her and opening his physician's bag which was always slung from his belt. "I've clean lamb's wool here and linen thread for stitching. You need not ruin your scarf and, indeed, 'tis best the wool be very clean . . . I know not why."

Deftly he dabbed the blood away, fitted the jagged edges together, and then, with a clean bit of lamb's wool, patted the contents of a bottle onto the wound before stitching it.

"The ointment will ease the pain as I sew, oh Breeca," he said.

The old woman nodded shortly, looking at him with grateful eyes. They were swimming with tears before he'd finished, despite the pain-easing ointment. Keagh inspected the repaired cut with an air of satisfaction.

"It will heal now," he said.

"Keagh, you have put yourself in jeopardy in my behalf," Marda said as she gathered up the bloody rags Breeca had been using on her lip. She threw them into the smoky fire in the center of the tiny room where they flared up and were consumed.

"I'm not afraid of that great bag of foul wind," Keagh said contemptuously.

Breeca watched the two of them shrewdly.

"You are the ardri's physician, then," she said, rather stiffly because of the newly repaired lip. She glanced at Marda. "He it is you fancy, girl, he you would not let me obtain for you with a charm."

Keagh's hands, busily gathering up the materials he'd used to treat Breeca, stopped suddenly. His eyes flew to Marda's face.

She felt the warm blood flood upward from her breast to flush her face with embarrassment. She put both hands to her cheeks, not meeting his eyes.

"Is that true, Marda?"

She nodded briefly, still not meeting his eyes.

Breeca laughed hoarsely. "An honorable lass, that, boy. A

shame to waste her on the likes of Lucat-mael. Let me prepare a poison potion for him . . ."

Keagh chuckled. "I'll pretend I didn't hear that, old woman." He handed her a small jar. "Put this on the cut each night, Breeca, and I'll return in three days to remove the stitches."

Breeca stared at the jar uncertainly.

"I've remedies of my own," she said proudly; "yet, you've done well and I'll use yours, physician. But I've nothing to pay you except Marda's brooch, which she gave me for making her the charm."

"The charm didn't work, Breeca; he's hot for her as ever," Keagh said with a laugh.

"Then I must return it to her." She groped within the folds of her dirty clothing and extended the little gold brooch to Marda.

Shaking her head, Marda folded Breeca's skinny old hand around the brooch. "You keep it, Breeca," she said. "Perhaps the charm didn't have time to work."

But the old woman assumed an air of dignity and extended the brooch to Keagh.

"Doubtless you are right, Marda. Keep repeating the charm I gave you and perhaps it will still prove efficacious. I will pay the physician's fee, then, with your offering."

Keagh drew his hands back, eyes twinkling.

"Nay, Breeca, you have paid me adequately already by telling me Marda refused to have me with a charm."

The old woman smiled impudently at him, wincing at the pain.

"Perhaps that only meant she didn't want you," she said primly.

"Did it?"

"Nay, she fancies you, physician. The girl's worth the having. Let me make you a poison potion for the druid."

But Keagh only laughed, patting the old woman's skinny arm. He pulled Marda to her feet and held the hide back to allow her to exit from the hut.

"We'll be back in three days, Breeca," he said gently. "Peace be under your roof."

"Thank you, lad," Breeca said gruffly. "And may you have your heart's treasure. I'll entreat the magic ones to obtain it for you."

Outside, they breathed deeply of the fresh air for the smells of the tiny hut had been oppressive. Keagh took Marda's hand and led her back to the bank above the magic spring.

"We'd best get back," she said nervously. "I would not get you into further difficulty in my behalf."

Keagh only smiled and pulled her down to sit beside him on a wide, sun-warmed rock.

"Don't try to elude me, Marda. We have to talk. Indeed, 'tis talking we should have been long since, it seems. I've been a great fool."

Marda looked at him uncertainly. Her heart had been quickening ever since he'd arrived and, indeed, the expression in his dark eyes when Breeca had told him that she, Marda, fancied him, had made it lurch painfully as if it wanted to cry out her love for Keagh.

"Tell me, Marda, did the old woman speak the truth? Do you want me?"

"I am only a charioteer's daughter," she said quietly.

"That is not what I asked, Marda. Do you love me, girl?"

Marda lifted her chin pridefully. "And if I do. What then? You are the ardri's own physician and son of a great chief. You would not be refused if you asked for the king's own daughters. Two of them are of an age—Ethnea the Fair and Fedelma the Ruddy are fostered with Daneen's father, the king of Connaught. Ardri Laeghaire has sent two brothers, wise druids, with them to be their tutors and men say there are no women in Ireland more beautiful and accomplished."

Keagh grinned triumphantly.

"Say it, then, beloved," he murmured.

Marda gasped at the endearment. Her eyes flew to Keagh's and clung. Humor and tenderness mingled in their dark depths. "Aye, little one, I will say it first," he chuckled. "You would have had no need of love charms anyhow, Marda, for I love you with all my heart."

A sharp, honey-sweet delight filled Marda and her happy cry startled a togmal—a tiny ground squirrel cleaning his whiskers on a branch above the spring. She smiled happily, and when Keagh opened his arms to her she flew within their circle and clung as if coming home after all her years of fosterage.

For a long time they embraced, exchanging many an inexperienced kiss that warmed and filled them with wonder. Marda rested her cheek against the clean expanse of his white tunic, inhaling deeply of the fragrance that seemed to cling to the immaculate cloth.

"Cedar," she said dreamily. "I've just realized 'tis cedar, that scent that seems always to cling to you."

He laughed and stroked her cheek gently. "From my coffer, it is. My father's carpenter made me a coffer of cedar before I left home."

"Where is your home, Keagh? I know only that it's in the south."

"I lived where the river Shannon flows into the western sea, Marda," he said. "But now my home is where you are."

He kissed her lips softly, filling Marda with a sweet, unfamiliar fire that eased and comforted even as it excited. She gave herself up to his embrace for a long moment.

Then she remembered Lucat-mael.

Sighing, she drew away.

"What are we going to do, Keagh? The king has promised me to Lucat-mael."

Keagh released her, sobering. "Aye. And devious is the man," he said angrily. "He must have known as I did not that Laeghaire had given you leave to stay unwed until you're seventeen as your father wished. He heard me asking Dubhtach yesterday morning why the comeliest lass at Tara hadn't married though sixteen years old. Dubhtach teased me, asked if I intended speaking for you. Then, when I replied that I certainly would if you'd have me, Lucat-mael must have gone straight to the king, fearing I'd ask first." He shook his head angrily. "I think he must have threatened any others who showed interest in you."

"I don't know about that. There's been no one *I* was interested in, so I've discouraged the ones who did approach me."

Keagh laughed silently. "And you think *that* would have kept them away from one so fair? Nay, Marda, I think he had you staked out for himself all along. And I think he knew threatening me would do no good so he ran hot-footed to the king, forcing Laeghaire to promise you."

"The king is so afraid of his spells," Marda said miserably.

"His 'spells' are the fear he strikes into men's hearts," Keagh said scornfully. "They let him frighten them into succumbing to his silly maledictions."

"Nevertheless, Laeghaire honors Lucat-mael as his chief historian and brehon, allowing him even the power of judging Laeghaire himself. Once Laeghaire has made his promise, heaven and earth won't change it."

"Lucat-mael shall not have you," Keagh exploded.

"How can we prevent it?"

"I don't know yet, but we will. I promise you, Marda." He sighed and drew her to her feet. "I suppose we must return to Tara, else the king will be sending his hosts to find us. Why don't we just leave, Marda, right now?"

"Where in Ireland would we go, Keagh? Lucat-mael would force the ardri to search the length and breadth of the land for us, and any who sheltered us would suffer," she replied sadly. "And if we were fortunate enough to escape to Britain or Gaul, would you be happy for long among the strangers?"

He held her gently, his chin resting on the top of her head.

"I think I would be happy anywhere with you, dear little Marda, but why should *we* be forced to flee our home when our only fault is loving each other? Nay, we'll stay and fight for each other! Laeghaire likes me well, I know it. And the ardrigan dotes on you. Let's go back and boldly present our suit to him. Perhaps when he knows we love each other, he'll reconsider."

"Aye, he must, Keagh," she said, turning purposefully back toward Tara. "Come, then, hurry."

The sweet April morning was glorious with warm beauty as they walked hand and hand through the forest. All around them the world spoke of beauty and renewal and youth. The thought of Lucat-mael was like some dark presence from a fairy mound, so they banished him and as they neared the great hill of Tara with its several huge raths and the enormous banqueting hall, Keagh began to sing. His voice was as sweet to Marda as the call of the meadowlarks.

"You might have been the king's poet, Keagh, as successfully as his liaig," she said contentedly.

"My poetry is only for you, beloved," he murmured, kissing the tips of her fingers. "I think I have loved you since my first day at

Tara when you came in to dinner in your green dress. You are all that is lovely and pleasing and fine to me."

"The blessings of the good fairies are mine," Marda cried happily, "for you love me. Oh, Keagh, we must be together. Fortune could not intend that we part."

"We'll be together, Marda, somehow, I promise," he said as they approached the outer ramparts.

The great grassy hill rose before them, standing 200 feet above the surrounding forested plain. The double ramparts that surrounded each of the magnificent raths had a water-filled ditch between them. Rath Righ, the fort of the kings, which occupied the summit and southern slope of the hill and reigned protectively over all the other lis or homes, was by far the biggest. Inside it lay the Forrad, or public meetinghouse, and the Duma nan Giall or mound of the hostages. A little to the south of it lay the magnificent rath Laeghaire was constructing which, eventually, he and his family would occupy separately from the rest of the court. To the north lay the great long many-doored banqueting hall which was used only for great state occasions. West of that lay several other raths, some dating back almost two hundred years to the time of King Cormac mac Art. Spilling down the hillside in all directions were the houses of Laeghaire's higher household officials. Marda sobered as she noticed the fine timber house where Lucat-mael's poor beaten-down wife, Gaida, lived. They crossed the outer rampart of Rath Righ and walked across the bridge. Keagh held her hand tightly.

Colmagh the plowman was waiting for them at the great double doors of the hall. He smiled broadly. He'd always reminded Marda of a luchorpan, the tiny brown-haired wrinkled shoemakers of the fairy folk. His round, humorous face was crisscrossed with as many furrows as his fields during spring plowing.

" 'Tis relieved I am that you're safe, lass," he cried. "Do you hurry, now, t'hall. Laeghaire's as agitated as a disturbed bee."

Marda tried to smooth her rumpled dress and scarf. The three of them entered the hall together, Colmagh going to his place among the servants. Keagh took her hand encouragingly, and, together, they made their way to the ardri's high chair. Marda was deeply aware that the entire court watched their progress

and Lucat-mael glared from his place beside the king. She threw
a quick glance toward the ardrigan, who smiled encouragingly.

But Laeghaire's stern countenance showed no sign of relaxing.

She and Keagh stopped before his chair and bowed respectfully, waiting, as was the custom, for Laeghaire to acknowlege
them. But, of course, even the ardri couldn't speak before his
chief druid gave him leave so the silence grew heavy; Lucat-mael
seemed to be enjoying everyone's discomfort. Marda watched
him covertly through her lashes as she stood, head bowed, before
the king. Slowly the druid chose from the joints of meat offered to
him a thigh piece, as was his prerogative, being of station as lofty
as the ardri. While his lips assumed a satisfied smile, his eyes
glittered balefully. She shuddered. Why did he want her so
when, from his expression, he despised her?

The druid motioned impatiently for a gilla who brought a basin
of water in which he washed his hands, his eyes still on Marda. An
eternity, it seemed, passed before he cleared his throat to speak.

"As you can see, oh Laeghaire, I've fetched back the thankless
girl you fostered in your own home. Certain you are to punish her
for her foolish flightiness."

Marda lifted her eyes to Laeghaire's, not daring to speak. The
druid played skillfully on Laeghaire's pride before the entire
court. The ardri would have to censure her now, or lose face with
his people. Yet she knew Laeghaire was fond of her, not only
because her father had saved his life but because she'd been with
them almost from her babyhood—indeed since he'd married
Angas, who was his third wife, the first two having died. She held
herself with dignity, watching him solemnly, willing him to remember the affection that was between them.

Laeghaire, released from the bond of silence now that his
druid had opened the discussion, surprised her by motioning her
to her place and Keagh to his.

"You must both be hungry," he said gruffly. "When we have
filled ourselves will be time enough to speak of this."

So, reprieved for the moment, Marda bowed and slipped into
her seat beside Daneen. She saw the ardrigan, on Laeghaire's
other side, lean toward her husband and speak softly and earnestly. Lucat-mael stopped her angrily and poured a tirade into

Laeghaire's ear. Keagh dropped into his accustomed place at the higher table, throwing her a look of encouragement.

"You look different, Marda," Daneen whispered as a servant handed them each wooden bowls of samit and crimmes which was a mixture of curds, butter, milk and the wild garlic that was just beginning to grow in the fields. It was Daneen's favorite morning food and she dipped into it eagerly. "I'm as empty as Finn's cauldron after dinner," she remarked. "What happened? Did that beast really hurt old Breeca?"

Marda nodded. "He hurt her enough," she said bitterly, "but Keagh stitched her torn lip. He says she'll be all right."

"He was brave, standing up to Lucat-mael as he did," Daneen said, reaching for a bit of bog cheese and a small barley loaf.

"Aye," Marda said proudly. "Brave and wise and kind."

Daneen smiled. "You have lost your heart to him, haven't you, Marda? And I think he must feel just so about you, for how else explain that misty, magical look you have."

Marda filled her spoon with the samit and then dumped it out absently, the tugging around her heart easing a little as she thought of Keagh's declaration and his ardent embrace. Despite the gravity of the situation, she smiled gently. "Aye, Daneen, he does. And what have I ever done to have such good fortune?"

Daneen patted her back covertly. "Nay, sweeting, what ever has *he* done to deserve you? Yet I think he deserves you better than that damned goblin," she muttered vehemently.

At last the meal was over. Laeghaire motioned his trumpeter to sound the signal for the court to depart to their various pursuits, but he beckoned for Marda and Keagh to attend him.

Daneen gave her hand an encouraging squeeze as she rose to leave.

"Good luck, Marda," she whispered.

At last only the ardri and ardrigan and Lucat-mael sat at the high table. Keagh came to stand beside her so that they were like two criminals being arraigned. Deliberately he took her hand in his and smiled at her.

"She is my betrothed, Laeghaire," Lucat-mael hissed. "Order that pup to release her hand."

Unexpectedly, Laeghaire frowned and shook his head.

"By my vow to her father, she cannot be anyone's betrothed

until after Samain, oh worthy shanachie and brehon," he said stoutly. "I have given you my word she will marry you when she's reached that age her father stipulated."

"Oh Laeghaire, forgive me, but I think you fulfill the letter of your vow to my father and not its spirit," Marda cried, clasping Keagh's hand for courage. "He would surely not want me wed to one like Lucat-mael who beats his cetmuinter and keeps many concubines in various places."

"Marda, have a care," Laeghaire cried angrily. "If your father were here to state his will, I would honor it if I could. You are but a slip of a girl. How dare you challenge my right as your foster father and king to choose your husband for you?"

"Forgive me, my lord, you did not choose him. He chose me."

Laeghaire flushed darkly; a pulse beat furiously at his temple. Marda wanted to weep with agitation but she wouldn't let the hated druid see her tears. She lifted her chin proudly.

"That is true, Marda," Laeghaire said with an air of trying to control his temper. "And you should thank the goddess Ana that I have so done for you. My brehon has pledged as high a marriage portion for you as Fiacc has for Daneen, a king's daughter." His blue-green eyes flicked nervously toward Lucat-mael who glowered triumphantly. Angas lowered her eyes and Marda watched fascinated as two dark spots formed on the rich blue-and-yellow gown stretched over the ardrigan's taut belly, Angas's tears.

Laeghaire noticed, too. He patted his wife's knee comfortingly as his gaze met Marda's.

I would save you if I could, Marda, the sea-colored eyes seemed to say. *Yet I cannot risk being struck blind or dumb by a malediction.*

"Your leave to speak would I have, oh Laeghaire," Keagh said respectfully.

Laeghaire nodded shortly. "Speak, oh liaig."

"I believe that your chief druid has asked for Marda before the time her father stipulated to thwart me, my king. For he was present when I asked Dubhtach about her and knew that I loved her and planned to ask for her. Since she is not yet of the age her father received your promise about, I request that you set Lucat-mael's demand aside as unworthy. I love Marda and she has honored me by returning my feelings. It is only right that her happiness should be of prime importance in this matter. As she pointed out, *that* is what her father had in mind when he requested you allow her to remain unwed until she was seventeen."

Angas emitted a short, happy laugh, then, glancing at Lucat-mael, she stifled it with a smooth hand placed across her lips. Her soft eyes danced merrily above it, teardrops like crystals edging the dark eyelashes. Laeghaire, too, seemed to soften for a moment. Marda held her breath as Keagh held her hand confidently. Only Lucat-mael was displeased. His face was like a lowering cliff as he rose in his place, leaning menacingly over the ardri.

"No! By Dagda, I will strike you all with a plague of urtrochta—evil sprites! You will never find rest again. You won't be able to eat or sleep or enjoy each other's bodies! You, oh Laeghaire, will be no better than the ancient prince Comgan, for I will make a magic wisp—a dlui fulla—to transform you into a madman." He whipped around and pointed at Marda. "You too, girl!"

Laeghaire blanched and Angas began to weep softly. Marda felt her own blood run cold at the horrible threat.

Keagh laughed scornfully.

"And what benefit would there be to you in wedding a madwoman, then? Release her, Lucat-mael; no good will come of trying to hold her."

Lucat-mael was shaking with fury. Marda stared at him, deeply frightened, as he seemed almost to swell before their eyes.

"You dare to lecture me?" His voice echoed thunderously in the vaulted room. "Be warned, liaig, you tamper with power you'd be wise not to."

Suddenly he raised his long arms and extended them toward Keagh, his sleeves sweeping majestically. Smoke seemed to emanate from his fingertips. Laeghaire gasped in superstitious awe.

But Keagh laughed contemptuously.

"You don't frighten me, Lucat-mael. You prove only that you've spent your time learning magic tricks instead of our ancient history as you are pledged to do."

The big druid lowered his arms slowly. "I know every detail of our sacred history by heart," he snapped. "And I know our history that hasn't even happened yet, for the magical sidh dwellers, they of the fairy mounds, are my informants."

"To foretell the future, now, that would be a feat of note," Keagh scoffed, "but never have I known you so to do."

"Oh, no? Hear you! The ardri himself knows that for months I have been prophesying the coming of a great enemy to Ireland." His eyes took on a fanatical glow as he gazed off into the reaches of the hall. He intoned:

"Adzehead will come over a furious sea,
His mantle hole-headed, his staff crook-headed.
His dish in the east of his house.
All his household shall answer
Amen, amen!
Adzeheads will come who will build cities,
Who will consecrate churches, pinnacled music-houses,
Many conical caps a realm round crosiers."

Keagh chuckled.

"You can prophesy until your toes fall off; that signifies nothing. Only when what you predict comes true can you crow, Lucat-mael."

The druid turned his eyes back to Keagh's where they bored into his maliciously.

"Soon, soon," he chanted. "Then you will understand the power of Lucat-mael."

"And this invader will come over the sea?" Keagh persisted, laughing. "Then our ardri would be advised to gather his hosts."

"The hosting is begun," Laeghaire said shortly. "You know the troops gather, Keagh."

"Because of this man's prophecy, oh Laeghaire? I thought surely you had other reasons for suspecting invasion."

Laeghaire made an impatient gesture.

"Marda's transgression is the matter at hand," he said uneasily, for Keagh's lack of respect for Lucat-mael's powers seemed to trouble him.

"What transgression is it for a young girl to walk in the woods on a spring morning?" Keagh demanded.

"She sought a charm against me," Lucat-mael thundered.

"Nay, I did not," Marda said spiritedly. "I but sought one to make me loathsome to you. I never sought to harm you."

Angas made a pitying sound and Laeghaire flushed.

"You are rebellious. You defy me and your king's directive!"

"I am sorry for that," Marda cried. "Never before have I questioned any command my lord gave me. I have served his household with all my love. But I swear, I will never marry you, Lucat-mael!"

"You will do what I tell you," Laeghaire thundered, shaking off Angas's gentling hand. "Leave me, now. I've had enough. You too, Keagh. On pain of my displeasure, abandon your infatuation for Marda."

Keagh bowed, but his eyes met Laeghaire's boldly.

"I obey your first directive, oh King; I can never obey the second," he said, and before Laeghaire could answer, he took Marda's elbow and led her to the big double doors.

The sun, bright as midsummer, had climbed high in the eastern sky now, and Marda felt the warmth on her cold skin gratefully. Keagh smiled encouragingly.

"Don't worry, Marda, it will be all right; I know it will. We will wear Laeghaire down. Angas will gladly help."

"He's so afraid of Lucat-mael," she said sorrowfully. "He *does* have much power, Keagh."

"His power lies in the way he frightens people," Keagh said dryly. "I will not let you go, Marda. We will find a way." He leaned over and kissed her lightly on the forehead. "I must go, beloved. Old Lochru relies on me, now, to teach the pupils; I am long overdue. Come, sweetheart, give me a smile; I swear to you, Lucat-mael shall not have you."

Marda kissed him and watched him walk away to the schoolroom. With all her heart she wanted to believe Keagh was right about Lucat-mael's power, but she was filled with deep foreboding. The events of the last few hours had been almost overwhelming, learning that Lucat-mael had demanded her hand, the trip to see Breeca, and then, against all hope, learning that Keagh loved her as she did him. She felt worn and troubled.

As always when she sought peace, she made her way to her garden.

As she knelt among the tender shoots in the soft, rich earth, her natural optimism and happiness crept slowly back to fill her. She had never dreamed of such happiness as to know Keagh loved her and wanted to marry her. In all her life she'd never had a home, for her mother had died at her birth and her father before she'd reached the age of two summers. Hence she'd been fostered with the ardri several years before most girls were sent to foster parents, and had been with him several years longer than the age most were married into their own homes. Although kind Angas had been like a mother to her, and indeed Laeghaire too, a gentle father as far as his position gave him time to be, always she'd been aware they were not her own people and felt the loss thereof. If she'd even had a brother or sister, cousin or grandparent . . . but there'd been no one. And making a home with Keagh seemed to her like a dream of the blessed isle.

She labored most of the morning in her lubgort—kitchen garden—pulling out weeds, loosening the earth around the tiny plants and carrying water to pour into little trenches she made near the plants, for the weather had been unusually dry and warm for April. Near noon, Keagh and Colmagh sought her out.

"Colmagh has something important to tell us, Marda," he said excitedly. "I've been recounting to him Lucat-mael's prophecy . . ."

The old man snorted inelegantly.

"Prophecy, is it? Be damned if it is! *I* could prophesy that. And many another could, too."

Marda plunged her hands into a pail of water to wash them clean of the moist earth, waiting quietly for Colmagh to explain.

"Sit down, Marda—you look tired," the little man said.

"You don't believe Lucat-mael is a prophet, Colmagh?" she asked as she sank down on the sun-warmed grass.

"All the bothach and sencleithe—the herdsmen and laborers—of the tuath know of this man Lucat-mael calls 'Adzehead,'" Colmagh said contemptuously. "He so calls him because of the sharp-pointed hood he wears. He's been here in Ireland for some time. Indeed, he was a slave here, named Succat, in his youth."

"Then he's already here? And Lucat-mael knows it?" Keagh prompted.

"Certain I am that he knows. There is nothing going on in Ireland that he doesn't know. He's unlike the rest of the flaith in that," he added, glancing apologetically at Keagh who was also of the nobility.

"How do you know of this Succat, old man?" Keagh asked, not taking offense.

"News travels," Colmagh said cryptically. "What do you want to know?"

"Well, what about these cities they will build? And what is a church?"

"A church is a building where they worship their god."

"But the gods don't live in buildings," Marda said in bewilderment.

"They only have need of one god," the old man said, sifting the dirt absently through his gnarled fingers. "Let me tell you what I know. In my own way, maiden. Perhaps, after all, this man Patrick can help you."

"Patrick. You just called him Succat," Keagh said patiently.

Colmagh threw him a glance. "I will explain, my lord, only rest easy," he said.

Keagh nodded and sank down beside Marda.

"Patrick is an old man now, of more than sixty years. But many years ago, when he was but a stripling, he was captured from his homeland in Britain and brought to Ireland by pirates. He was named Succat then. He was sold into slavery to Miliucc, a chieftain in the north. He tended Miliucc's swine for seven years, then, at the bidding of an angel, escaped and found a ship to take him to Gaul."

"An angel?" Marda asked wonderingly. "What manner of being is that?"

"A messenger from his god in heaven. And before you ask me where heaven is, 'tis a wonderful kingdom of everlasting life, somewhere off in the sky. Anyhow, Succat wandered many years in Gaul and learned more of his religion—the story of his one god who was born long ago of a virgin. His father was in heaven and came to her spiritually, as a third person of this god. Then he was born and was named Jesus Christ."

"Then his god is like our Dagda, who also has sons and daughters," Keagh began, but Colmagh shook his head.

"He is nothing like Dagda, Keagh," he said patiently. "Let me finish. Succat went to Rome where the leader of all the Christians

—they call him the Holy Father—gave him a commission to come to Ireland. And gave him the name of Patrick which signifies 'father' in their language, for a father Patrick was to be to the Irish. He is here, now; he went first to Miliucc to pay him because he ran away. . . ."

"He was enslaved and brought here against his will and yet he paid the man who put him to herding swine?"

"Because he believed in justice, you see," Colmagh said patiently. "And Miliucc had lost money he paid for a slave when he ran away."

"And did he then pay for his bondage?" Marda asked.

"Nay, for Miliucc had heard of the miracles Patrick's god could perform and he feared him. He shut himself and all his household up in his house and set it afire. All died."

"The man was mad," Keagh said incredulously.

Colmagh nodded. "Aye, for Patrick would not have taken vengeance. He is the kindest and humblest of men."

"You know him, Colmagh?"

Colmagh stared down at the dirt that he continued to sift through his fingers. He seemed to struggle with himself. Then, finally, he looked up and met their eyes, looking searchingly from one to the other.

"And if I do, what then? Will you tell Lucat-mael where you have gotten this information?"

Keagh snorted. "I will tell him nothing. But what does it matter, Colmagh? You may know who you want."

Colmagh shook his head. "Nay. Patrick has brought the greatest blessing Ireland will ever have. But it will not root peacefully. All that his god stands for wars against our ancient ways. The druids will never, never accept him."

Keagh nodded thoughtfully. "They would not take kindly to a god who performs miracles," he said dryly. "That is *their* prerogative."

"Miracles! Rather, trickery," Colmagh snapped. "Yet, Keagh, you are not like the others. You cast no spells nor speak maledictions against us."

"I have no need of spells," was the reply. "Those I can heal, I do. Those I cannot, I don't. I don't know whether that's the will of one god or a hundred; it just is."

"Where is this Patrick now?" Marda said after a pause.

"He's at Strangford Lough. I have been to hear him preach twice."

"But that's a hundred miles by land," Marda said in surprise.

"Aye. My daughter who lives there sent me word to come hear him." He laughed shortly. "Ever am I ready to go see my grandsons, so gladly did I go. And gladly did I receive Patrick's message, too."

"So, if you know, many know of him," Keagh said slowly.

"Aye, many. He has consecrated many churches in the north and those who came with him—priests of the church, they are called—are spreading the news of this kind god wherever they go. And in these churches there is always a table—an altar—with dishes, where he turns bread and wine into the body and blood of Jesus."

"So much for Lucat-mael's prophecy," said Keagh. "This god strikes me as eminently sensible. A sacrifice of bread and wine is less wasteful than the firstborn of each animal that Cromm Cruach demands. At least Laeghaire won't allow the firstborn child to be sacrificed to him anymore."

"But men say Lucat-mael and some of the others still do so on feast days," Marda said. "Children have been missing."

Keagh frowned. "I'd thought such practices a thing of the past but, though 'tis hard to credit, Lucat-mael's implacability where you are concerned, beloved, makes me attend your words. One thing is certain, you cannot be given to that man!"

Marda leaned her head against Keagh's shoulder for a moment, and he put his arm around her; the contact was warmly comforting.

"I see why you think this man might help us, Colmagh," she said slowly. "His magic must be powerful indeed, if Miliucc so feared it that he was willing to die! Perhaps 'tis because it is good magic. He even wanted to pay—came back voluntarily to the place of his captivity."

"There is no magic, sweetheart," Keagh said kindly, stroking her hair. "If there ever was, it is dying."

"Still, Patrick can help you," Colmagh said stubbornly. "For he and his priests have the power to perform a marriage between a man and a woman that none on earth can break."

"That is what I want more than anything," said Keagh. "Whether he would perform such a marriage or we just vow together, nothing on earth will separate us, though."

"Marda will only be safe from Lucat-mael until she is seventeen," Colmagh said with an air of practicality. "Are you just going to sit here and wait until that time?"

"No, by Dagda and my medicine bag," Keagh said urgently. He turned to Marda, grasping her upper arms. "What do you say, Marda? Would you run away with me?"

"To Patrick?"

" 'Tis as good a destination as any," he replied with a shrug. "Certain I am that there's no future for us together here. We will join this man's company, his people, whatever they be."

Marda stared into Keagh's eyes with tears starting in her own. "You would leave your own class for me, Keagh? For, the flaith would think you foolish to risk your position with Laeghaire for a charioteer's daughter."

"I would give all I have for you, beloved." He kissed her gently.

"You haven't much time," Colmagh said worriedly. "Lucat-mael will never stand for you billing and cooing like this. He'll try some underhanded trick to separate you."

Keagh turned quickly, as if making a decision.

"Can you guide us, Colmagh, now?"

"Certainly. I was hoping you'd say that," the old man said with a laugh. "But, look you, we'd best gather some food, for Lucat-mael will no doubt follow and 'tis best we take some back ways. Nor could we easily stop at hostelries, for there he would find word of us."

"Then each of us will leave separately and join somewhere."

"Breeca's hut," Marda contributed. "You promised her you'd take the stitches out in three days, Keagh. If we are not going to be here, you'll have to tell her how to do it herself."

Keagh nodded.

"Then it's agreed. Each of us will gather what food we can and meet at Breeca's hut . . . one hour after the noon meal. Bring a warm cloak, too, beloved, for if we must spend the nights in the woods, you'll have need of it."

"Look there, on the rampart," Colmagh said in disgust. "The fox is watching us."

They followed his gaze and saw Lucat-mael glaring down on them. He started toward them menacingly.

Marda stood up and began sauntering casually back to the rath.

"I'll have Daneen get Fiacc to distract him when I'm ready to leave," she said in a low voice. "May Patrick's god be with us."

Later, when they'd gathered at Breeca's and explained they were leaving Tara to find Patrick, Breeca insisted on coming with them.

"My magic may not be as strong as it once was," she said grimly, "but I have lived in the woods for many a day, and I know ways to hide the trail so not even a hound could follow it. Believe me, this old man's a fool if he thinks he can get you to Strangford Lough without Lucat-mael finding you!"

And in the end, mostly because they hadn't the heart to leave her behind, they agreed.

When sunset came, they'd traveled more than ten miles toward Patrick, and Breeca had bullied them into streams for at least half of that and the other half they'd gently brushed away any sign of their passing with the feathery branches of the hemlock. Even so, Breeca wouldn't allow them to light a fire that first night. Huddled into their cloaks, they slept close together for warmth.

CHAPTER 3

Just before dawn Marda was awakened by a soft quickening of
the breeze and a sound, soft as a sigh—the ruffling of forest birds'
feathers as they withdrew sleepy heads from under their wings
and watched the eastern sky for the first tentative lightening.

Marda eased herself out from under the cloak she'd been shar-
ing with Breeca who slept on, snuffling softly like a sleeping baby,
her worn face gentled by slumber. Keagh and Colmagh had
assumed positions flanking the women and slightly apart from
them, both facing back toward Tara as if to protect them from
pursuers.

Her stomach growled insistently and, for the first time since
Lucat-mael had demanded her hand in marriage, she felt genu-
inely hungry. She stretched quietly and crept off into the woods
where she and Breeca had fashioned a makeshift latrine which
would be well covered and hidden when they left the campsite.
Then she moved silently to the little stream, a bit above her
sleeping fellow travelers so as not to awaken them, and washed
herself as best she could.

Faint fingers of light had been filtering through the thick oak
forest above her and they grew stronger as she moved silently
along the bank, searching for anything they might eat, for although she'd brought a fine pork joint and several barley loaves,
bounty of the cook who was used to her begging food for Breeca,
and the others, too, had brought food, several days would be
required to reach Strangford Lough and she thought it wise to
eke out their provisions as best she could. Keagh had a small sack
of apples, withered now, in the spring; Colmagh had brought a
quantity of oatmeal and a cauldron to cook it in, and Breeca had
emptied her shelves of dried game and fish, carrying it in the
folds of her tattered clothing.

She found a fine patch of watercress and many clumps of the

pungent crimmes. Quickly she lashed together a makeshift basket of reeds and, washing the cresses in the running stream, laid them on the basket to carry back to camp. She was about to return when Keagh found her. He smiled and opened his arms to her. Joyfully, she flew into them and nestled against his heart. As he kissed her, the very birds of the forest seemed to erupt into a joyous uproar.

"You look like the loveliest of water sprites, Marda, graciously accepting the offering of the waters," he said, nodding toward the basket of cress.

"Colmagh says the Christians don't believe in deities of the waters and earth and heavens but only in one God, creator of all things," she mused. "Do you think that's likely, Keagh?"

He paused, released her, then leaned over the stream, splashing water into his face and running his hand over his now stubbly chin. Keagh, unlike many of the Irish, was clean-shaven. He looked up at Marda thoughtfully; then, shaking his hands, returned to stand beside her.

"Ever have I considered the hosts of gods and fairies and demons worshipped in Eire to be silly and impotent," he said honestly. "The ancient tales are unbelievable to a reasonable man, my darling. Do you honestly believe that Laeghaire's father, Niall and his brothers actually confronted an aged hag in the forest who demanded that they kiss her and, when only Niall complied, she turned into a lovely young woman with the power to make him ardri? The druids tell such tales, but none but them have ever witnessed such wonders. Magic harps that come off the wall and play by themselves. Rocks that scream out in triumphant concord when the ardri of Ireland sits upon them. Men who disappear into the fairy sidhs and don't return for a hundred years. Nonsense, Marda. They are but tales to entertain the simple."

Marda smiled in spite of herself. Until recently, she'd believed in the magic of the gaels completely. Until Breeca's spell had failed.

"But, yet, all this," she said slowly, motioning to their surroundings where lush bracken clustered under soaring oaks and life abounded, "how did it all come into being, then? How did we, men and women with minds and wills and hearts to lose in love . . . how did we come into being?"

"I know not," Keagh said slowly. "Who can explain the existence of the world? I only know it's not as the magicians and soothsayers claim."

"Colmagh says Patrick's god is different, Keagh," Marda said hopefully.

Keagh drew her head against his chest.

"Marda, I don't think you should get your hopes up. No doubt he is just another clever druid who knows how to play on men's fears and uncertainties in this life."

Marda drew back and looked up into his eyes.

"Why, then, Keagh, have you suggested we come to him?" she cried. "If he can't help us—if his magic be not stronger—then we have only angered Laeghaire and Lucat-mael the more."

"We have escaped them, Marda," he said quietly. "We will exchange our vows before this Patrick and then we will take ship for Gaul. I should not have given you any hope that this Christian priest would somehow enable us to live peacefully in Ireland. For as long as Lucat-mael lives, we never will."

"Oh, Keagh, wrong you were to deceive me," she said sorrowfully. "I—I thought somehow he'd help us. Oh, perhaps he *is* different. I do not want to leave Ireland. Angas loves and needs me. The child is big, Keagh, I think bigger than it ought to be when she lacks more than two months of term."

"She will have others to care for her, Marda." He kissed her lips tenderly. "I know you could not bear to belong to Lucat-mael."

She nodded agreement. "Never could I live with him. Or without you. But I would have told my lady I love her. And bid her goodbye had I known we were leaving. She would not have betrayed me."

Keagh smiled. "Not willingly, dear one, but Angas would have wept and the signs of her grief would show for the sharp-eyed Lucat-mael to read."

"Someday, when he is dead, we will return, won't we, Keagh?"

"I promise," he said. Then, peering up at the sky which was glowing a soft peach through the trees, "We must be under way, Marda. Come."

Together they returned to camp and wakened the two old

people, who were stiff and chilled from the night on the cold ground. Since there had been no sign of pursuit, they concluded Breeca's wiles had confounded any pursuers and so lit a fire with Keagh's flint, feeding it with small fallen branches. In a little while, fed with a warm meal, their bodies warmed, they obliterated all signs of their first night's camp and continued north.

For two more days they traveled, lighting fires at night now, for there were wild boars and other beasts in the forests. No one from Tara seemed to be in pursuit, but nevertheless, now that they had fires they took turns keeping watch by night. On the fourth day, just at dusk, they reached Strangford Lough.

Footsore and filthy, they entered the little settlement built around the chieftain, Dichu's rath. The entire place was surrounded by a double rampart as at Tara, and indeed was much like the ardri's establishment though far more modest in scale. Wearily they approached the gate where Colmagh answered the challenge and, the gatesward recognizing him, they were admitted.

Colmagh led them along a cobbled path lined with decent lis, dwelling houses of varying sizes. Women were calling children home to supper and their beds and doors were being closed over firelit interiors. They stopped in front of the last house before a small stream on the bank of which stood a mill; Colmagh knocked, then entered, motioning them to follow, without waiting to be bid.

The modest lis was dirt-floored and partially underground. It consisted of one great room, perhaps forty by twenty, with several wicker compartments along the walls, sleeping accommodations for the family and visitors. A welcoming fire burned in the pit at the center of the room, the smoke escaping inadequately through a hole in the roof. An iron frame supporting a large brazen cauldron hung over the fire and a pretty, dark-haired woman, her hair escaping from her linen coif, leaned over it, ladling out wooden bowls of the contents for herself and the small boy at her side. She looked up when they entered and, dropping the ladle into the cauldron, flew to meet them with a happy cry. She embraced her father; her hands on either side of his face, she leaned back to look at him.

"It's not expecting you I was, Father," she said. "You've not brought my mother . . ." She looked uncertainly at the others.

"Nay, sweet Gulda, for we left silently and secretly. Your mother would not have been up to the journey we've made. Next time I'll bring her. 'Tis others I'm recommending to your fine hospitable heart."

He introduced them, explaining their reasons for leaving Tara so precipitately.

"Come, rest ye by the fire," Gulda said kindly, helping Breeca down the ramp and to a spot on one of the benches flanking a low table that sat before the fire. "Had I expected you, a better meal than mutton and carrots would I have cooked you. Still, there's aplenty of it and new-baked wheat loaves to go with it."

Keagh sniffed appreciatively. "Were it the sweetest of pork, 'twould be no more welcome," he cried. "Kind your words and your open door to receive the stranger."

They sat on the benches, their tired and battered feet resting among clean rushes as Gulda served them with the stew and bread and her own well-brewed ale. The little boy, a merry-faced child with innumerable dimples, who was named Tadgh and had completed four winters, promptly climbed into his grandsire's lap.

"Where is Luigh?" Colmagh asked.

"Helping the ri's men with the planting," Gulda said. "He'll be home shortly." She smiled at Marda and Keagh. "Luigh is my older son."

"He's the man of the house now that his father's dead," Colmagh said proudly. "And fine the job he does of it, too, though he's but twelve."

"How long have you been widowed?" Keagh asked.

"Since just before Tadgh was born," Gulda said with a sad smile. "The lad never knew his father, yet the image of him he is."

"Aye. We wanted Gulda to return to Tara with the boys, yet the north is her home now, she told us. And a true home she's made of it, though with no man to help her."

"Why do not you and Mother come to me, Father?" she asked with a smile. "Let me help *you*, now, who've ever done so much for me."

"When I'm old, daughter," the old man said with a laugh. "For now, though, 'tis helping these youngsters you can be, by giving them shelter. And Breeca, too—she's been ill-used these many years."

Gulda looked pityingly at the old woman who was now snoring, her hunger satisfied. The torn lip, from which Keagh had removed the stitches that morning, glowed red against the pale old face.

"Anything I would do for your friends, Father, the giving of food and shelter but the smallest part of it," she said kindly.

"Tomorrow, then, you can take them to Patrick, for they've a fancy he might be able to help them—if not by magic, then perhaps by helping them find a ship to take them away from Ireland."

"Unless he be afraid to offend the ardri and his druids," Keagh said diffidently.

Gulda smiled and shook her head.

"He fears no man," she said emphatically. "Aye, you shall meet him tomorrow. It is the sabbath, the day holy to Almighty God for, after laboring six days to create the earth and all in it, he rested on the seventh day, and so we make it holy to God."

Colmagh chuckled softly.

"Then you have accepted the faith entirely, my girl," he said, stroking her hair.

"Aye, Father. As have you, in your heart. Although you have not yet been baptized."

"What is this baptized?" Keagh asked, staring from Gulda to Colmagh.

"Cleansed of all sin, that which we received from our first father, Adam, and mother, Eve, and that which we were guilty of ourselves before Patrick's coming to us with the word of God."

"Sin," Keagh said cynically. " 'Tis the likes of Lucat-mael who should be cleansed of sin, good Gulda, not one such as you."

But Gulda smiled serenely. "You will understand, Keagh, when Patrick has explained." She rose and lifted a large cauldron of water to the framework above the fire, Keagh jumping to help her.

"Soon there will be warm water that you may bathe, and I will find you clean clothes though they'll not be so fine as your own," she said. "While you take turns bathing in the last cubicle there, I'll borrow more pallets from my neighbors that you may sleep warm and comfortable in my lis this night.

"And on the morrow, you shall see the blessed Patrick for yourselves."

Marda's head had scarcely hit the straw-filled pallet when she was deeply asleep. It was the first time since she'd left Tara that she'd been warm and safe at night. Nor did she awaken until birdsong filled the rath of the ri, Dichu. Gulda was up before them, boiling goose eggs and stewing meal for them to eat. They ate heartily, feeling rested and grateful for clean clothing. Even Breeca was decent in a woven wool failainn of brown with a matching lummon, or cloak, over it. Keagh had been given a lend —a coat of white wool and brown woolen trews that hung a little loose from his waist for they'd belonged to Gulda's husband who'd been, apparently, a much bigger man. Marda wore one of Luigh's lummons over Gulda's dress of gray linen. They were prohibited by law from wearing the many colors the flaith were allowed. Even Marda, although she was only a charioteer's daughter, was allowed to wear bright colors, though no more than two at a time.

At last the tolling of a bell in the little settlement told them it was time to attend church, the saying of Mass, Gulda called it. Strangford Lough shimmered in the early morning sunlight, the rath lying along its edge like some enchanted village. Dichu's fort or dun rose above all the other dwellings, the fine oak doors carved and painted in intricate patterns. Beyond the dun, on a slight knoll, stood a new oblong timber building with a sharply pitched roof like nothing Marda had ever seen before. It had double doors, like Dichu's dun, and a strange wooden cross on the roof tree—a symbol, no doubt of that cross upon which their god's son, Jesus, had died. The roof was of thatch. The entire building was perhaps forty feet by twenty, without windows. As they approached it, the smell of new wood still clung about it. The entrance doorway, which was slightly wider at the bottom than at the top, was in the west of the building.

Others of the rath were assembling also, and as Gulda intro-duced them to various acquaintances, Marda clung to Keagh's hand. Suddenly she wondered why they were bothering with Patrick. Keagh did not believe he could be of any help to them, and indeed she felt in her heart he was right when he said the only way they could be together was to leave Ireland.

Yet the little church with its stark, simple cross on top drew her irresistibly. All that Colmagh had told them of this new god, of his love and mercy to the people he'd created, appealed to her. She felt instinctively that the laws this god laid down were just and true. She looked up at Keagh. His face was uncharacteristically solemn and inscrutable. He squared his jaw, lifting it a little as one does upon going into battle, and stepped through the doorway behind Gulda and Colmagh. Breeca, flanked by the two boys, Luigh and Tadgh, brought up the rear.

There were backless benches lined up on either side of an aisle the length of the building, and at the end of the aisle stood a table of the finest hazelwood. It had a sort of apron carved with crosses along the front and a snowy linen cloth covered it. Above this table hung another rude cross with the figure of a man, arms outspread, nailed to it. It was carved from pine and painted to resemble blood around the nail holes on the hands and feet, and from a crown of some thorny plant as well as a cut in the right side. Marda gasped. It was a cruel death, this, that Patrick's god's son had endured.

They took their places on one of the benches near the back of the church where they could watch as others filed in. Dichu and his family, resplendent in scarlet and green and gold, came in and occupied the first bench near the altar to the god. He was a burly middle-aged man whose hair seemed stiff and wiry, probably from the lime washes warriors used on their hair to make it stand out in battle. Some of his household, flaith and servant, occupied the seats behind him, those of lowest degree being the farthest from him while the rest of the people of Strangford Lough occupied the seats to the left side of the aisle and in the rear of the right side. The church was soon filled to capacity and as the people came in, Marda was struck by the bright look of expectancy they wore which lighted their faces to beauty.

Presently a young man in a dark, roughly woven robe, unlike those of the Irish, came in and lit many candles on the altar, filling the small, dark building with golden light which reflected off the new-sawn oak walls and lingered on the upturned faces. The man knelt on one knee before the altar, bowing his head reverently. His robe had a cowl or hood lying loose on his shoulders and he was tonsured. A round spot as big as a man's palm had been shaved at the crown of his head. It was unlike the druids' more rectangular tonsure. He arose and retired behind a screen to the side of the church from whence he'd come. In a few minutes another man came from behind the screen, a covered utensil of some sort held reverently between his hands, the first man at his heels. The congregation sighed and stood up.

" 'Tis Father Patrick," Gulda whispered.

Marda stared at the slight man who was bowing very deeply before his altar. He put the burden he carried on the altar just under the figure on the cross, drawing his hands away from it as if reluctant to lose contact with it, and folded his hands as he bowed over them and began speaking quietly in a tongue Marda recognized as Latin, having heard the druids use Latin words sometimes, but did not understand.

Patrick was smaller than Keagh, who was short and slender for a Gael. His hair was about equally composed of dark brown and snowy white; it hung down on his back, covering the shoulders of his coarse robe. He was bearded heavily and his nose was long, elegant and very slender. She could not see his eyes clearly from her place, since he'd been mostly turned face away from the congregation, but when he turned to face them in the course of his ritual, he held his hands up and looked searchingly and slowly around the room so that Marda felt he'd seen deeply into every set of eyes turned toward him. Then she was aware of a dark blue gaze under heavy brows not yet gray.

Keagh was watching him as raptly as she, and after a time Patrick motioned the people to sit down and he came to stand facing them, where he folded slender hands and tucked them within the folds of his long sleeves.

"My beloved people of God," he began, "by the grace of God, and through the generous piety of your ri, Dichu, our church is nearly finished now. But although he it was who gave the land and materials that we might build, each of you helped in the building. So good, you have been, so kind—" Here his voice cracked as if he was deeply moved. "My dear friends, many years ago I was brought as a slave to Ireland. I ran away from my master, Miliucc, and escaped. But there was no escaping my love for you. A quarter of a century and more and still you spoke to my heart; you called me back.

"And so I am come to share with you the dearest treasure of the world. I wanted to give it to Miliucc and to pay him my slave price which I'd stolen from him by running away. Great grief it is to me that he would not receive me but rather died by his own hand. Great grief to God, my dear folk, for He wants you. Each of you. He longs for you as if each were His only son. You have seen His power, many times since I am come among you, when I healed your sick, not of my own power but of God's. Through Him I can do all things; without Him I am as nothing, of no more account than the lowest slug.

"Today, my children, is Passion Sunday. Today we commemorate the time when Jesus approached His death for love of us, those of us who'd died before His time, those of us who were living then, those of us living today and the countless souls who are yet to live. So great is God's love that He sent this dearly beloved son among us to win us all as His brothers and sisters. He came to preach life not just for the three or four score years even the strongest of us may expect on earth, but life forever. The dark grave, silent and cold, is not the end but only the gateway to eternal life for those whose hearts are full of the love of God and His creatures.

"In two weeks we celebrate Easter, the Sunday when Jesus, so cruelly put to death by those who did not yet understand His father, left the grave and arose, glorious and whole, to walk among us. He proved then, once and for all, that selfish, evil men, the Sanhedrin—like our councils of druids—could not kill Him, could not stop His glorious message of love."

Marda listened entranced, thinking how tender, how loving were the voice and the message the humble little man offered. How kindly this god seemed. She thought of Cromm Cruach, the dread and ugly stone idol, representative of the god who delighted and feasted on the blood of babies. Beside her Keagh listened too, although from the cynical expression on his face she could tell he didn't truly believe this Jesus had actually risen from the dead.

"Some of you have asked me as I instructed you," Patrick continued, "why it was that God did not rain down thunderbolts on those who seized His son to do Him violence."

Keagh nodded shortly. Patrick, catching the motion, smiled gently.

"Verily, He could have done so. Many, many years before Christ, when men were even harder to convince, He caused the sea to open to allow His people to escape from their tormentors, the Egyptians, and when the Egyptians pursued, the seas closed upon them, drowning them all. This He did in the olden times.

"But once He'd sent His son to us, He had no further need to smite evildoers in this way. By His resurrection, Jesus showed us all that His love triumphs over the evils of the world. He showed us the world of the spirit. He said, 'Don't worry for a moment about those who can kill your body for you will live forever, whatever happens to the body. Worry only about those who would destroy your soul by making you do evil.'

"Oh, He could do wonders. Were He to walk among us today, He would show you He had the power to change one salmon from the Boyne water and two oaten loaves into enough to feed all the people of Ulster. He did it when those who'd come to hear him preach were faint with hunger. But 'twas the bread of eternal life, His own precious body, which he came to give us.

"Before He was conceived in His mother's womb, before the time of the prophets of old, it was ordained by God that His son would come among us and die and rise to show us the way to heaven.

"Soon I must leave you. I must go south to bring the word of God to the rest of the Irish. Father Segetuis will stay to minister to you. Before I go, I want to tell you about the most wonderful sermon Our Lord Jesus ever preached. Some of you, 'tis true, have already heard it when we had lessons each morning. These will continue on the field below the church, my dear friends; as long as I remain among you, I will teach them. Then Father Segetuis.

"Even so did Jesus teach our forefathers on the sunny mountains of the south. He spoke simply for us, the lowly ones, the millers and weavers and tillers of the soil and the shepherds, as well as for the learned. He called us the salt of the earth and said 'twas such as we who would spread His kingdom. He opened His mouth and taught them, saying:

" 'Blessed are the poor in spirit, for theirs is the kingdom of heaven.

Blessed are the meek, for they shall possess the earth.

Blessed are they who mourn, for they shall be comforted.

Blessed are they who hunger and thirst for justice, for they shall be satisfied.

Blessed are the merciful, for they shall obtain mercy.

Blessed are the clean of heart, for they shall see God.

Blessed are the peacemakers, for they shall be called the children of God.

Blessed are they who suffer persecution for justice' sake, for theirs is the kingdom of heaven.

Blessed are you when men reproach you, and persecute you, and, speaking falsely, say all manner of evil against you, for my sake. Rejoice and exult, because your reward is great in heaven; for so did they persecute the prophets who were before you.'

"Nor are we to seek vengeance against those who wrong us," Patrick continued. He grinned suddenly. "You know how dearly do I love the tales of Ireland's ancient ones. Do you remember the story of Queen Maeve stealing Connaught's brown bull? She started a war that lasted for years as each side tried to get even. All because of one woman's greed and pride. We must not so do.

"And 'tis loving our enemies we must do. Jesus said that *anyone* can love his friends; we know that even the druids do that. But it takes a Christian—a godly man—to love those who hurt him, who wrong him, who maledict against him. We must be perfect as our heavenly father is perfect."

Keagh sniffed at that. Patrick, who seemed to see everything, smiled slightly, his blue eyes twinkling.

"Dearly does God love the man who does His will and greatly does He bless that man with His grace to help him. He tells us ask Him for anything good and He will give it. He will withhold no good thing from those who serve Him."

Marda clasped Keagh's hand tightly. Timidly, in her heart, she began forming words of supplication to this kind God. She would have to ask Patrick to speak to God for her. For surely, there must be some magical words he used to get such a powerful God's attention.

He spoke a bit more to them of God's loving kindness and care of the people He had created. Then he turned back to the altar and began doing something, most reverently, with the utensils he had brought with him.

At last he came forward to the people with a chalice and a loaf of bread. They arose from their places reverently and went to kneel before him. He handed the loaf to the first in line, an elderly, somewhat stout woman, who broke off a tiny bit and passed the loaf to the next in line. Dipping the bread in the chalice Patrick held, she consumed it, then sketched an awkward sign, roughly the shape of a cross, on her head and body and stood up to return to her place. Marda thought her face seemed strangely transfigured. She remembered Colmagh saying Patrick changed bread and wine into the body and blood of Jesus. She stared at the chalice and loaf in awe. Truly, it looked like ordinary bread to her.

She and Keagh, Breeca and Colmagh, remained seated as the others filed forward to receive the bread and wine. Marda looked at Keagh. He smiled at her and leaned over her to whisper, "I have no quarrel with the philosophy of this god of Patrick's but what nonsense. A man rising after days in the tomb!" He shook his head incredulously.

Marda was not so sure. Of course, no one of them living now had seen this thing happen but Colmagh said that many of those who'd served the lord Jesus swore that it had. And they'd spent all their lives thereafter telling others. Even though they were put to death they would not recant their stories of Christ dying, being buried and rising again. They'd seen Him ascending into heaven. No man would continue to swear to a lie even though he could save his life by telling the truth, she thought. Only for the truth would men be willing to go to their own deaths.

And only because they had real evidence that it would not be the end!

When all the people had received the bread, Patrick consumed the rest of it, including the dregs remaining in the chalice. Very carefully he cleansed the vessels that had held the food, covered them with the linen cloth, his thin hands squaring the corners precisely, and left them on the altar. He turned to face the congregation again, blessing them and dismissing them. Reverently they got up and filed out.

Gulda stopped, motioning them to wait with her for Patrick. When he came out, she introduced him to Marda, Keagh and Breeca and invited him to return home with them for dinner. Patrick accepted at once.

"For I know that you have many questions, my son," he said to Keagh later as they finished a plate of small honey tarts Gulda had brought at the end of her excellent meal.

"Aye, Patrick, I have questions. But there are no answers save in the pretty tales you told. Insubstantial and unprovable as any threatening saga told by Lucat-mael!"

"Lucat-mael?"

"Ardri Laeghaire's head druid," Keagh said dryly. "He has bullied our king into giving Marda to him in marriage although he cannot claim her until Samain for 'tis geis—forbidden among us to thwart a dying man's wishes, and that she remain unwed until she is seventeen was her father's last wish."

Patrick's gentle mien grew stern. "I know about druids," he said ironically. "How they have enslaved the Irish!"

Keagh looked at him with grudging respect.

"In that we agree," he commented.

Patrick contented himself with a smile. Tadgh, Gulda's littlest son, came to lean against his side and Patrick took the child upon his knee. He popped a bit of honey tart into the child's mouth and Tadgh chuckled, showing a dozen dimples in his rosy cheeks.

"You are all of the ardri's household, then?" Patrick asked, patting Tadgh as he slid down from his lap and headed out the door.

"Not I!" cried Breeca. "Once I served kings. No more. Never will I serve any man again."

"Then perhaps you will serve God, good Breeca," Patrick said mildly.

"I will serve him if his return is more gracious than what I have hitherto known," she said bitterly. "What magic powers does he grant to those who serve him? Colmagh says you have the power to turn ordinary bread and wine into the body and blood of this

Jesus. Now, dearly would I love having the power to change Lucat-mael's flesh into food, though 'twould be fit food only for battle ravens."

"There is no magic, old one, but only God's loving kindness to His people. The food value of the bread and wine is small indeed when applied to the body. But it feeds the spirit. It strengthens each of us to endure the vicissitudes of life."

"Then your god doesn't promise a better life for those who follow him," Keagh said slowly.

"You are right, Keagh," Patrick replied. "Often, indeed, He has only torture and pain and finally death to offer His followers. Yet, when this earthly course is run, He promises eternal joy and peace in His presence in heaven!"

"A poor exchange, say I!" Keagh leaned back on his elbows. "Our ancient Irish gods offered eternal life in I-Brasil, the blessed isle. And they did not demand a life of suffering to secure it. Only that we sacrifice to them."

Patrick stared at him thoughtfully.

"And you are thinking that what my God promises is more reasonable, that men should earn their bliss by good works," Patrick said evenly.

Keagh flushed. "Does your god give you power to read men's hearts, then?" he challenged.

"I hope so. For, else, why was I called back here to Ireland? My children from the wood of Focluth called me back as if Ireland were the land of my birth. I could not ignore the call. I could not." He lifted shaking hands to his forehead as if, even then, he could hear it. "I tell you, Keagh, that God has willed me to return to Ireland to bring His holy word to the Gael. Someday this fair isle will be the citadel that guards His faith. Since the time of Christ, men have come to Ireland with His message but their words were like seed that fell on barren ground. Here and there have I found a Christian, a faithful one. But I feel His power within me. I know that He walks with me and talks through me. All hearts hear His words, now, and turn in peace and love to serve Him. I say to you that the time of enchanters and murderers and idolators is ending in Ireland. This will be a blessed land. All men will turn to the one, true God and creator of all things!"

"And will people be allowed to live as they chose? To marry

with the one they love in this paradise?" Keagh asked ironically, reaching for Marda's hand. "For, certainly, now they can't. I do not wish to be contentious, Patrick, but I believe only what I can see. What you offer seems to me little better than what we've always had. I believe in myself. In my skill to heal. I can't heal every illness, that is true. But it is in man's nature, after all, to die in time. Most of the misery in Ireland is caused because people rely on unseen beings instead of themselves. I will grant you that this one of yours seems intent on justice and good for the people. And because of that—because you seem not to prey on their miseries and fears—I respect you."

Patrick grinned. "You are not shy in proclaiming your own arrogance, boy. But then, you are a flaith—a druid, too."

"My druidism has nothing to do with it," Keagh snapped. "You know as well as I that the only schools in Ireland are druidical. In order to learn medicine, I had to be a druid. But I learned early that much of what passes for magic is only trickery. Before we left Tara, Lucat-mael astounded the ignorant with his 'magic mist'—forest spores concealed in tubes hidden in his sleeves, I'd guess!"

"If you think their magic is *all* trickery, you are a fool, Keagh," Patrick replied. He frowned and brushed absently at his dark robe. "There is evil in the world as surely as there is good. Long, long ago God banished one of His own angels from heaven for presuming to power he didn't deserve. This dark angel, Lucifer, has much power that he once received from God, though it is not equal to God's. Yet he does much evil with it and many, including some druids, follow him for the power he gives. Lucifer destroys souls, leading them to everlasting suffering and darkness."

"Then this great god you champion must be no more powerful than the evil one he banished. Else he would have destroyed him! Patrick, Patrick, little difference do I see between you and the druids."

Marda gasped and touched Keagh's arm, breaking her silence.

"No, Keagh, you should not speak so to him. Truly, a great difference there is, for Patrick's god is good. Were he to destroy his enemies, then all the things Jesus said would be a lie!"

Patrick looked at her approvingly. "You understand, little one," he said softly.

Keagh looked contrite and grasped Marda's arms, turning her to face him.

"I'm sorry, my heart, he is a good, harmless old man. I have no cause to offend him. Or you. But we waste time, Marda. No miracles will he perform to free you from the druid. We must leave Ireland; there is no other choice."

"I don't know, Keagh," she said hesitantly. "I have listened to all you have said to him. But I—I don't think you're right. You classify him as a teller of falsehoods, like the druids. Or, at best, a befuddled old man . . ." She looked apologetically toward the little priest who was watching her intently, a slight smile on his lips. "I tell you, Keagh, I have felt something—such a yearning—as I listened to him talk. He doesn't talk of his god's power but of his love. He urges a life of service, of kindness and justice to all. . . . Don't you see? 'Tis what you have ever believed!"

Keagh took her hands in his. "What would you have me do, beloved? I cannot believe in his god—"

Just then someone kicked furiously at the outer door and it flew inward, revealing a tall, gaunt man, his face ravaged, with little Tadgh's body in his arms. The child's head lolled backward over the sinewy arm as if it were a daisy broken from the stem but yet hanging there. Water kelp hung from his wet blond hair and his skin was nearly as blue as the sky at Brom Trogan. Both his body and the tall man who held him were dripping puddles on the floor.

Gulda took one look and screamed. Luigh, too, his boy's voice cracking as he flew toward his little brother.

"I found him in the millrace, Gulda," the man said. "But I had heard the splash many, many minutes before and thought it was one of the older lads who swim there. Forgive me for not investigating immediately."

Keagh sprang up and pulled the child from the miller's arms, pushing Gulda and Luigh roughly aside.

" 'Tis no use, I know it's no use," he cried as he turned the limp little body onto its stomach across his knee and tried to pump water from the lungs. Marda's own eyes were swimming with tears and she flew to Gulda's side, taking the poor mother into her arms. She looked back at the boy over Gulda's shaking shoulder. He was quite blue and dead; his lips and fingernails were like beeswax.

"How long in the water, man?" Keagh demanded, not ceasing his pummeling of the tiny body. The precious, lively face was stilled.

"Twenty, thirty minutes—at the least."

Keagh stopped sorrowfully. Tenderly he turned the boy around, laid him gently on one of the benches, and folded the tiny hands across the chest.

"Once I saved a child who'd been in the water one fourth of that time," he said sadly. "I lived to wish I had not, for the poor child was witless and paralyzed for the rest of his days which were not many. Yet, his poor family suffered. Never has one been known to live who was submerged so long. Gulda, bring me your polished brass mirror."

Gulda left Marda's arms and obeyed Keagh. He held the brass disc to the boy's lips and nose but no sign of breath disturbed the shiny surface. Keagh drew Gulda's cloak from its peg on the wall and started to cover the tiny body with it. Gulda sobbed heart-brokenly while poor Luigh beat impotently at the wall. Colmagh wept unashamedly.

Patrick sank to the floor, his eyes upraised in prayer. Then, very slowly, he crossed the room and drew the cloak away from Tadgh's face.

"Be of good cheer, Gulda," he said gently, "your son will rise by the power of God." He took the tiny hands in both of his. "Tadgh, hear me," he began.

"No—you will not torment this poor mother, Patrick!" Keagh shouted, seizing Patrick's arm as if to pull him away from the dead child. Patrick flicked his arm backward negligently, as if swatting at an insect, and Keagh went flying against the wall, the breath knocked out of him. Marda's mouth flew open in disbelief as she ran to his aid. Who would have thought the old man so powerful? She was bitterly disappointed that he was insisting the child would rise from his wet deathbed; anyone could see that he was dead, cold, going rigid. Keagh gasped, unable to draw himself up from his position on the floor.

"Tadgh-een! Attend my words," Patrick called loudly. He held the little hands tightly, his eyes lifted. "Almighty Father, by the power You have promised those who love you through Your son, I humbly beg you to return this child to us, living and whole, that Your servants may believe that You are the resurrection and the life. For Your glory, then, I command—

"Tadgh-een, arise and go to your mother!"

Keagh had partially recovered himself. He lunged forward, Marda holding him, helping him. "By my strength, old man, you are cruel," he cried.

But Marda's eyes were on the child's body. The little face was changing. Like the rosiness of the dawn, pink color was flowing back into it, chasing the gray-blue before it. The pale lips assumed delicate color, like apple-blossom petals, and, incredibly, they curved upward in a smile.

"Look, Keagh," she screamed. She felt his indrawn breath against her hand. His eyes followed hers. A light seemed to glow around Tadgh's body. He stirred, yawned, opened his eyes and smiled, looking around the room until his eyes found his mother. He rolled off the bench, hit the floor running, and threw himself into her arms.

"Tadgh-een, Tadgh-een, my baby," Gulda cried, hugging him in an ecstasy. Her face seemed as bright as the light that had been around Tadgh.

Marda's heart was pounding so furiously that she felt as if it would leap right out of her chest. The child had been dead, she would have sworn it. He was flushed and happy, holding his mother's face between his two little hands, kissing her lips.

"Mother, I saw Our Lord Jesus and a bonny man with him, too," he cried happily. "Black and curling as the hair of a spring lamb was the hair of him, and his eyes like those flowers I like that you call forget-me-nots. He said to tell my mother that he loved her still and waited for her. He said he was your Cucuillin. . . ."

Gulda's face drained white. She sank to the bench, Tadgh still on her lap. She raised shaking hands to her lips.

"Father Patrick, he's just described his father who was dead before he was born. And—and always, in our private times—I called him my Cucuillin for he reminded me of the brave, ancient king. . . . Father Patrick, no one ever, ever, ever knew that; 'twas private!"

Tadgh patted her cheek comfortingly, nodding. "Jesus said,

'You must return, Tadgh, that Patrick may convert the Irish.' "
He laid his head against her breast; she was drenched, now, from
his sodden clothing. "Happy I am to be back, Mother," he added.
"Yet, oh, I wanted to stay with Jesus, too!"

They all stared at him. His little face was radiant and no one
could deny that he spoke the truth. Slowly, one by one, they sank
to their knees. Old Breeca was sobbing in great, tearing gasps
that shook her aged body with emotion. Marda bowed her head
as tears ran down her cheeks.

Keagh was the last to fall to his knees. Shudderingly, a great
sigh escaped him.

"I did not see your Jesus rise, oh Patrick," he said hoarsely.
"But I am a physician and I know this boy was dead. By the
power of your god, you have brought him back."

He lowered his head to the old man's hands in a gesture of
submission and humility.

"I believe, Patrick," he whispered.

CHAPTER 4

Although Patrick had been healing the sick in the name of God and had even restored sight to a blind man before Marda and Keagh's arrival, his restoring Tadgh to life brought the druids of Dichu's court to humble acceptance of the gospel Patrick taught. The miller, like those from Tara and Gulda's family, knew the child had been truly dead and, at Patrick's word, had lived. He was known as a truthful man who'd hitherto refused to have anything to do with Patrick and the new religion.

Marda's joy was boundless.

She had been drawn to Patrick's words almost instinctively, feeling in her heart that his god was truly He who'd created the world and all in it, and that He'd sent Jesus to show His people the way He wanted them to live. But, like Keagh, she'd had reservations. Perhaps it was Patrick himself who'd formed a sensible philosophy of life out of his own kindness and "invented" a god so that he himself might grow powerful.

If Lucat-mael had such power, she knew he'd have used it to enslave the ardri's people, whereas Patrick declared that he himself was powerless. Any wonders he performed were only by the grace of God.

Keagh had examined Tadgh as soon as his mother had rubbed him dry and dressed him in warm clothing. Marda watched his expression grow ever happier and wondering as he questioned the child about his experience and drew more detail of the appearance of his father. Of Jesus he was less detailed in his description, speaking of his kind smile and that he seemed to shine. Gulda cried softly as the boy talked, declaring that she had never spoken of the things Tadgh told her. But Keagh said he'd not have needed such testimony from the child to believe he'd been brought back from death; he knew a dead child when he saw one.

And Breeca and Colmagh nodded vigorously, the old man hugging Tadgh warmly.

"Oh, Patrick, in all my life I never dreamed I could know such a wonder," Keagh said humbly. "As a physician, I know that death is not always the horror men think; sometimes it comes as a friend. Yet, truly, do all men fear their own end. With my own eyes, I have witnessed one returning from that unknown place and speaking only of great joy to be had there. What, then, have men to fear?"

Patrick nodded, smiling. "You are like Jesus's disciple Thomas, my friend, who would not believe until he had put his hand in the wound in our Lord's side. But greater is the testimony of an unbeliever who has become convinced than of a score of believers."

"That is true, Patrick," Colmagh remarked thoughtfully. "And well is it known at Tara that Keagh is no man to believe in anything he sees not with his own eyes. Therefore even the ardri would believe him if he told of Tadgh's resurrection."

"Oh, but he dare not return," Breeca cried. "Laeghaire would surely imprison him and force Marda to marry Lucat-mael."

Keagh turned to face Marda.

"Would you risk that, my Marda?" he asked gently. "You could stay here so you'd be in no danger, but if Laeghaire didn't believe me, well might I be imprisoned or even killed."

Marda clung to his hand and her eyes met his, clinging fiercely.

"Keagh, you will not return without me," she said quietly. "But, with all my heart, I believe God wants us to be together and no harm will befall us. We have seen His power. If He can deliver a child from the grave, He can protect us from harm."

Patrick seemed to consider that. He cleared his throat, frowning a little.

"From what you tell me of Lucat-mael, he is a powerful enemy. And he has much influence with the king. 'Tis true, my child, that God protects us from all mortal harm do we but believe in Him, but He is not some powerful druid who smites His enemies or always lets His people triumph. Indeed, in the beginning of the church when He was just risen from the dead, many Christians were put to death. I think you and Keagh would be powerful voices for God, and no doubt He has chosen you for just such a task. But I want you to know there is danger. If you chose to return to Tara, it must be with a clear understanding of the danger."

Keagh and Marda looked at each other for a long time.

"You spoke just now of the joy you feel in knowing death is not the end, Keagh," Marda said at last. "I feel it, too. All of my life I have believed in goodness and kindness and love, instead of power and hatred of those who are different. And now Patrick comes to tell us that this is God's will, and he proves it to us by restoring Tadgh. Oh, Keagh, I want to marry you. To love you all my life and grow old with you. But it is more important that we tell the people at Tara—Laeghaire and Angas, my dear foster parents, and all the others what we have witnessed that they may come to God, too, than that we should have all our own dreams of marriage come true."

Keagh smiled and drew her into his arms. There were bright tears in his eyes that he dashed away, but without shame.

"Even so did I know you would speak," he said softly. "When will we start?"

"Bide with me awhile," Patrick said, "for there is much more I would tell you. I will baptize you next Sunday with the other catechumens who are ready. And then, Tuesday after, I too will accompany you, for I always intended going to Tara when God gave me a sign that the time was right." He paused. "*You* are my sign. And next week is Holy Week when we commemorate Jesus's last passion suffering on the cross, dying and rising. We will go to Tara for Easter, which is two weeks from today."

"But that is Beltane!" Breeca cried, blanching. "The day of the spring fires to the god Bel. There is much ceremony and worship of the god . . ."

"So it is," Patrick said thoughtfully. "I remember from my days of captivity the custom of the ardri's druids lighting the Beltane fire at his order. All fires have been previously put out so that the kingdom is dark. When the ardri's fire is lighted, men bear torches to runners waiting all over Ireland so that, shortly, all fires are relighted from the one great Beltane fire at Tara. And then the wicked and licentious Beltane rites begin with folk coupling in the fields and woods and sacrifice to the god, Bel. Oh, indeed, God has ordained that I should go to Tara just at this time. God's blessed Easter fire will replace the evil one's fire henceforth!"

"If you fear not the god Bel, surely you'll have a healthy fear of Laeghaire and his druid," Breeca said cynically. "For, good Patrick, I know them both and I doubt you will ever convert them."

"If God wills it, I will convert them," Patrick said firmly. "But I fear them not."

Indeed, it seemed he feared nothing.

Each morning Colmagh, Breeca, Keagh and Marda joined the class of catechumens on the heather-strewn field by the church. Marda and Keagh would sit side by side, hands enclasped, listening with steadily increasing joy to Patrick's accounts of God and the earthly life of His son. They came to know the villagers and Patrick's household.

He'd brought many a priest with him to Ireland—Auxilius, Iserninus and Segetius in whose care he'd leave the church at Strangford Lough. Already he'd ordained a native priest, Sinell. There were others—priests and those studying for the priesthood; Comlach, who was a leper Patrick had healed, Athcen, his cook, Mescan, his brewer, Odran, his charioteer, and a great, redheaded bear of a man, MacCarthen, who was Patrick's self-appointed champion. He actually insisted on carrying the old man across streams so he would not wet his feet and risk illness, despite Patrick's vehement protests. Most of them usually spent the lesson mornings in the meadow, too.

They were all gathered there the Friday morning Lucat-mael and ten of his pupils appeared at the edge of the wood.

"It is the druid who wants to make Marda his wife, Father Patrick," Keagh said grimly as the party of men advanced toward the group in the meadow.

Patrick nodded, watching the progress of the eleven. "I've been expecting him," he remarked matter-of-factly. "Little is there in Ireland that he does not know within days."

"He has come to drag me back to Tara," Marda said steadily.

"That he will never do," Keagh cried, putting his arm around her shoulders. "When you go, it will be with me."

"And with me," Patrick added. "Let us hear what this Lucat-mael has to say."

They watched in silence until the druid had covered the remaining distance and stopped before them, folding his arms across his chest.

"By the great cauldron of Dagda, you are here. With Adzehead. Just as I saw in my vision these twelve days gone," he cried.

"Vision!" Keagh said contemptuously. "Your spies were fleet, Lucat-mael."

Lucat-mael turned and glowered at Keagh. His eyes sought Marda's and penetrated. She thought they were like those of the serpent pictured in Patrick's Bible. They were close-set and malevolent. She lifted her chin proudly and met his gaze, willing herself not to show the fear he aroused in her despite all her resolutions against being afraid.

"Why have you followed us?" she challenged him.

"To return you to Tara."

"I will return to Tara as I left it; with Keagh. And, now, with Patrick."

"You will return *now*." As if unable to contain his frustration, he reached out and seized her wrist, pulling her roughly toward him.

Keagh leapt forward and slapped angrily at the druid's hand.

"Always, I am ordering you to take your hands off her," he spat. He pulled Marda away from the druid and pushed her behind himself.

Lucat-mael's followers and pupils, strong young men all, moved forward menacingly. Marda, holding fast to Keagh's upper arms, felt his muscles tense but he stood his ground.

In an instant MacCarthen and Odran, who was nearly as tall as the big champion and considerably stouter, came to flank Keagh. Others in the group stood up as if to lend their support.

"Come, come, my dear ones, we will be fighting soon," Patrick said conciliatingly. "Our Lord commands us to peace! I am Patrick, sent here by Celestine, the Vicar of Rome. Welcome to Strangford Lough, Lucat-mael. You may tell the ardri that we will be at Tara within the week. . . ."

"I am not your messenger, priest!" Lucat-mael snarled. "You are not wanted in Ireland. Return across the seas from whence you came."

The congregation began rising, buzzing angrily, moving toward the druid menacingly.

"Speak for yourself," MacCarthen growled. "We love Father Patrick. *You* go beyond the seas, bald druid."

Patrick shook his head reprovingly.

"Nay, good MacCarthen, I have come to bring God's love to all —druid, flaith, and all the people of Ireland in every tuath. . . ."

"You prating Christian eunuch! We want none of your God at Tara."

MacCarthen muttered menacingly and moved forward. He grasped Lucat-mael's shoulders and shoved him backward, sending him sprawling on the grass.

"Nay, nay, 'tis not our Lord's way to smite those who offend us," Patrick said mildly, running forward to assist the fallen druid.

Lucat-mael shook him off angrily, standing up and smoothing his robe. His followers pressed forward, their low voices like the first rumbles of thunder on a summer day.

MacCarthen looked at Patrick beseechingly. "Surely, Father Patrick, even almighty God cannot stomach the gall of him! Were He here Himself, surely He would smite the godless cur for villifying you. I but do His will in the matter."

"He but called me a Christian eunuch and so I am for the love of God," Patrick said, smiling.

Lucat-mael smiled evilly. "Perhaps you are not a eunuch. Perhaps I should have brought you a diseased ewe since you have forsworn women," he taunted.

MacCarthen roared and launched himself at the druid. But Patrick, more nimble than he appeared, thrust out his arm and held MacCarthen in check.

"Don't mind him, dear friend. His maledictions and insults are but the product of his anger and they hurt me not," he soothed. "Remember that Jesus bids us be meek and mild as He Himself is. To pray for those who maledict us—"

"By the wind, and earth, and fire and water, did he so?" Lucat-mael interrupted. "Then I should send the ewe to him, for he is no man but a cringing milksop!"

Patrick's conciliating smile disappeared as if it had never been there. His blue eyes blazed like a bonfire when straw is thrown on it. He snatched up his crosier which was never far from his side and, roaring like a warrior going into battle, charged the druid.

"You may insult me, ridicule me, maledict me. You may even kill me before it's all done! But by the bloody crown of Christ, you'll speak no ill of my Lord," he cried, knocking Lucat-mael to the ground.

Lucat-mael, taken by surprise, stared up at the little priest. His pupils belatedly pulled their master out of his reach, sitting him up against a big rock in the field.

"When you have rested, let us leave this place of madmen, master," one of them said fearfully.

At last Lucat-mael struggled to his feet. He shook his fist at Patrick.

"I will tell the Ardri Laeghaire to assemble the hosts against you," he cried furiously. "We will drive you and all your crazy followers from Ireland, depend upon it."

Without another word, he whipped around and led his men back to the forest.

"He is not a coward, that must be conceded," Keagh remarked as he turned and drew Marda into his arms. "We are at least three to his one, yet he tried to take her."

Marda tried to control her trembling. Despite her eagerness to go to Tara, to help bring Laeghaire and his court to God, she felt a powerful fear as she watched the druid's retreating back.

Beside her, Patrick sighed.

"I must learn to control my temper," he said ruefully, "but by my God of doom, he angered me! A wonder it is that God has chosen a flawed vessel like me for this work. I have come to Ireland to bring the joyous news of Christ to Ardri Laeghaire and all the Gael and sorry will be the impression he gets of me from Lucat-mael."

"We will explain to Laeghaire how he baited you and insulted the good and gracious God, Father Patrick," Marda said comfortingly. "The ardri will understand why you defended God; shameful would it be if you had let Lucat-mael continue to revile Him."

"And when I have told him how you brought Tadgh back from the realm of death—" Keagh began but Patrick interrupted him, shaking his head.

"*God* sent him back, Keagh, never forget that. I have no power except what God graciously grants me." He brightened a little.

"Nevertheless, when you tell him how God returned the little one to us, surely he will welcome me for God's sake."

Keagh nodded confidently. "Well does Laeghaire know that I am not a weak branch, blowing in the wind. If I tell him something is so, he will know it is for never have I knowingly told an untruth."

Patrick smiled and clapped the young physician on the back. "Aye, my son, there is nothing to feel anxious about. Ever have the Irish listened to my words and believed."

"Miliucc did not," Odran said gloomily.

Marda glanced at Odran, frowning.

"Miliucc had not Keagh to tell him of the wonders God can do," she said quietly. "Father Patrick is right, there is nothing to feel anxious about."

Nevertheless, in the following days as they made their confessions and were baptized, she began to feel a certain anxiety about returning to Tara.

When she and Keagh were alone, they discussed it.

"If we were married, Marda, even Lucat-mael would have trouble separating us," he said thoughtfully. "Why don't we ask Father Patrick to marry us before we go to Tara?"

She shook her head sorrowfully.

"Don't you see, Keagh? We cannot do that. We must not defy his authority over us if we have any hope of being able to influence him. Besides, Patrick has taught us that God commands we honor our parents. I could not deliberately disobey my father's wishes for me, or anything I should say about God's laws would be suspect." She gazed at the cross atop Patrick's little church. "Laeghaire is no fool, Keagh. He will understand that we could have escaped had we desired. He appreciates courage and honor. I don't know why I should feel so apprehensive about it, for surely God will protect us in every way."

"Aye, my darling, I'm sure He will," Keagh said comfortingly. " 'Tis only our inexperience as Christians that causes uncertainty. All will surely be well for us. For all our lives."

And as he embraced her, she gave herself up to the sweet, soaring joy she felt in his arms. With Keagh to love her and God to protect her, Lucat-mael could have no power over her.

They sailed to the mouth of the Boyne water in three large curraghs, for many of Patrick's household accompanied them. Odran had gone with some of the others toward Tara with Patrick's chariot, insisting it was only meet for the representative of the Holy Father in Rome to enter Tara with dignity. He was to meet the others at the home of Sesgne, a minor chief who had already met Patrick in the north and offered him hospitality on his way to Tara.

Patrick preached the gospel of Jesus to Sesgne's people and agreed to leave one of the younger priests with them so that they could learn more. He promised to come back and himself baptize anyone who desired it.

Sesgne had a five-year-old son named Benen who reminded Marda very much of Tadgh. He had the same myriad dimples when he smiled and his eyes were of an even deeper blue than little Tadgh's. Benen promptly attached himself to Patrick, and even when the old priest went into Sesgne's garden for a short rest before their departure for Tara, Benen was at his side. When Odran arrived with the chariot and MacCarthen went to the garden to summon Patrick, he found the little boy carefully strewing the old man's recumbent form with flowers, his tiny hands as gentle and silent as the kiss of a butterfly.

Patrick, hearing MacCarthen's footsteps on the paved path, sat up, sending flowers flying. He rubbed his eyes, laughing.

"Have I died and gone to paradise, then?" he asked whimsically.

Benen smiled shyly.

"I thought you could smell them in your sleep, Father Patrick, and be happy," he said. "The flowers are to thank you for telling us about Jesus. Did he really say, 'Suffer the little children to come to me'?"

Patrick leaned over and hugged the child. "Indeed he did, Benen. Jesus loved children. If you will go to the classes for the catechumens each morning, I'll baptize you, too, when I return so that you may be even closer to Jesus."

"You are going away?"

"Aye, child, we are all ready to start for Tara to tell the ardri, too, about Jesus."

Patrick got up and started toward the courtyard where the

chariot waited, but Benen clamped his little arms and legs around the old man's knees, nearly upsetting him. Marda ran to steady Patrick, and then leaned over to soothe the little boy. But Benen was almost sobbing.

"Take me with you, Father Patrick," he cried. He looked around wildly, catching sight of his parents who'd come into the garden for farewells with the rest of the household. They were a handsome couple, Marda thought, both tall and fair with the same blue, almost black eyes of their little son. Benen's mother looked deeply hurt by the child's outburst. She came forward and knelt beside him.

"You'd leave Mother, my son?" she said softly.

Benen turned to her, keeping one small hand tightly entwined in Patrick's robe. He put the other around her neck and laid his little cheek against hers.

"Don't feel sad, Mother," he said solemnly. "None the less do I love you, but I—I just know I must go with Patrick. I *know* it, Mother. It is as if Jesus said to me that I should go with him and learn to be a priest, too."

"But you haven't even reached the age of fosterage," she cried, stroking the fair hair. "When you are seven, if Father Patrick agrees . . ."

"I am past five, Mother, and you yourself told your maid that I am five, going on twenty-five; I heard you say it. I am ready to be fostered now, Mother. Please, please let me go with him. For I feel that if I cannot learn from him about Almighty God and His Son, I'll die. I tell you, 'tis the will of God."

The woman looked at her husband dazedly. He came forward and took her hand, laying his other on Benen's head. Silently they gazed at the boy, then looked up to meet Patrick's gentle eyes.

"You have not yet made any fosterage arrangements for the lad?" he asked.

They shook their heads.

"He is bright for his age," Sesgne said at last. "Would you consider having him as foster son, Father Patrick?"

"He's a foster son any man would be proud of," the old priest said warmly. "And I understand the great honor you do me to offer him to me in fosterage. If his mother agrees, I will be happy to have him."

"There is none I'd consider more worthy," Benen's mother said faintly, "yet, I'd thought to have him for almost two years yet. He is but a little lad; often he still creeps into my room for a last hug and kiss at night . . ."

Patrick smiled gently, shifting his gaze to Marda.

"If a woman's tenderness be still needed, Marda will supply it for the time we're biding at Tara, good daughter," he said reassuringly.

Benen was watching the interchange carefully. Smiling, he released his hold on Patrick's robe and pulled on Marda's that she would kneel down as his mother had done. Slowly she did so and the little boy seized her around the neck, pulling her close and smacking a kiss on her cheek. She was almost nose to nose with his mother.

They started laughing together.

"A cheeky lad," said Sesgne. He reached down and gently disengaged Benen's arm from his mother's neck and pulled her to her feet where he enfolded her in a tender embrace, leaving Marda in Benen's.

"Well, wife, what do you say? We have accepted Patrick's God and, it seems, already He has asked us to make sacrifice to Him by calling our son."

The woman smiled, a little sadly, but she nodded and touched her son's blooming cheek with her fingertips as if in farewell. Benen released Marda, his face splitting in a wide grin.

"God will bless you, Mother and Father," he cried. "There will be another son soon to take my place. No later than midwinter."

His mother gasped and put her hands to her lips. "It is so. I had told none, yet. Not even your father," she cried.

"How did you know that, son?" Sesgne asked, his own face showing his joy as he held his wife.

Benen shrugged. "I just knew. When Mother touched me, I knew."

"Ri Sesgne, God has indeed chosen your son," Patrick said solemnly. "I am honored to be his foster father."

Sesgne shook his head wonderingly.

"*I* am honored, oh Patrick," he replied. "I grow weary of the old ways. The killing and constant strife between chiefs and families. Glad I am to listen to the counsel of your God who urges us to peace and love. He has taken my first son and he shall be a sign of Ireland's conversion. Yet, he has graciously given me another son to follow in my footsteps as ri of our clan. And never will my people leave His service. We will delay your departure only long enough to prepare Benen's clothing that he may accompany you. Come, my son, bid your mother farewell properly."

They camped that night at a hilltop site overlooking Tara far off down the valley. The River Boyne lay behind them and the little settlement called Slane lay in front of them. Here, the ancient warriors of Ri Fiacc who'd fallen in battle had been honorably interred and the site was still a place to be revered.

Patrick, Benen at his side, surveyed Tara shimmering in the late afternoon sun as Keagh and Marda helped prepare a bough bed for him before turning to their own beds. He seemed greatly tired by the short chariot ride, yet as he gazed down at Tara, his lips moving in prayer, strength seemed to flow back into him.

Their meal that night was only a few cresses and a small loaf each for it was Good Friday, the day Jesus's death on the cross was commemorated.

"This is propitious," Patrick said, smiling, as they finished their meager meal. "Here, tomorrow night, I will light the first Paschal fire in Ireland."

Breeca shook her head, muttering.

"You are troubled, good Breeca?" the old man asked politely.

"Aye, Father, for tomorrow is Beltane eve. It is geis, forbidden, for any but the high king's druid to light the Beltane fire. Lucat-mael will consider it a great insult that you should light a fire on Beltane eve."

"Yet God bids me light it," Patrick said stubbornly. "I have put myself in peril before by obeying the inner urges He has sent me. There is not a subtle way of bringing His word to Ardri Laeghaire; I must show him that God's way, not the druids', will henceforth be the law in Ireland."

Marda listened quietly. She couldn't help but feel some of Breeca's trepidation, but to her surprise Keagh spoke up, agreeing with Patrick.

"Aye, Father, you are right. When a man's leg turns gangrenous after a wound, there is only one way to cure him. The leg must be cut off, the stump cauterized. Lucat-mael will howl, that's sure. But there is no more dramatic way to prove to Laeghaire that he is a slave to the druid than for you to light the fire and still live to tell about it. Always the druids have made men fear that Bel would strike them dead or send the Morrigan to feed on their flesh if they anticipated him. What time does he usually light the fire, Marda?"

"Just as the sun goes down," she replied.

Patrick considered for a long moment.

"Then I will light my Paschal fire just before sunset," he said. "We will spend tomorrow gathering brush and wood that my fire will be the biggest and brightest Ireland has ever seen."

"Marda and I will go alone to Tara tomorrow noon, Father Patrick," Keagh said thoughtfully. "We will be there when your light flares up. If you will stand out before it, holding your crosier and the great cross, Laeghaire will see that you have not been struck dead or attacked by demons. And I will tell him of Tadgh's resurrection. He will believe. God willing, Lucat-mael will too, but that I must doubt. He is an evil man."

Patrick nodded. He reached inside his robe and withdrew a small silver crucifix on a slender chain.

"Nevertheless, my son, carry this symbol of our Lord with you," he said.

"I need no symbol, Father Patrick; our Lord abides in each of us," Keagh said solemnly. But he took the crucifix and put it around his neck where it lay just beneath his gold muince, or necklet.

"Come, my children, tomorrow is a day that will change Ireland forever," Patrick said, getting stiffly to his feet. "Let us go to our rest."

Marda helped Benen, who'd fallen asleep with his head against her knee, and he shared her bed of boughs that first night of his fosterage. Keagh lay nearby. She was just falling asleep when she felt him bend over her, his lips moving softly over her cheek. She opened her arms to enfold him and, for a long moment, they clung together, their hearts hammering in unison.

"I had to say good night to you in private," he said against her ear. "Why could you not have been born after Beltane instead of after Samain? The six months I must wait for you will seem more like six years."

She smiled and snuggled against his chest.

"Laeghaire will allow us to marry, won't he, Keagh?" she whispered.

"Aye, Marda. For surely God will grant us strength against Lucat-mael's evil power." He kissed her once again and drew away reluctantly. "Sleep well, little beloved. Tomorrow will be an arduous day."

She heard him lie down on his own bough bed and, shortly, could hear his even breathing so she knew he slumbered. She cuddled Benen close to keep him warm. Only a few weeks ago, none of them had even heard of Patrick. Or God. Yet already their lives had been touched and they all belonged to Him. With all her heart, she prayed to Him that Laeghaire's court would come to Him as surely and joyfully as they who'd already encountered Patrick had.

But Lucat-mael's malevolent face kept intruding.

"We will see you in Tara on Easter morning, Father Patrick," Keagh called jubilantly as the two of them set out shortly after noon the next day.

"Be sure to give my honor and best regards to the ardri," Patrick called after them. "Tell him I will bring him God's blessing."

The morning was warm, threatening rain. Keagh took Marda's hand as they turned onto the fine, wide chariot road called Slige Midluachra which connected Tara to the north country.

" 'Tis easier going than the trip north when we had to avoid the chariot roads," he remarked. His dark eyes smiled warmly at Marda. She gazed up at him, pleased by the way his brown hair curled wetly over his ears, for he'd bathed in the river just before they'd left, donning his newly cleaned druidical clothing he'd worn when they'd left Tara. "Great is my joy that we will have a hand in bringing the one, true God to Tara."

"Aren't you even a little afraid, Keagh?" Marda asked musingly.

He smiled and squeezed her hand. "Nay, not even a little," he said confidently. "I have seen God's power and never will I be afraid again. Lucat-mael is but a trickster, Marda. He will fall like a punctured bladder before God."

Marda stared at the dusty road before them. Their feet made little slip-slapping sounds as they walked and the dust felt silky as it settled on their feet and ankles.

"Patrick warned us that Lucat-mael may have powers from the evil one—the angel God drove from heaven long ago," she said worriedly.

"True. But God *did* drive that fallen angel from heaven. His power cannot be as strong as God's. Don't be afraid, beloved."

She thought about that for a moment.

"You're right, Keagh," she said at last. "If God is for us, who can stand against us?"

He nodded confidently.

"When Laeghaire sees Patrick standing triumphant in front of his Paschal fire unharmed, nothing Lucat-mael can possibly say will do him any good. Laeghaire will thank us with all his heart for helping him to throw off his druid's thrall."

"And we will be free to marry as Christians, Keagh," she said softly.

He stopped and drew her into his arms, kissing her, first gently, then with rising passion. Marda clung to him happily as the sweet, slow, now familiar joy of his touch flowed through her.

"We were meant to be together, Keagh," she breathed happily. "Were ever man and woman so suited to each other?"

He nuzzled her neck dreamily.

"I suppose, from the beginning of time, lovers have always felt that way, Marda. As if they were made for each other."

"Aye. In heaven. By Almighty God we were made. For each other." She smoothed his cheek, savoring the clean skin, freshly shaven.

"I will build us a fine timber house at Tara, Marda, but also a cottage in the hills where we can be alone with our own children from time to time," Keagh said as they drew apart and continued walking toward Tara.

"And will you object to me gardening?" she said pertly, laughing for the pure joy of being alone with him, walking through the sweet April morning. "Or will you tell me solemnly it is beneath a liaig's wife?"

"You know I care nothing for 'seemly behavior,'" he said fondly. "You may grow enough vegetables to feed all of Munster if you choose, beloved. But you must have help. You work too hard. And you will have our babes to occupy you as well."

"A boy, like Benen," she agreed happily. "Another, like Tadgh."

"Aye. And girls, too, fair and generous as their mother."

"We will have a happy life, my Keagh."

"Aye, beloved. Happier even than I'd dreamed before we met Patrick and accepted God. Do you feel it, too, Marda? This . . . oh, a sort of intensification of love, I guess you'd call it, because you are not only my dearest love but beloved of God, too."

"Yes, Keagh. It is a proud and solemn thing to know He purchased us with His own life. I don't know exactly how it can be, but we will live on, together, forever because God so wills."

Her eyes felt misty as she clung to his hand, her joy growing. It was true. She felt an ever deepening love for Keagh, and it was all mixed up with the knowledge of God who'd sent His son to earth and had sent Tadgh back to those who loved him. All the dreams of love and yearning were being satisfied at last. God was a constant contentment to her and she would marry Keagh . . . bear him children. She would have a home of her own. There would be other children, too, those Keagh would take in fosterage. He would teach them the skills of a liaig and she would comfort them because they missed their mothers. Their home would be a haven of love and friendship and hospitality. Patrick would come to them sometimes as would Daneen and Fiacc and Dubhtach and Angas and Laeghaire.

Determinedly she pushed Lucat-mael and the other druids who would support him in opposing Patrick out of her mind.

It was late afternoon when they entered the great hall at Tara. Only a little gilla had been present to admit them; the others were already preparing themselves for the Beltane rites, he explained.

"The lady Angas is keeping to her own grianan in the new house," the lad volunteered. "Her time is too nigh for her to participate."

"Oh, is she well?"

The boy shrugged. "She comes not to the hall, now. The ardri ordered the workmen to hurry with her own quarters that she might be in more comfort when her child is born. Yet, her liaig seems not alarmed."

Keagh frowned. "He should be. The child is not due for more than two months. She's too heavy for such a small woman, her ankles too swollen—" He left off, shaking his head. "We'll deal with that later, though. We must reach the hill of the Beltane fire before Patrick lights his Paschal fire—to explain."

He took Marda's hand and drew her with him.

"You are worried about Angas, then, Keagh?" she said as they hurried toward the hill. Late arrivals were ahead of them on the path to the great banqueting hall before which the fire was traditionally lighted.

"She's going to bear a large child, Marda, that I've known all along. There could be no mistake; the child isn't due until late in the summer, a little after Brom Trogan, August first, yet she's heavier in the womb than many a woman at term."

"Could it be twins?"

"No. I have examined her and the outlines are clearly that of a large child—a single child. Marda, I'll be here with her, don't worry. That old fool Lochru puffs himself up, declaring he's responsible for this fine, strong baby because of the potions he's had her drinking, and that's about all he'll contribute to her safe delivery. She'll be all right, I promise you. Hurry, sweetheart, it's growing late."

The hillside before the hall was crowded with people. Everyone except the sick and very old or very young had come to Beltane. Next to Samain, the first of November, when the sidhs opened and the fairy folk ventured forth into the world of men, it was the most important festival of the year. Men and women worshipped Bel with wild couplings and much eating and drinking of the fermented honey. Marda herself had never attended the celebrations, although she would have been expected to once she'd become adult and married. Her father's request that she stay single until she was seventeen had saved her.

"Look, it's the ardri's liaig and Marda," someone in the crowd said, breaking the expectant silence as everyone stood looking toward the great heap of wood and kindling, waiting for Lucat-mael's spark. The sun hung over the western horizon like a great orange ball. Marda's heart began hammering as if in unison with the quick, nervous breathing of the assembled people. All heads turned to look at them and, almost unconsciously, the people fell back, forming a sort of aisle for their progress toward the ardri and Lucat-mael.

Marda lifted her head slowly and she and Keagh strode in step through the crowd, hurrying now because of the rapidly descending sun.

"Oh, Laeghaire, I bring you blessings from Patrick, representative of the Holy Father in Rome," Keagh said. "He is even now at Slane waiting to light the fire of everlasting life. . . ."

"He would dare light a fire on Beltane eve?" Lucat-mael roared, towering over them.

"Aye, my lord," Keagh said boldly, ignoring the druid. "You will see, any moment now, that Patrick will light the fire. And he will stand before it, holding his crosier, his symbol of office so that you may see for yourself that no harm has befallen him. Always the ardri's druids have told their masters that Bel would strike them dead if anyone lit a fire before the chief druid of the ardri on Beltane eve. You will see for yourself that it isn't so."

Suddenly a woman screamed, and throughout the vast crowd a heavy, ominous muttering began.

"By the Dagda, look yonder," shouted Lochru, the queen's druid liaig. His bony finger pointed to a great rosy light on the hill of Slane. For one confused moment Marda thought the sun itself had decided to jump to the north, but of course it was Patrick's fire. He'd timed it so that it flared up minutes before Lucat-mael would have lighted the fire at Tara. The sun dropped, almost as if hurrying to escape the fire, beneath the western horizon. Marda realized her heart was pounding almost too rapidly to count, and at the same time she'd forgotten to breathe. She drew a long, shuddering breath and looked at Laeghaire.

He stood motionless as a statue, his body touched with fire itself, then falling into dark shadow as the sun left. He was staring intently at the opposite hill. Lucat-mael, his mien furious, threw the tinder and kindling box at the prepared brush impotently.

A figure appeared, silhouetted against the rosy fire. Patrick's form, holding aloft his crosier with one hand, the great processional cross with the other, seemed outlined with glory.

"They must have gathered every bit of dry wood on the mountain," Keagh murmured delightedly.

But Lucat-mael was rending his garments, gnashing his teeth.

"Oh, Laeghaire, unless that fire be put out this night, it will never be extinguished in Ireland until the end of time," he screamed. "By the Dagda, it burns me; it burns me!"

"You see, oh Laeghaire, Patrick is triumphant," Keagh cried. "There is no punishment! The fire of his God is good—beneficial to men. Aye, Lucat-mael speaks true: It will never be put out in Ireland. Nor should it be. For God, the true God that Patrick champions, can give life to men though they be dead. . . ."

"They say this carpenter they call God came back to life after three days in the tomb, oh King," Lucat-mael snarled, "but no one has ever seen—"

Keagh grinned mischievously.

"You seem to know a lot about it, Lucat-mael! Are you prophesying as you did about Adzehead?"

Lucat-mael threw him a murderous look.

"Seek not to throw aspersions on me, boy," he spat. "I was speaking of their claim that their god rose from the dead. This religion is for gullible children!"

"Nay, for I myself have seen Patrick restore a drowned child to life!" Keagh began. But Laeghaire, speaking for the first time, made a sound of disbelief and disgust.

"By the Dagda, Keagh," he shouted. "How dare you come here to disturb our sacred rites! How dare this Patrick light a fire on this night! And you must have had your wits stolen by a wisp to talk of drowned children coming back to life. Even mighty Bel can't do that."

"It is true, my lord," Marda cried passionately. "Oh, you know that never have I lied to you, not even to save myself from chastisement when I was but a little maid. I saw it, too. The child was growing stiff. Keagh, your own liaig, examined the child and pronounced him dead. Yet, Patrick invoked God to restore him and the child jumped up and ran, laughing, to his mother. . . ."

"He has bewitched you both," Laeghaire shouted. "And Bel will surely strike him dead for his blasphemy. Only my druid, at my command, may light the Beltane fire. Since time out of mind, 'tis geis for any other. . . . He will die, I tell you."

The crowd moaned softly, watching the gaunt figure silhouetted against the flames.

"He is not being struck dead, oh Laeghaire," Keagh cried triumphantly. "See? He holds the cross of Christ aloft. Bel, that demon-god, is powerless against the true God. Lucat-mael, explain if you can how it is that this demon you serve hasn't struck Patrick with fire and wind and water!" He didn't even try to keep the irony from his tone.

Despite his bravado, Marda saw a tremor of doubt cross Lucat-mael's sinister face. Laeghaire blanched, hesitated.

"The night is not over! Bel will smite him!" Lucat-mael snarled. "Of more immediate concern is your defiance of Laeghaire, oh liaig! My King, he has ignored your wishes. Insulted you. And me. For he has dragged my promised wife off into the wilderness in the most dishonorable way. Don't you see? They've fled to Adzehead because he is your enemy. They pretend to believe in his god—bring these wild tales of a risen child because they seek to thwart your will that Marda marry me."

Laeghaire's jaw tightened in fury. Marda shook her head vehemently. Always, Lucat-mael preyed on the ardri's pride.

"We would never align ourselves against you, my foster father," she said scornfully. "Nor is Patrick your enemy. He comes to you with the deepest love. Christian love, my lord. To bring you God's word that you and your people may have everlasting life. As for Keagh and myself, why, we were safe away. We could easily have taken ship for Britain or Gaul. We returned freely, as Patrick's emissaries. We are Christians now, my lord. We believe with all our hearts in the God who so loved His people that He gave His son to die for them."

"Perhaps this new god is more powerful than Bel," said a voice from the shadows and Dubhtach Maccu-Lugair stepped forward. Marda saw that Fiacc, as always, stood right at his elbow. The younger druid grinned and winked reassuringly at her. "What the maid says makes sense, my king. If they had wanted, they could have been far away from Ireland by now. And," he added, gesturing toward Patrick who still stood silhouetted against the flames although he'd lowered the cross so that it stood in front of him, just projecting above his cowled head, "Keagh speaks truly. Bel has not stricken him dead. Which can only mean Bel has not the power to do so. On the other hand, if Keagh attests that Patrick brought a dead child back to life in his god's name, then it seems wise to me that you listen to what he has to say of this powerful god."

"No one is more powerful than Bel. For ages past, he has blessed us. This foreign holy man has insulted him on this most sacred night. Send the hosts against him, oh Laeghaire. Destroy him," said Lucat-mael.

"When has the ardri of Ireland ever done such a thing?" Keagh said contemptuously. "Hospitality to the stranger who comes in peace has ever been a sacred duty to the Irish. And Patrick comes in great peace and love, my lord. He will come himself, voluntarily and with great concern for all the Gael, tomorrow morning at sunrise for it is the day Christians commemorate Jesus rising from the dead. It is the greatest feast day of the church. You have no need to raise the host against a gentle old man and his handful of clerics!"

By now the hilltop was nearly dark. The only light came from Patrick's fire. Nearly the entire population of Tara had assembled on the hilltop and they pressed in around the group in front of the ardri. Furiously Lucat-mael knelt and struck at his tinder. After a few false starts, the kindling flared and he lighted a waiting torch, then thrust it into the waiting bonfire. His face stood out, bold and sardonic, in the swift conflagration.

But the Beltane fire seemed anticlimactic and diminished.

Keagh took Marda's hand, grinning. "He must have gathered half the trees on the mountain for that fire," he whispered admiringly.

The druid, hearing, whipped around furiously.

"I have spoken," he said, his voice sinister. "If that fire be not put out this night, it will never be extinguished in Ireland. And by Bel, I will put it out! Patrick comes in the morning? Good, we will meet him. My lord, give me leave to station a large party to ambush them at that curve of the stream, just north of Tara. We will drive them into the ravine, kill them to the last man. Then we will see how powerful his god is."

Keagh sprang forward, his hands up.

"Nay, my lord, 'tis not worthy—" he began.

"You have been telling me a great deal about what is 'seemly' and 'worthy' for me to do," Laeghaire thundered. "And how dare you approach me so familiarly? We will do as Lucat-mael counsels. I want no part of such a necromancer!"

"You can't, my lord!" cried Marda. "Oh, my lord . . ."

Lucat-mael reached out and grabbed her wrist angrily. "By the goddess Morrigan, I will tame you, girl," he snapped, jerking her sharply around and grabbing her hair in his other big fist.

Keagh, seeing that, roared and sprang at the druid.

"Seize him," Laeghaire ordered, and before Keagh could touch Lucat-mael, he'd been grabbed and clubbed into submission. Marda screamed and struggled to escape the druid. "Put him into the strongest cell of the Duma nan Giall, the house of hostages," Laeghaire commanded, and two husky young druids lifted the limp body between them, striding off toward the hostage mound.

The ardri turned toward Marda, towering over her, his voice quivering with anger.

"You, girl, will surely marry Lucat-mael at Samain. I have been patient with you because of my fondness for you and for Angas who cherishes you. 'Tis weakness and I'll be guilty of it no more. Put her under guard in the queen's grianan, oh Lucat-mael! When I cleanse my court of the arrogant physician, she will be biddable as a good foster daughter should be."

Marda wouldn't stop struggling. Keagh had looked so white, so still. "Let me go to him," she shouted, distraught.

This only seemed further to infuriate the druid who jerked mercilessly at her, half dragging her down the hill toward Laeghaire's unfinished dun.

"You will be released when Keagh and the holy man are dead," Lucat-mael said, pulling, bullying, pushing her until she thought there wouldn't be an unbruised part of her body.

All around them the crowd, as if somehow relieved to see that Keagh had been seized without the wrath of his new god falling on the ardri, turned laughing to the wild rites. Young druids grabbed the first comely girl who came to hand and, shouting victoriously, the king's brewer unstoppered a cask of fiery mead. Marda felt tears rolling down her cheeks but she lifted her chin proudly, with an effort keeping from sobbing aloud. She would never give Lucat-mael such satisfaction. He summoned a young kern who turned reluctantly from the pursuit of a girl and fell in step beside them.

In a few minutes Marda had been confined in a small room of the queen's quarters. Indeed, it wasn't yet finished. Lucat-mael, eager to go back to the Beltane rites and to direct the laying of the ambush, barred the door, speaking to her through the closely woven wickerwork panel at the top.

"Tomorrow morning, the holy day Adzehead reveres, will be the last he will ever see. And if Laeghaire listens to me, Keagh also," he said with grim satisfaction. "The guard is right here, Marda; you can't escape so don't waste time trying."

She heard him turn and walk away. Sliding back the wicker panel, she saw the big guard, blond hair and beard brilliant in the torchlight, lounging disconsolently against the wall opposite her door.

"Close the wicket, lass," he said gruffly. "Best rest if you can; you look like to drop," he added with awkward kindness.

"Can you . . ."

"Don't think to wheedle, lass," he sighed. " 'Twould be worth my life to cross the king's druid."

Marda sighed and slid the panel back into place.

It was no use. She was a helpless prisoner, Keagh was hurt and, if Lucat-mael had his way, would be put to death.

And Patrick and his followers—MacCarthen, Colmagh, Breeca and even little Benen—were walking into a trap.

CHAPTER 5

Within a very few minutes of quiet exploring, Marda found that there was no escape from the little cell. There was iron grillwork over the one window, and although had she been alone she might have been able to work through the wickerwork panel on the interior door, the guard would certainly not allow it. The room, though unfinished, was furnished with a comfortable pallet and a small table. Lucat-mael had even left a torch on the wall outside the door so that there was faint light through the wicker. She was so weary she could hardly keep going, yet her apprehension for Keagh and the others wouldn't let her rest. She paced nervously back and forth, pausing to look out of the window where the night was bright with light and frantic activity. There were shouts from the revelers on the hill and the fire, constantly fed, blazed bright as day, throwing fitful light all over Tara.

Yet Patrick's light blazed brighter still.

The old man no longer stood outlined against the fire. She could see much movement, though, as if the very trees had developed wills and swayed in a rising wind that seemed to howl as if the banshee had come out of the hills around Tara to protest the coming of Patrick. Marda shivered in spite of herself. It was a night of ancient evil.

Soldiers, too, mustered, ordered by Laeghaire or Lucat-mael to forgo the reveling so that they would be ready to spring the trap on Patrick in the morning. If only there were some way she could warn him! Impotently she gripped the iron grillwork and pulled, but of course she might more easily have budged the dread idol of Cromm Cruach at Mag Slecht.

There was nothing she could do! Just then a gaunt form, Patrick again, moved momentarily across the faraway fire. His crosier, never far from his hand as if he gathered his very strength from it, was outlined for a brief moment. The simple cross atop seemed to call to her. Wordlessly she sank to her knees. There was, after all, *one* thing she could do. She folded her hands and bowed her head in prayer.

The words Patrick had taught them had never seemed so eloquent.

". . . Deliver us from evil," she prayed silently. Slowly a sort of quietness crept through her mind. "See to Keagh, heavenly Father," she prayed confidently, "since I cannot."

There was a sound of footsteps approaching the door outside.

"What are you doing here, my lady?" the guard said.

"I have been told Marda is here." Angas's voice, gentle and high-pitched, came to her through the door. "I have the king's leave to visit with her, bring her a meal. Open the door."

"No one told me not to admit you, my lady," the guard said with cheerful resignation. "Enter, then."

The door swung inward and Angas, her form enveloped by a long, dark, cowled cloak, came in, carrying a laden tray against her swollen belly.

Marda took it from her, set it on the table and turned to embrace her.

"How kind of you, my lady," she cried. "Do you know if Keagh is all right?"

Angas shook her head and shut the door behind her. The guard, unconcerned, walked away and they heard a soft bump as he resumed his post against the opposite wall.

"He is under heavy guard," Angas murmured. "But they allowed me to speak to him for a moment. I knew you'd want to know how he is."

"He was unconscious when I last saw him. Oh, is he all right, then? You say you spoke to him."

"He isn't seriously hurt, my child," Angas said soothingly. "But he is greatly concerned about this Patrick—your new friend. Rightly so, too, for they're sending many men to intercept him when he comes in the morning." She shook her head, her form shadowy against the faint light from the doorway.

"How did you know about all this, my lady?"

"Dubhtach came to tell me. He has ever been fond of you and Keagh and he thinks my lord is wrong to be contemplating such a dishonorable act against Patrick. But no one can reason with him when Lucat-mael has gotten him so stirred up."

"Lady, they say they'll kill Keagh," Marda said and the tears she'd been withholding rolled down her cheeks. In a moment she was enveloped in Angas's soft arms as her foster mother murmured soothingly. "Is there nothing you can do for him, Angas?"

"Child, I have already done all I could. I got Laeghaire to see that someone looked after him, brought him food and drink. But you know how it is. No one will he listen to when Lucat-mael is in control." She sighed softly, stroking Marda's tear-wet cheek. "Keagh told me to tell you he loves you and you must not be afraid. He says you must contrive somehow to warn Patrick of the ambush."

"I have already tried to get out, my lady, but there is no way I can get through the window. And the guard let me know I cannot get past him, either."

Angas chuckled softly.

"There is a way, darling. But first you must eat what I have brought you."

"With all that's on my mind? I cannot think of food . . ."

"You will. You must or I won't help you, Marda," Angas said firmly. "Come, eat. Every bite." She took the linen cover off the tray and went to the door, pushing the panel back. "Give me the torch," she said imperiously to the guard. "This child can't see to eat."

"Nay, Lady, I can't do that," the soldier said apologetically. "Leave the wicker open and that will give her light from without."

Angas sighed and closed the wicker sharply.

"I thought to get that torch out of the way," she said softly. "But at least he has given me a reason to be miffed with him. When I leave, he'll not be surprised that I refuse to speak to him."

Marda began eating the small loaf and duck breast that Angas had brought for her, washing it down with cool ale that heartened her in spite of herself. Her hunger surprised her and she didn't stop until the tray was empty. She wiped her hands on the napkin.

"I have eaten it all, my lady. Tell me, now, how can I possibly escape? How can I warn Patrick?"

"*You* cannot, but *I* can," Angas said cryptically.

"My lady! You must not even think of such a thing," Marda cried, remembering Keagh's fears about Angas's state of health. And if Keagh were not to attend her when her time came, she'd be doubly periled. "You must not—you could not walk through the forest to Slane."

Angas laughed and put a finger to her lips, her eyes dancing. She reached up and unfastened her brooch, shrugging herself out of her cloak. "Did you not wonder why I wore such an all-enveloping cloak?" she whispered. "Here, darling, put it on." She helped Marda fasten the brooch in place and pulled the cowl up around her face. "Now hold your arms out in front of you, under the cloak, so you look as vast as I do."

Wonderingly, Marda understood Angas's purpose. She hugged the other woman warmly.

"Dearest Mother, you would do this for a priest you don't even know?"

"Aye, Marda," she said soberly. "For I like not my lord's agreeing to an ambush. 'Tis more Lucat-mael's way than his. And, should it succeed, a bad taste will be in his mouth forever."

"But what if we are caught, my lady? The ardri will be furious with you."

"No doubt he will," she said serenely. "Yet, he would not chastise me now while I'm great with his child, and by the time the babe is born he'll have calmed down and will thank me for not letting him so dishonor himself as to ambush and kill peaceable men."

Marda nodded. "I had best go then, my lady Angas." She rounded her arms and leaned back as if she were carrying a baby in her own womb. "Think you the guard will be fooled?" she asked softly.

Angas smiled wryly. "Not for long. Keep your head down as if you are angry with him and move swiftly away from the torch. And try to be back by morning."

"Won't your women note your absence?"

"I have allowed them all to go to the Beltane rites except for Daneen, and she adds her good wishes to mine for your success, Marda."

Marda hugged her again, kissing the smooth, round cheek and

then Angas, standing close beside her, called out, "Open the door, guard, I wish to leave," in an imperious, aggrieved tone. Marda had to suppress a laugh in spite of her worry about Keagh and the others. When the guard opened the door, Angas stood back in the shadows while Marda moved quickly through the door, imitating as best she could the queen's awkward, late-pregnancy gait. The guard, a bit sheepish because of refusing the ardrigan's request for a torch, locked the door quickly, avoiding looking at her. Marda sighed in relief and went quickly into the queen's quarters.

She paused there only long enough to hug Daneen and assure her that she was all right.

"Do what you can for Keagh, Daneen, for love of me," she whispered, hugging the younger girl.

"Marda, how exciting . . ." Daneen cried, blue eyes dancing, but Marda hushed her by laying her fingers gently against the girl's lips and slipped through the outer door, making her way to the spot on the ramparts where she'd slipped away before. If anyone saw her they'd think it was Angas, taking a late night stroll, but in truth most of Tara was reveling at the Beltane fire.

She clambered across the ramparts in the dark, cincturing Angas's cloak up about her waist so she'd not fall over it. Within minutes she'd gained the edge of the woods. But it was so dark that only Patrick's fire, which she glimpsed intermittently through the trees, guided her on her way.

She stayed to the woods along the edge of Slige Midluachra. Once she had to drop down as a chariot came down the road. Peering from cover in the fitful light, she saw two shadowy figures in white druidical robes in the chariot. Her heart turned over at the sight. Always, the druids' traditional white garb would make her think of Keagh. Silently she prayed that God would protect him. Her heart ached with the knowledge that Laeghaire had imprisoned him and that he was in grave danger. If only she could think of some way to free him . . . to get him clear away from Ireland. If only they'd stayed away, sailed off to Britain. Their reasons for not going had been honorable; they'd wanted to help Patrick bring the Christian faith to Laeghaire's people. But in her heart she knew she'd somehow expected that God would solve their problems, hers and Keagh's as well. Now, despite her dread of what would happen to Keagh, she knew he was right. She *had* to get to Patrick, warn him so that he didn't come in solemn procession on Easter morning to certain death.

As the druids in the chariot rattled off toward Tara, she got up and continued north. Her only hope was still with Patrick. He had restored little Tadgh to life and he'd told them of how God had delivered Saint Paul from prison. Maybe, somehow, he could ask God to deliver Keagh, she thought with the simplicity her new faith had given her.

Something small and winged flew at her face. Stifling a scream, she ducked and, from long habit, folded her fingers around her thumbs as a charm against the night raven, the Morrigan.

You are acting like a pagan, she told herself angrily. *It is only a bat.*

Yet, the forest seemed steeped in malevolence. Even Patrick acknowledged that Lucifer, the fallen angel, took many guises to lead souls to destruction. *Deliver us from evil,* she prayed silently.

Suddenly, without the slightest warning, a cold drizzle started falling, not sufficient to put out Patrick's beckoning light, but enough to soak Marda to the skin and add to her miseries by making the bracken beat wetly at her legs and the soft ground turn to mud. She had to get out of the thick woods. Determinedly, she climbed down the bank onto the cleared roadway. At least, she prayed, the rain would keep the druids and soldiers under cover.

The way to Slane was easier on the road. She began to run unhurriedly now, glad for the fire ahead that summoned her onward.

As the night wore on, the fire became more than a beacon—it was a quest for shelter, warmth and comfort. Only a little way more, she told herself wearily. Patrick and Breeca, Colmagh, MacCarthen, Odran, Mescan, Athcen, and little Benen were all waiting at Slane for Easter morning when they'd blithely walk to their deaths.

But she would be there in time to warn them. That thought strengthened her as memories of the happy moments she'd shared with Keagh warmed her. Right now their prospects seemed as bleak and black as the surrounding night. But with God's help, somehow they'd overcome all the terrible difficulties.

As she struggled on, Angas's cloak as heavy as lead from the rain, she comforted herself by thinking of God's power. If He could defeat cold, grim death, what power did the evil Lucat-mael have against Him?

The night was well advanced when she finally broke through the trees and entered the clearing where Patrick's party had camped.

"It's Marda!" cried Colmagh, who'd been feeding the fire. The others had taken shelter from the drizzle under lean-tos of woven reeds and boughs, Breeca and little Benen in the one closest to the fire.

They all came to greet her, Patrick's face concerned as she sank, exhausted, to a log. Benen crawled out of the lean-to and hugged her.

"You're all wet, Marda," he said sympathetically.

"Here, lass, shed that wet cloak and get into the lean-to," Breeca cried, reaching toward her. But Marda waved her away.

"They've imprisoned Keagh, Father Patrick," she gasped, "and even now, they lay an ambush for you. The ardri wouldn't listen . . . he's planning to kill you . . ."

"My poor child. You've come all the way back to warn us," he said kindly, but he seemed unafraid.

Colmagh brought her a cup of warm ale which strengthened her and drove the chill from her numb hands. She drained it gratefully and handed the cup back to him, stretching her hands to the blaze.

"You must not go to Tara by Slige Midluachra, Father Patrick," she said urgently. "They lie in wait to kill you."

"And Keagh is in prison? The ardri would not accept him, then, as my emissary."

"Oh, he accepted him as your emissary," she said bitterly. "That is partly why he's in prison. They hate and fear you. They will stop at nothing to kill you. And they say they'll kill Keagh, too."

In spite of herself, she faltered and began crying.

"You are a brave woman, Marda," the old priest said comfortingly. "Many a strong man would hesitate at starting through such a night on so long a journey alone. How is it you got away from them?"

"They don't know I've gone. The ardrigan, who considers her husband's duplicity shameful, has taken my place. I slipped away, wearing her cloak. And no one noticed; they all revel at Beltane. But I must start back, right away. I would not have her in trouble on my account."

Patrick stared thoughtfully at the fire.

"As soon as we have thanked God with the Mass for bringing us safe so far, we will all go to Tara." He smiled at Benen. "Well, child, you would learn to be my acolyte. Go then, bring the Mass vessels. Remember, you must carry the Blessed Sacrament reverently."

Benen bounded out of the shelter of the lean-to and ran off, returning in an instant with the things Patrick had requested. He set them down carefully beside the log that would serve as the altar.

"Father Patrick, I don't think you yet understand," Marda said worriedly. "They are lying in wait. They will kill you."

"Nay, child, they will not. For God did not deliver me from slavery nor guide my steps through all these years of study and prayer to have me die at the ardri's hand." He lifted his eyes to the cross on his staff, smiling confidently. "It has been revealed to me that I am to win Ireland for God and somehow, even now, He will show us the way. Come, my children, let us kneel and offer the Mass together."

The rain stopped as Patrick reached the Consecration. Marda saw him smile as if it was only what he had expected. Yet, the air was cold and a white miasma crept from the wet ground, swirling mysteriously about them. Day was still far distant but she fancied there was a lightening of the swirling, black clouds above them.

They rose together as the Mass ended when Benen cried out in excitement.

"Look, Father Patrick, by the fire!"

Marda gasped. A large buck deer, several of his does, and a fawn stood watching them within the circle of firelight! That they were unafraid of the fire was startling enough, but when Patrick turned and gazed at them and the buck bowed his head as if in greeting, she felt she was witnessing a miracle.

"By my God of judgment," Patrick breathed, "and so that's

how it is to be done. Eight of them there are, and a fawn. Eight adults of us and a child."

The deer moved silently and sure-footed around the fire and came to stand among them. Patrick folded his hands together and lifted his eyes to the dark skies.

"You are most gracious," he said simply. "Thank you."

He patted the buck's flank absently, as if it were quite the usual thing to have wild forest creatures cavorting about him, and turned to Marda. "Tell me where the ambush is to be laid."

She took up a stick and traced a crude map of the road into Tara on the wet ground. "Just before the hill on which Tara sits, there's a smaller rising. To the left lies a fairly sharp rise, wooded and affording much cover, while to the right there's a sharp drop to the Boyne. If they trap us in there, there's no escape. They can stone us to death or leap down with their axes if need be."

Patrick nodded. "And on this wooded rise, would there be footing for us to pass behind them?"

"Aye, Father Patrick. The woods are thick but the undergrowth is not heavy and the land is flat. The road turns a bit so that you could get back on it and walk straight up Tara hill just beyond the pass."

Patrick grinned, looking like a mischievous boy for all his hoary beard and hair.

"Won't the ardri be surprised to see us all walking up the hill? We will sing the lorica against evil that I taught you. Remember: 'I bind myself today to a strong virtue, an invocation of the Trinity.

'I believe in a Threeness with confession of a Oneness in the Creator of the Universe. . . .'"

"But we can't get the chariot through the woods," said Odran indignantly.

"Odran, Odran, do you not know yet that we must go afoot? With these gentle creatures God has sent us as protection?"

"Protection?"

"Disguise, then," Patrick said patiently. We will pass the soldiers, each of us crouched down behind a deer. Thus will we go through the forest." He looked contemplatively at the mist, like thin oatmeal now. "They will see only a herd of deer, moving at first light through the woods."

Marda suddenly felt reassured. All would surely be well. God was strongly on their side.

"Come," said Patrick, and men and deer fell into place around him. Together they moved off through the forest. Birds, sensing the coming day, sounded sleepily.

The way back to Tara on Slige Midluachra seemed much shorter with loving friends around her, Marda thought. The mist grew ever heavier, yet the world lightened perceptibly as the sun rose above the rain clouds. When they were just north of the pass, she stopped them, raising a finger to her lips to silence the prayers they'd been saying.

"Here we take to the woods," she whispered.

"Each of you stay to the left of your deer," Patrick added. "Put your arm around its neck so you stay close."

Benen's blue eyes were dancing. Indeed, he'd been playing with the fawn all the way from Slane. Now, he kissed it between its bright eyes and the little deer reciprocated with a long-tongued salute to Benen's chin. The little boy clapped his hand over his mouth to keep from laughing aloud. MacCarthen, being the tallest among them, chose the buck as his. Each of the others put his or her arm about a doe's neck, crouched down, and entered the wet bracken. They stopped reciting the lorica aloud, now, but Marda knew that everyone, like her, was praying silently. Her arm tightly clutching the deer, which browsed as casually as if it were alone, her heart beating furiously against her rib cage, she moved quietly through the bracken with the others.

"What's that?" she heard a hushed voice off to her right cry. Benen, clutching the fawn beside her, looked frightened.

"Shut up, you fool. 'Tis only a herd of deer, coming back, no doubt, from their morning watering," came the whispered reply.

"Captain, I have a taste for deer meat. And, by Dagda's cauldron, that buck would feed a-many of us. Let me launch my spear—"

"Put your eyes back on the northern road! Would you have the holy wizard slip by us while we chase deer?" came the imperious reply.

The buck lifted his head, as if scenting danger in the soldiers. Mist swirled around him. Marda stole a glance across her doe's back. Kern—foot soldiers—were massed all along the roadway, concealed behind every tree, phantasmagoric in the foggy air. Had Patrick and the others marched boldly along the Slige Midluachra, they'd all be dead by now. She felt a high pride that she had warned them.

They moved slowly beyond the soldiers' station, no one paying much attention to them, for the deer seemed to be just a normally cautious herd making their way through the woods. When they were far enough away, they came out on the road again.

"There lies Tara, yonder," Marda said. The great rath mound seemed to rise shining through the pearly mists.

"Come, my children; by my God of judgment, we have fooled them," Patrick cried exuberantly. "Let us enter Tara in triumph as Christ entered Jerusalem."

The deer looked at Patrick as if for a sign.

"Thank you," he said simply, and they moved off into the woods, the fawn pausing long enough to lick Benen's hand.

"I must go, Father Patrick, for I would not have Angas suffer on my behalf. Be careful. Though the ambush has failed, Lucat-mael is exceedingly treacherous."

"God be with you, my daughter," he said, making the sign of the cross on her forehead. "Fear not; He will protect us all."

As she slipped into the woods, they started singing the lorica, exultantly;

"... God's Might to uphold me,
God's Wisdom to guide me ..."

"By the fairy mounds!" cried a soldier's voice. "Look! The holy wizard! How did he get by us?"

"He is a wizard in truth!" cried another voice. "For I myself saw that only a minute ago, there was only a herd of deer! It was Patrick and his followers in disguise!"

"It's so, Captain—you saw them yourself," came a third voice and then all was a babble of confusion as Marda sprinted through the wet forest for the back ramparts. She grinned in relief. At least, with such a wonder to discuss, no one would see her reenter the rath. By the time word reached Laeghaire of Patrick's arrival, the men would swear that they had *seen* the deer change into men.

She went back into the queen's grianan as she had left it. By now, the morning was full-blown but foggy. Daneen hugged her in delight and she told her quickly that Patrick was even now knocking at the gates of the rath, having been warned in time to elude his would-be murderers. Then, shaking out the cloak and hoping the guard wouldn't notice its condition, she assumed Angas's gait and stalked back to the little room where she'd been confined last night.

"Let me in; I want to see how my foster daughter fares," she mumbled, and the guard, sleepy, unlocked the door without comment, no doubt thinking she was still angry with him. She went through and shut it quickly behind her, taking off the wet cloak.

"My lady," she whispered. "Are you awake?"

Angas, who'd been lying on her side, her back to the door, rolled over and struggled upright, smiling radiantly. Marda thought with alarm that her eyes seemed more deeply shadowed than ever after the night. She embraced her warmly.

"You reached him in time?" Angas asked anxiously.

"Aye, my lady. I will tell you all about it later. But, for now, Patrick is at Tara's gates. Please go to the king. Beg him to release me for maybe I can be of some help. And find out how Keagh is if you can."

Angas ran her hands over her braids to order them and, without wasting time in questions, took her cloak from Marda and, throwing it over her arm, knocked for the guard to release her. As the door shut behind her, Marda began praying the lorica passionately:

> ". . . God's Host to secure me
> Against snares of demons . . ."

It seemed like an eternity but was in reality no more time than was required to complete the long song when the guard, accompanied by another soldier, opened the door and motioned her to go with them.

"The king commands you be present when he receives the wizard," he said. He led her out of Laeghaire's new rath, around the perimeter of the main rath with the Duma nan Giall where Keagh was imprisoned, and to the smaller Rath na Seanaid, which was the council chamber where Laeghaire sat in judgment or welcomed visitors of an official nature. She wondered grimly which it would be with Patrick. She looked longingly at the hostage mound, hoping Keagh would be at one of the windows, but they remained empty and bleak. God forbid that he was too ill or injured to watch from the window!

She caught a glimpse of Patrick and the others, waiting under guard in front of the great banqueting hall. She raised her hand in salute and they called encouragement to her. She entered the Rath na Seanaid. Laeghaire, sitting in the great king's chair, motioned her abruptly to come stand behind Angas's place.

"He is within our ramparts, oh Laeghaire," Lucat-mael said urgently after a swift, baleful glance at Marda. "Kill him! And all his tonsured followers."

But Dubhtach strode forward, his hand out beseechingly toward the king.

"You cannot behave so ignominiously, my lord," he cried. "This man is gentle and elderly. He comes unarmed, saying he brings you only love and blessing. I have talked with him already this morning. And, you yourself heard the captain of the company you sent to intercept him. The men all swear that he and his people passed them in the fog, magically transformed into a herd of deer!"

Laeghaire nodded abruptly. Marda thought he looked strained and angry.

"Well have I attended them, oh Dubhtach. For this reason, I have decided to receive them honorably as if they were any visitors."

"Honorably? My lord! Is it honorable to have your men all seated thus, their shields beneath their chins? 'Tis an insult to this old man!"

Marda realized with a start that Dubhtach was right. It was customary for each of the courtiers' servants to precede his master ceremoniously into the hall and hang his master's shield on the wall above his place of honor around the great council table. As of old, if they retained their shields, sitting on the edge of their seats, the shield held at the ready under their chins, it was a sign that they neither honored nor trusted the visitor to Tara. They should all be standing under their shields!

Angas reached up and took her hand, squeezing it in encouragement.

"For fear of his magic, I am receiving him," Laeghaire snapped. "But, by the Dagda, I'll show him no honor further than merest courtesy."

"You will live to rue the day you received him," Lucat-mael shouted.

But Laeghaire, although he seemed to pale even more, motioned his chamberlain to open the door and summon the newcomers.

The men all sat stolidly, staring at the great, magnificently painted double doors. Presently they opened and Patrick, his crosier held proudly before him, entered, MacCarthen and Benen walking a bit behind him, flanking him. The others came too, looking around curiously at the stately hall.

Patrick, unsmiling, stomped up to the place before the King's.

"I have been scandalized to learn that you imprisoned my emissary and laid a snare for me and my people, oh Laeghaire of Tara," he said solemnly. "You have sent your own sons against me!" He looked around the hall where several of Laeghaire's grown sons and sons-in-law sat, chins jammed down on their shields, their beards hanging over them—Feidlimid, Coirpre, Dricrui. "Never will they sit on Tara's chair!" *How had he known them?* Marda thought.

"You dare to curse my blood, then, oh holy man?" Laeghaire shouted, his words tumbling over themselves. Marda could see that he was in great dread of Patrick. Ever, he had been terrified of anything he considered supernatural.

"I do not curse them, oh Laeghaire," Patrick said patiently. "I but prophesy. No son of yours will sit on Tara's chair, for you have taught them fierce anger and hatred. I tell you, Ireland is destined to be a Christian nation!"

"Christian!" Laeghaire spat. "How long, think you, Adzehead, would Ireland survive if we gave up fierce anger and hatred? The invaders would destroy us."

"You will never be destroyed, no matter what disasters strike you, no matter how many invaders despoil you, if you but put Almighty God as master over your land. You know not the might of His love!"

"I don't want to know of him, either," Laeghaire cried. "Go back beyond the seas from whence you came; I want you not, nor your dead-yet-living god."

"It matters not what you want, Laeghaire," Patrick said as if explaining to a spoiled child. "The God of Hosts desires that you all come to love and serve Him. He has sent me to teach you."

All at once a murmur spread through the hall. Marda looked around the room. Dubhtach and Fiacc had stood up!

Patrick saw, too. He smiled, his eyes meeting Dubhtach's deep blue gaze. He opened his arms as if to welcome them.

"*We* would learn of this god, oh Patrick," Dubhtach said boldly. "For I have talked to Keagh. I know that rather would he die than let a falsehood cross his lips. And he swore that you, by the power of your god, brought a dead child back to life."

Patrick nodded, his bearing dignified and calm. "Gladly do I welcome you to my first catechumen class, good druid," he said.

"*I* would learn of your god, too, oh Patrick," said Angas unexpectedly. She threw a defiant look at Lucat-mael, who was clenching his fists, glaring at Patrick. "And then, perhaps, *this* son of Laeghaire's," here she laid a soft hand on her belly, "may be worthy to one day be ardri of Ireland."

Patrick smiled at her, his expression soft.

"I have no doubt of it, my lady," he said.

"Dubhtach Maccu-Lugair, you deliberately set yourself against me," shouted Lucat-mael. Marda noticed that, uncharacteristically, he looked rumpled and sweaty. He seemed oddly excited. She knew that he and Dubhtach had always treated each other with antipathy, and if there were ever any currents of discord at court, Dubhtach was certain to be on the opposite side from Lucat-mael, whatever the cause. She supposed Dubhtach was only too happy to take advantage of Laeghaire's obvious fear of Patrick since it was sure to annoy Lucat-mael.

"I but set myself with Patrick," Dubhtach said imperturbably. He straightened his immaculate robe. "I but offer him the courtesy a druid of the ardri's house should," he added pointedly. "And I will listen to tales of his god."

Lucat-mael clenched his fists impotently. "You are as mad as Keagh," he muttered. "For *he* listened to the holy man's words and look what it got him."

"What did it get him, Lucat-mael?" Patrick demanded, his eyes intent on the druid.

Lucat-mael seemed to swell in triumph. His thin lips split open in a grim smile and his face gleamed in the growing light.

"A watery grave! I have just returned from the sea where I saw him bound, sewed into a sack, and thrown overboard several miles offshore."

"How dare you!" Laeghaire shouted. "I told you to put him aboard the first ship leaving Ireland. I but meant to exile him!"

Lucat-mael laughed unpleasantly. "You are too kind, oh Laeghaire, and I must protect you. . . ."

Keagh was dead!

Marda felt herself swaying, desperately retreating from the unthinkable which was racing toward her from all directions like druid mist.

"Holy man, catch the girl for she is fainting," screamed Laeghaire and that was the last thing Marda knew.

CHAPTER 6

Keagh awoke, head aching as if Patrick's chariot had been driven over it, in the Duma nan Giall. He was lying on the floor of one of the cells used for recalcitrant prisoners and, through the bars in the door, torchlight revealed that he was guarded by at least one big soldier. As he lay there quietly, he realized that the guard he could see was conversing with at least two others.

He pulled himself erect, suppressing a moan, for he had many aches from the beating Lucat-mael's followers had administered before he fell unconscious. Thinking of it, fury filled him. He would have expected little better from the powerful druid, but never would he have believed that Laeghaire, who'd always been a friend to him, would have allowed it.

"You will let me in," came an imperious feminine voice from without. "The ardrigan still has rights in Ireland. And gillas who tell her what treachery is afoot!"

He smiled broadly, wincing a little at the pain. Angas, sweet-tempered though she was, was capable of great anger, and the guards, apparently apprehensive of arousing her, opened the door and let her enter his cell.

"My lady, where is Marda?" he said, helping Angas to the one small stool in the room.

"She's being held in my grianan, Keagh. She is all right," Angas said softly. "I am going to her as soon as I have seen for myself your condition. You have recovered consciousness, then. Are you hurt?"

He felt gingerly of the spot from which his headache seemed to radiate and was surprised to feel the warm stickiness of blood.

"Not too seriously. A few cuts and a headache."

"I will leave orders with the guards that you are to be cared for, given food."

"That is not the most important thing, my lady," Keagh said, thinking of Patrick at Slane, unconcernedly preparing to walk into an ambush. He hesitated, wondering how far he could trust the ardrigan who, for all her love of Marda, still adored and obeyed her husband.

As if understanding his fears, she laid a soft hand on his shoulder. "You want me to warn Patrick," she whispered. "I will, Keagh, for I won't have my lord guilty of cold-blooded murder! But only Daneen can I trust among my ladies and she knows not the way. I must find a way to free Marda."

Keagh nodded. "He must be warned. And, in truth, I would be relieved to know Marda is safe from Lucat-mael. Tell her she must not worry about me and that warning Patrick must take precedence over everything. Tell her I love her."

Angas arose. "I'll manage, Keagh. I'm glad you're not hurt too badly. And don't worry. Laeghaire won't let Lucat-mael really harm you."

She kissed his cheek softly and he helped her rise. She called for the guards to open the door, instructing them that Keagh was to be fed and his wounds attended to.

But she had scarcely gone when Lucat-mael arrived. He snatched away the tray of food one of the guards had fetched and pulled Keagh roughly to his feet.

"Bind him," he ordered.

Before Keagh could protest he'd been seized, his arms lashed tightly behind him and the napkin from the tray thrust into his mouth. It seemed to absorb even his saliva and his thirst became as great a pain as that in his upper arms where the ropes cut. Lucat-mael smiled, his eyes glittering maliciously.

"The chariot is waiting on Slige Dala. Hurry," he said urgently.

The two druids who'd dragged Keagh from the Beltane rites came into the little cell and took him from the guard. Lucat-mael's pupil, a young man named Crunnmoel, opened the door for them. Together they carried him from the mound of the hostages, keeping to the shadows, and ran to the ramparts where they lifted him over. Lucat-mael kept looking behind him, so Keagh knew he was being abducted without Laeghaire's knowledge. Desperately he tried to summon voice, but the huge linen napkin effectively silenced him. Indeed, he felt as if he would surely smother. They hauled him along the ramparts, past

Laeghaire's unfinished dun where the queen said Marda was being confined. He was thrown into a waiting chariot. Crunnmoel took his place at the reins and Lucat-mael, kicking Keagh furiously until he drew himself into a ball, climbed in beside his pupil.

"See to the ambush," he said to the two druids—the oldest of his fosterlings, Keagh knew. "The holy man must never reach Tara alive. I will be back before morning."

He motioned to Crunnmoel and the lad plied the whip over the horses. They sprang forward, throwing Keagh sharply against the back of the chariot. Pain shot through his shoulder and became part of the rest of his miseries. He'd not had a chance to eat of the food Angas had ordered sent to him and had taken only a short drink of the ale. His thirst was very great and weakness from his long fast wore him down. Where was Lucat-mael taking him? Dazedly he felt himself losing consciousness again. He shook his head furiously. No! Somehow he must stay alert, watch for a chance to escape, for by Patrick's crosier, he knew Lucat-mael never meant to let him live.

They rode furiously through the night, eastward toward the sea. He felt the soft, moist air surrounding him and presently it began to rain. Lucat-mael cursed softly and urged Crunnmoel to beat the horses harder.

At last they ground to a stop and the two men jerked him erect, pushing him furiously from the chariot. He sprawled, his cramped legs refusing to hold him, and he felt as if he had a thousand bruises from the cobbles where he'd landed.

"You, here, help us with this prisoner," Lucat-mael called out to a form, slightly darker than the night. Keagh could hear the sea beating against the rocks. "Bring a torch. By Dagda, 'tis black as the inside of a mound."

Shortly, as his vision cleared a little, Keagh could see that he was lying on a jetty. A fisherman's shack loomed above him and presently light flared up as someone struck a tinder and ignited a torch. By its light he saw a gnarled little man with a fisherman's cap who held the torch and stared down at him pityingly. Beside him a little girl, obviously just awakened from sleep, rubbed her eyes and stared wonderingly at the newcomers.

"You have a coracle," Lucat-mael observed, nodding toward

the outline of the fisherman's vessel. "Get a length of canvas and sew this traitor into it. Then you will take us out to sea and throw him overboard."

The old man stared at Lucat-mael defiantly.

"Ordering me, you are? And why should I obey you?"

"Because I am the ardri's druid," Lucat-mael snapped.

The old man leaned over and pulled the napkin from Keagh's mouth.

"No need to torture the boy," he drawled. "There is none here to hear his cries except me and my granddaughter."

Keagh gagged, immensely relieved to be free of the choking napkin.

"Thank you . . ." he gasped.

"I'll not be drowning a bound man as if he were an unwanted cat," the old man said stoutly.

Lucat-mael jerked his dagger from his belt and grabbed the little girl, slicing at her finger from which blood spurted.

"Ready the canvas and your boat or I'll draw more of the child's blood," he shouted.

"Looks as if you've drawn enough as it is," the old man cried above the little girl's frightened sobs. "Look at it pour forth."

"Put pressure on the inside of her forearm," Keagh yelled. "Tie the napkin tightly around it for a few minutes and it will stop."

The old man snatched up the napkin, wet from Keagh's saliva, and did as he was bid. The bleeding eased to a slow ooze. "Good," Keagh said. "It will stop now. Release the napkin slowly in a few more minutes."

"And get your canvas and a needle while you wait," Crunnmoel said laconically.

"Aye, or I'll cut deeper next time," said Lucat-mael.

Sighing, the old man turned to his hut, taking the torch with him as he rummaged for the canvas and needle. He came back carrying the torch in one hand and the needed material in the other, and handed the torch to Crunnmoel while he released the napkin from his granddaughter's arm. "See, Bridey, 'tis stopped now," he said kindly. "Thank you, boy, for she's all I have in the world."

"Sew him up," Lucat-mael ordered angrily.

The old man sighed and rolled the canvas out on the sand. Lucat-mael pushed and kicked Keagh over onto it and the fisherman started sewing it around him.

"Sorry, boy—you see how it is," he muttered.

Keagh nodded. He closed his eyes as the canvas was drawn over him. His heart beat as if it were in his throat instead of his chest and he fought to keep from vomiting in the blackness. He forced himself to try to gain some serenity, some acceptance of what was happening to him. Patrick had convinced him that God could do anything. He'd sent Tadgh back to them. Yet, he knew that Tadgh's resurrection had been for a purpose, but Christians must die in this life, same as men had always done, and no one ever knew the hour of his death. So he was to die as a young man, without ever having possessed his Marda. His heart turned over painfully. It was bitter hard to accept. And yet, what right had he to expect any better if God willed that he die? He would spend his last moments of life praying for her and for the others. Surely, though he must die, God would not ordain that she must submit to Lucat-mael. With all his heart he loathed the druid.

"Don't damn me for that, Heavenly Father," he whispered softly, "for even now, I cannot help it."

Suddenly the old man, having almost completely enclosed him, began tugging awkwardly at the unwieldly burden that he had become.

"Move the torch—ye're blinding me," he said. "Get the boat ready."

Lucat-mael moved to do so and Crunnmoel held the torch aloft so his master could see. Swift as the tongue of an adder, the old man slipped something into Keagh's hands, bound as they were behind him, then finished the last stitches. He felt himself picked up and carried to the coracle where they threw him roughly to the bottom of the boat.

"You wait here, Crunnmoel," he heard Lucat-mael say. "Keep the child at your side and if the old man tries to thwart me or even refuse to help me, kill her."

The boat was shoved off into the sea. The wind and rain lashed at them and Keagh grew more sodden and paralyzed in the smothering sack. Cautiously, knowing Lucat-mael couldn't see in the dark, he worked his fingers along the object the old fisherman had put into his hands until he determined that it was a sharp knife. Indeed, he cut himself a little on it but if he could only get some feeling back into his hands, he might be able to sever the ropes that bound him. They'd been looped around his wrists, then his arms. The blade of the knife seemed just at the ones that had been put around his chest and upper arms. Gingerly, he started sawing at them.

They sailed for what seemed like a long time to Keagh. He was sweating furiously now, fear and yet wild hope coursing through him. He cut at the ropes, trying not to make any noise that would be heard above the wind and rain, praying intensely that he would be able to free himself. So far out they went that surely he would not be able to get safely back to shore even if he managed to cut himself loose but at least he would try. And he would not drown helplessly bound in a canvas sack. Then, as Lucat-mael ordered the old man to help him throw Keagh overboard, the ropes around his upper body gave way. He gulped air into his lungs just as he hit the water.

The sack sank slowly while Keagh worked furiously to free his arms. He finally got his wrists free of the rope and pulled his arms around, holding tightly to the knife as if it were a lifeline. He managed to pierce the canvas with the point. His arms were numb and weak from the long confinement and he thought he'd never summon strength to slit the sack. Yet, Almighty God had helped him so far by providing the little fisherman who was grateful enough for his granddaughter's life to help him and he would do all he could to save himself.

Help me!

It was the most intense prayer he'd yet said to God. He felt strength fill his hands and he brought the knife up in a long slash that parted the canvas. He kicked himself free from it and headed desperately to the surface, breaking through into the black and rain-dashed night just as his lungs threatened to draw in the killer sea. He gulped the good clean air gratefully, retching, crying, thanking God.

He could see nothing but blackness all around him. Waves high as Laeghaire's banqueting hall crashed over his head and threatened to drown him but as he was borne aloft on one of them, he saw, at least, the direction of the shore for the old man's torch still burned. He turned toward it, trying to ride with the waves. It was a long, long way off; the torch, visible only intermittently, seemed no more than a pinpoint. There was no sign of the coracle and he supposed it had already headed back to shore.

For what seemed like hours he swam and floated on the waves, keeping his eyes on the dot of light as if it were heaven itself. Slowly, he felt that he was making headway. He saw the little boat reach shore and the druids shoving the little girl and the torch toward the aged fisherman. Then a wave would drop him again and he would come up, sputtering and struggling ever shoreward, to catch another glimpse of the torch.

The old man stayed on the beach, holding the torch aloft.

It was nearly morning before Keagh, spent and sickly retching seawater, stumbled, almost fell in the shallow edge of the sea.

With a glad cry, the old fisherman threw the torch down just as the Easter sun appeared on the eastern horizon. The little girl slept on the sand, the napkin wrapped around her hurt hand.

"By the Dagda, you made it and grateful I am to have thwarted that cold bastard of a druid," yelled the fisherman. He jumped into the waves and helped Keagh, getting himself hunkered down and putting his frail arms around the physician's torso.

Keagh was too weak to do more than grin and they'd barely managed to stagger beyond high-tide mark when he collapsed.

Marda awoke in the small grianan room just as Keagh finally regained consciousness in the old fisherman's hut.

She remembered Lucat-mael's gloating words as consciousness returned and she cried out in a great agony of the soul.

"Keagh's dead!"

Her scream startled Breeca, who'd been tending her and had dozed off, her head against the wall.

"There, there, there, child," the old woman soothed, tears standing in her eyes. She drew Marda into her arms where the girl clung, shaking with bitter sobs. "A scandal and a sorrow it is. That druid is nothing but evil and, no matter what Patrick says, I can love and forgive him not! There, little one, there."

Angas and Daneen came to her bedside, too, having been listening for her to awaken from her faint. They patted her ineffectually, their silent sympathy apparent in their faces, Angas's worried and flushed and weary, Daneen's habitually sunny demeanor grave. The other women were nowhere in evidence, all sleeping off the effects of the Beltane rites in their various chambers. Even the workmen hadn't resumed their labors on the new rath, this day after festival.

"He's gone, Breeca," she sobbed. "Gone out of Patrick's reach for surely he'd restore Keagh to life, too, if he could find him."

"Don't lose heart, Marda," the old woman said comfortingly, her eyes brightening at Marda's words. "For sure, I'd not thought of Patrick restoring Keagh as he did the child. Perhaps his magic even extends to the middle of the sea."

Marda drew back, shaking her head sorrowfully. "If only he could. If only he would."

"My lord has offered him and his people lodgings at Tara though Lucat-mael objects," Angas volunteered. "Laeghaire believes that he has much power and fears to anger him overmuch. Would you like me to send for him?"

"Oh, aye, my lady," Marda cried, hope rising.

Angas nodded to the little gilla, Tober, who ran off to fetch Patrick.

"Child, you must not get your heart set on the impossible," said Angas kindly. "After all, this child Patrick brought back may not truly have been dead whereas if Lucat-mael speaks the truth, Keagh lies at the bottom of the eastern sea, his hands bound and sewed into a—ah, dearest Marda, I meant not to grieve you still further. Ah, my poor child, poor, poor child. 'Tis mortal hard for you."

"Why did he have to kill him, my lady? Keagh never hurt him. And now, I swear I will die before I will wed Lucat-mael!"

Angas exchanged a bleak look with Breeca and Daneen.

"You will not have to marry him, Marda," she said grimly. "I myself will help you escape Ireland before Samain, but see that you don't let him suspect it. Since Keagh is—is—gone, he has removed the guard from you at least."

Marda lay back against the pillows, her eyes closed. She tried to close her heart, too, against the painful knowledge that Keagh had been sewn inside a bag and drowned. He couldn't be dead! Not her laughing, vital Keagh. She thought of their journey to Tara—was it only yesterday? He'd spoken of his love for her and his great happiness and of the house they'd build and the children they'd have. Because they'd found God, they'd thought everything would work out so they could marry and spend their lives together. How foolish they'd been! Patrick had warned them that, often, being Christian meant not everlasting happiness in this world but toil and sorrow and pain.

But never had she dreamed that God would demand this much suffering from her. Tears coursed down her cheeks.

A light tap at the door sent Breeca to admit Patrick. Marda turned her head to meet his gaze and, doing so, her chin quivered and she pulled the coverlet up to mop at her streaming eyes.

"Can you help him, Father Patrick?" she said, sobbing.

"Marda, Marda, I have not stopped praying since that evil man told what he'd done to Keagh," the old man said sadly, "but I can only ask of God, not command Him."

"God granted your request in Tadgh's case," she said hopefully.

"Aye. And, too, perhaps Lucat-mael lied in order to make you stop thinking of Keagh. Perhaps he really only sent him into exile, for to drown a helpless man is a grave and horrible deed. Surely no one could do such a thing."

"Lucat-mael could, Father," Marda said bitterly. "Keagh and I told you how fierce and evil he is. He hesitates not at any deed. Until Laeghaire forbade it, he it was who always sacrificed the children to Cromm Cruach as if he enjoyed it, Breeca says."

Breeca nodded vigorously. "Aye, Father Patrick. Lucat-mael and I are enemies of old," she remarked bitterly. "Before I became a Christian and learned that killing is wrong, I wanted Marda and Keagh to give me leave to poison him. I wish I'd done so. Before I became a Christian, that is," she added hastily as Patrick frowned.

"His hate will eventually consume him," he said reflectively.

"It has already consumed Keagh, Father Patrick."

"Have you prayed for him, Marda?"

"What good would that do? If God had chosen to deliver him from death as He did Tadgh, then surely He would have done so and Keagh would be here with us now. Instead, he lies at the bottom of the eastern sea. I . . . I am very angry with God. He is as cruel as Cromm Cruach."

"Never think that, Marda," Patrick said kindly. "You are struggling with grief, now, and so you are understandably bitter. Perhaps, child, God wants Keagh with Him. Perhaps Keagh's death will better serve His purpose to bring the holy faith to the Irish. You must, then, accept it and comfort yourself that Keagh was God's man at the time of his death. Even now, he may be happy in paradise."

"But I will never be happy until I join him there," she said, choking with grief. She thought of Keagh's sweet face, lit by his deep, dark eyes that almost disappeared into a dozen laugh lines when he smiled, the tumbling, curly brown hair and the cleft in his handsome chin. With all her heart and soul and mind and strength, she needed and wanted him. Couldn't God have found a better way to inspire devotion in the Irish than by taking Keagh from her?

"God has promised never to burden us more than we can bear, Marda," Patrick said gently.

"You are wrong, Father Patrick, for Keagh's death is more than I can bear. God must have made a mistake."

Angas took Marda's cold hand in hers and lifted it to her own cheek. There were pools of tears in her eyes as she looked sadly at the old priest.

"I would give anything if I'd been able to change my husband's mind. All this wouldn't have happened if Laeghaire had refused Lucat-mael's demand for her. But, she has walked the distance to Slane and back twice this day and she is very tired. We must let her rest."

"You are right, my lady." Patrick stood up and sketched the sign of the cross on Marda's forehead. "Rest, Marda, and lay your burden on the Lord for now." He turned his gaze to Angas. "You look weary too, Angas. Rest now—I'll return later."

Breeca closed the door behind Patrick, then sent for a bowl of hot broth which she proceeded to season and spoon into Marda. When the weary girl had finished it, the old woman tucked the coverlet up under her chin.

"Father Patrick would not approve, Marda, but I gave you a druid potion to ensure a quiet and dreamless sleep."

Marda nodded. Already her eyes were very heavy. Just before she dropped off to sleep she heard Breeca mutter, "And I only wish I'd fed a stronger one to Lucat-mael. Before I became a Christian, of course."

Marda slept for more than a day, thanks to Breeca's merciful potion. When she awoke, the knowledge that Keagh was dead struck her so forcibly that she lay gasping for breath. The grief was not a raging torrent now, but a deep, never-easing ache that she knew she'd never escape as long as she lived. Sighing, she rolled onto her side.

Angas was there, sitting on the little stool beside her bed, her head and shoulders resting against the wall in an awkward attempt to find ease. She slept, her dark lashes like black feathers against the pallor of her cheek. Marda stared at the dear face. The round cheeks seemed sunken and the eyes shadowed. Her baby moved visibly across the great mound of her stomach and, still sleeping, she put her hand on the movement, a slight smile on the pretty face. A great tenderness for the ardrigan filled Marda's heart, partially easing her own grief. She thought of Keagh's concern for Angas. He had thought she might very well have a hard time because of the size of her infant. Now he wouldn't even be here to help her. Marda's eyes filled with tears. Don't make me lose her, too, she prayed urgently. She reached out and touched Angas's hand, waking her.

"My lady, you should be in your own bed," she chided her. "You shame me that you suffer on my account."

Angas smiled.

"You look better, child," she said. "I've been so worried about you."

"Dear lady, you should be concerned for yourself." Marda swung the coverlet back and sat up. "Breeca and the others should have made you lie down. Come, now, back to your own room."

Angas stood up, nodding. "You *are* better," she said, laughing. "We tried to wake you because—oh, Marda, you're not as strong as you thought," she added as Marda clutched at the bedpost, for when she'd tried to stand up, a great dizziness had assailed her.

Angas called to Tober to bring a tray for Marda and gently

pushed the girl back down. "You've overdone for days, darling," she said, pulling the coverlet up over Marda's knees. "And eaten nothing but a small bowl of broth in two days. I was beginning to think Breeca had overdone her potion. . . . Oh, Marda, I'm so glad you're awake."

She clapped her hands together as if in barely contained excitement. Her eyes, circled with weariness though they were, yet sparkled. Marda stared at her soberly, hurt and angry that Angas, whom she had regarded as her own mother all her life, should seem to be exhibiting so little sympathy with her grief. She sighed deeply.

"I know that I must eat, my lady," she said. "Though, God knows, at this point I don't care whether I live or die. But that is really of no concern to anyone else and I shouldn't burden—"

Angas laughed and shook her head.

"Poor Marda, you think me unfeeling. . . . Oh, darling— we've been waiting for the drug to wear off—"

She was interrupted by a tap at the door and, moving ponderously, she went to open it.

"No doubt it's Tober with the tray," she said, chuckling delightedly. Marda's lips tightened and she felt hurt tears form in her eyes. Angas threw the door wide.

She saw the napkin-covered tray first and then, as the bearer, taller than little Tober, came into the room, she raised her eyes to the face.

It was Keagh.

He thrust the tray toward Angas who took it, laughing uproariously now, and deposited it on the table. By then Keagh had reached Marda's side and gathered her into his arms. Angas slipped quietly out and shut the door behind her.

"It's really you? Oh my darling, are you alive or have I just summoned you in my awful loneliness?"

Keagh was raining kisses on her wan face and hair and neck. She tightened her arms around him and gripped his neck and shoulder, pressing her fingers in, savoring the touch of him beneath her hands.

"I'm real, Marda, sweetheart. Thanks be to God, I'm real. Can't you tell?" He kissed her so deeply, as if he would draw her so close that they'd finally meld and become one, not letting her go, holding to her with all his strength, yet tenderly, too, that she could only answer with her happy heart.

"Did Patrick save you as he did Tadgh, then?"

"No, my darling." The kisses still fell along her chin and throat. Not only his touch and his own suspiciously wet eyes told her it was truly Keagh but the clean, cedar scent of him. She lay across his heart—weak, it was true, from overexertion and lack of food, but gathering strength every second because Keagh was alive and holding her in his arms.

"Did Lucat-mael lie, then, about having thrown you overboard sewed in . . ."

Keagh laughed tenderly. "No, Marda, he did it. He himself threw me overboard, at least a couple of miles offshore, bound and sewed into a length of canvas."

"Then . . . then God has granted us another miracle," she said humbly. "Oh, Keagh, I'm so ashamed for I said He was cruel . . ."

"It was a miracle," he agreed and told her briefly about the fisherman's help. "But it was not Laeghaire's idea," he added, "and, surely, when the ardri learns about the druid's duplicity, he'll cast off his hold."

"You're not going to walk back into their power, Keagh?"

"We were alone last time, Marda. Don't worry. This evening, Patrick and the others have been invited to dinner in the banqueting hall." He laughed grimly. "I can't wait to see Lucat-mael's face when he sees me alive and well. In just these few hours, Marda, Patrick has already gained many followers who are listening eagerly to his words about God. Everyone at Tara was greatly impressed that he was not struck dead on Beltane eve for defying Lucat-mael. Indeed, Laeghaire's own brother Conall has given him land to build a church. And the land was a gift to him from Laeghaire himself. We have friends at last, Marda, and neither Lucat-mael nor Laeghaire would dare try to murder me openly again."

She nodded thoughtfully. "I can see that you're right about that, Keagh," she said, "but no treachery is beneath Lucat-mael, so you must be careful always."

"We must convince the ardri that Christianity will be like the dawning of a bright new day in Ireland. He's a bold warrior, but ever he has lived in fear and trembling of the unknown and Lucat-mael has preyed on him by exploiting his fear. I want no such dark world for our children, beloved."

She smiled gently and traced the line of his jaw with her finger. He turned his face slightly until his lips met it. He kissed each fingertip, sending little shivers of delight along Marda's spine, then placed his lips softly in the palm of her hand, holding her transfixed with explosive new feelings. She drew her hand away and replaced it with her own lips against his. They clung together blissfully as Marda's grateful heart sang a song of praise for his delivery. If God had brought them so far together, delivered him from the devouring sea, then surely He would see them safely through the coming battle against the dark forces of Lucat-mael. They *would* ultimately be together. They were meant for each other.

There was a soft tap at the door and Marda drew away from Keagh as Angas came back, followed by Daneen who was smiling delightedly. She ran to embrace Marda and pat Keagh's shoulder roughly.

"You'll have to leave off embracing her until she can get dressed, Keagh," she teased. "And Breeca's coming with a bowl of soup, this time without a potion, for she says Marda needs some nourishment to tide her over until dinner."

Keagh rose reluctantly and leaned over Marda to bestow a last kiss.

"When you first go into the hall, Marda, don't say anything about me, for as yet Laeghaire and the others don't know I'm alive. They're planning new contests to test Patrick's power, of course, and while he wouldn't lie if put to a direct question about how I survived, he's not going to volunteer the information. The other druids and the king will think it's an example of God's power and, after all, so it is. But Patrick plans to use all the dramatic effect he can get out of my appearance. Until tonight, beloved."

The banqueting hall was already crowded when Marda and the other women of the ardrigan's household followed Angas into the great room. All the tables were covered with immaculate white cloths embroidered with ancient patterns around the edges. Servants were lighting rush lamps hung along the walls, for the evening was foggy outside and gloomy within.

Marda had never seen so many people at Tara in all the years she'd lived there. She'd known, of course, that Laeghaire had been gathering the hosts because Lucat-mael had prophesied about Patrick, telling the king he was a powerful enemy who must be dispatched. But from the excited snatches of conversation around her she realized that already his hosting had benefited Patrick as much as it had his enemies, for many were already attending Patrick's classes and there was a strong pro-Patrick party, led by Dubhtach and Fiacc, who thought the ardri's treatment of the old man had been shameful. Angas, Daneen, and several of the queen's women had also become Patrick's pupils and spent much time in prayer for Laeghaire's conversion, much to the annoyance of Lucat-mael. During the time Marda had been sleeping, the druid had continually been summoning magical spells, challenging Patrick to better him. Indeed, the courtiers kept saying, the fog that had begun as the sun drew west this evening was the dread ceo druidechta or druid fog, summoned by Lucat-mael to further test Patrick.

Marda had to remind herself to keep her demeanor sober as would be expected from a girl who'd just lost her beloved. But as she thought of Keagh's merry laughter and anticipated how shocked Lucat-mael would be to see him alive, she was hard put to keep her lips from twitching into a smile. She kept her eyes averted as much as she could and quickly took her place at the queen's table, for surreptitious glances told her that Lucat-mael was watching her closely.

At last Patrick and his household of priests came into the hall. They were shown to a place of honor near the queen's table and just below the ardri's, so that Lucat-mael and Lochru were almost opposite Patrick and MacCarthen where they glared fiercely at the imperturbable old priest.

When the many-coursed dinner was finished, Lucat-mael rose in his place.

"You are guests of the ardri of all the Scots, Adzehead, because, however reluctantly, we must concede you have a certain degree of magical ability. There is no doubt that we two cannot coexist in Ireland! My forebears have governed Ireland since your Christ was a puling child, and never will we accept this new religion of yours unless you prove it is stronger than the old religion. And so we have devised contests. For instance, I've summoned a magical mist. Let us see you dispel it."

Patrick laughed scornfully.

"Only the Lord God summons fogs and mists, druid," he said.

"Not true. For I have done it."

"Then *you* dispel it!" came the sharp reply.

Lucat-mael grinned, his lips drawing back from his teeth so that he looked almost foxlike.

"I thought you would evade me. I cannot dispel my own enchantments. I called the mist. But if you be the wizard you claim, you dispel it."

Patrick stood up casually and walked to the door of the hall which he threw open. To everyone's amazement, the mist was gone. The stars shone fair and bright in the sky. Marda lowered her head, smiling. The wind had been freshening when they'd entered the hall; it was only natural that the weather would change—any countrywoman knew that. But the court buzzed with wondering comments. Lucat-mael, who surely knew about such things but must have misread the weather indicators, glowered.

"Almighty God dispelled the mist," Patrick shouted above the hubbub. "In His time, all things are accomplished. You miscalculated, druid."

Lucat-mael looked as if he'd like to kill Patrick right then and there. His mobile face struggled with various expressions, but finally his arrogant pride seemed to win.

"You are right," he said, loftily, "I miscalculated. For I first summoned the mist on the night before Beltane and so much has happened since that I forgot this is the third night. I but summoned it for three days and so it was I, not your almighty god, who dispelled the mist."

Angas laughed aloud, clapping her hand over her mouth as she was wont to do when her sense of humor got the better of her at inappropriate times. Marda lowered her head to hide her own laughter. After all, she was supposed to be heartbroken because Keagh was dead. The thought of him, laughing, holding her but an hour ago, made her heart soar and she laughed silently into her napkin.

Lucat-mael's answer had only served to discredit him with many of the diners. He hurried to redeem himself.

"You speak of this god, holy man. That misguided young liaig, Keagh, even claimed that he brought people back from the dead. Only the fairy folk can do that, on Samain night."

Dubhtach rose, his blue eyes brilliant and intent.

"Don't claim the power over life and death for the fairy folk, oh Lucat-mael," he said icily. "For never have I seen them. 'Twas always only you who claimed that. And you have proved yourself treacherous and deceitful by your treatment of young Keagh."

Laeghaire had sat silent through the interchanges between Lucat-mael and Patrick, then Dubhtach. Now he shifted uncomfortably in his chair. "I have already reprimanded my druid for putting Keagh to death, for I liked the boy well. However, he speaks to the point when he doubts Patrick's ability to bring anyone back from the realms of death. I myself would like to see such a deed."

Patrick smiled warily.

"And, I am sure, you have a convenient dead person close by," he remarked dryly.

Lucat-mael smiled mirthlessly.

"Aye. An unfortunate accident occurred to my servant, Crunnmoel, this afternoon. While snaring pigeons on the palace roof, he fell to his death on the cobbles. I will have him brought in. Raise him, priest."

He motioned to two of his fosterlings who left the hall and returned almost immediately with a stretcher on which lay Crunnmoel. The huge hall was in a clamor as everyone noticed the gore about his head.

Patrick rose from his place and went to the youth's side. He bent over him, examining him carefully. Then, with a scornful laugh, he turned and stared at Lucat-mael.

"This boy is dead, all right. But he's been poisoned. His so-called wounds are only bread dough mixed with pig's blood!" He peeled off a section of the "gore," exposing Crunnmoel's unmarred forehead underneath.

"Aye, he's dead," Lucat-mael gloated. "Now raise him up if you can!"

Laeghaire blanched. "Are you sure he's truly dead, oh Patrick?"

"Aye, ardri. He is dead. Has been for hours. I will not test the Lord my God by attempting to bring him back and if you take that as a sign I am a trickster, so be it."

"You pick and choose who will be restored to life, then, oh priest," Lucat-mael shouted gleefully. "Christians you restore, but not druids. Yet, you claim this god of yours wants all of Ireland to be his loving children. No, you can't bring Crunnmoel back. You prove you care nothing for the Irish. No one but the fairies can rise again."

Laeghaire rose in his place, staring down at Lucat-mael accusingly. "You said you'd only instructed Crunnmoel to use his druidical powers to make his heartbeat undetectable, and when Patrick had failed to restore him you would apparently bring him back. Yet, you have killed this boy, entrusted to you by his parents, just to embarrass Patrick! You go too far, druid."

Marda noticed Patrick leaning over and whispering something in Benen's ear. The little boy slipped down and left the hall, unnoticed in the uproar. Patrick smiled imperturbably.

"I fear, oh Laeghaire, that Almighty God would not be pleased with any king who had murderers of the innocent in places of power and influence. You must understand that I come here in God's name, not to perform feats of magic. Not to restore the dead to life but to bring the word of God to you that you may have life everlasting. I don't promise men will live forever in this world, oh King, but if they open their hearts to God, love each other kindly in His name, they will live forever in heaven when they depart this life. Still, it is God's will, sometimes, that those who have been unjustly put to death should be restored to us."

He stopped talking and pointed toward the great double doors of the hall. Everyone followed his pointing finger.

Keagh stood there, immaculate, almost seeming to shine, in his druidical robes.

And Lucat-mael's frightened screams shook the ramparts of Tara.

CHAPTER 7

During the following weeks, a strained truce seemed to prevail although Lucat-mael spent much time in his own quarters, practicing imbas forosuai, which was the rite wherein he ate a raw piece of a dog after chanting an invocation over it, then going to sleep. His subsequent dreams, he believed, would tell him the will of the gods. He'd wake from these enchanted dreams more vehement against Patrick than ever, and would go to Laeghaire demanding that the old man be banished from Tara or, better still, destroyed, for his presence angered the ancient gods, he declared, especially the Morrigan who watched on the battleground and sent death and destruction to her enemies, then ate their flesh.

Laeghaire, although he'd been impressed and frightened by Patrick's wonders, would blanch at Lucat-mael's tirade. He was torn between his innate trust of Keagh's declaration that he'd seen Patrick restore a dead child by his god's power and his deep, lifelong fear of the old gods. As a warrior who'd only too often witnessed the ravens hovering over a battlefield, waiting to pounce on the newly dead, he was most frightened of the Morrigan. To have one's flesh rent from one's bones and eaten, never to be able to go to the Isle of the Blessed, that was fearsome indeed.

So, while he listened to Lucat-mael's interpretation of his godsent dreams and agreed that something would have to be done about Patrick, he avoided offending Patrick's god by allowing Angas to attend the daily catechism lessons under a spreading yew tree beyond the parade grounds and even agreeing to her being baptized.

"Women are certainly flighty creatures and the goddess would not hold me responsible for what you do, my Angas," he said smugly in the privacy of her grianan where he came each morning and evening to check on the progress of her pregnancy.

Usually, her girth and weariness increasing alarmingly, Angas would be lying on her couch, her women seated on cushions on the floor, sewing baby garments for the expected royal child.

"My darling Laeghaire," Angas cried fondly, "I have been baptized as have Dubhtach, Fiacc, Daneen . . . oh, so many others. Indeed, Keagh was saved from drowning and surely that was a miracle brought about by the protection of Almighty God. The Morrigan has not hurt us! Which proves she either doesn't exist or has no power against the true God. She is only a minor demon at most!"

"It may prove only that she waits!" Laeghaire said fearfully, glancing over his shoulder. "Lucat-mael thinks I should destroy Patrick."

Breeca, newly restored to a position of respect at court and decently clean in new white linen clothing, bit off her thread and smoothed a tiny shirt across her lap.

"But you won't do it, will you, my lord?" she asked complacently, "for then you'd have the Christian God to worry about. And, in your heart, you fear He is more powerful than all the ancient ones together!"

Laeghaire frowned at the old woman who'd been in his father's and kinsman Nathi's court all the years he was growing up. "Don't glower at me, oh Laeghaire; you look like you did at eight when I told your father to birch you for sneaking mead! An ardri of Ireland, my lord, must be willing to hear the truth!" she said.

"Take care I do not banish you again, old woman, no matter my lady Angas has taken a fancy to you!" Laeghaire said gruffly, but Marda could see his lips twitching as if he were trying not to smile. "I have followed the ancient ways of my people all my life and I do not change easily," he added stiffly. "Let it suffice that I have stayed my hand and allowed Patrick to bide here in peace."

"And will you allow Marda to marry Keagh?" Angas said daringly. Her wan cheeks flushed with excitement as she stared at him, waiting for him to answer.

"We'll say no more about it just now," he said gruffly, his big hand going out to stroke her cheek. "You've enough to do taking care of yourself, lady, and seeing that my child is safely born."

He leaned over and kissed her. Then, as they all stood, he left the chamber. Angas's eyes danced.

"Marda, he's weakening," she cried happily.

Marda dropped her sewing and clapped her hands together and Daneen hugged her exuberantly. Breeca beamed and nodded as if to say, "I told you so."

"I am beginning to hope, my lady," she cried in delight. "Oh, not that I don't believe with all my heart that Keagh and I will wed when I've honored my father's wishes that I wait until I'm seventeen. For even if we have to run away from Tara, we will, but I want to stay here with you, my lady."

Angas took her hand and drew Marda down to kiss her cheek. "He'll come around," she said dreamily. "If only Lucat-mael and the other druids would accept Patrick's teachings."

"You ask for the moon, lady," Breeca said, jabbing her needle at the embroidered bird on the little shirt as if she were angry with it. "Druids will never accept any teachings that take power from them. Oh, before you tell me that Keagh and I have, let me explain the difference between us and the others. I, a woman, tormented my druid father until he let me become a druid liaig for only in the druid school was the learning to be had. And much did I learn, too. Keagh is like me. He wanted the knowledge. Keagh scorns the power, though, and I do not. If Patrick makes one mistake, it is to underestimate the power! I never could command much, I grant you, but Lucat-mael does. Oh, he has power. Now I know it is from the dark demons and sorry I am I didn't give him a potion—before I became a Christian, of course."

"Breeca, you don't mean that," Marda chided. "Our Lord forbids killing and you have become a good Christian."

"Aye, Marda," Breeca said pensively. "Of course."

"Speaking of physicians, Keagh has been as closely involved with my pregnancy as Lochru although he says good red meat, cow's milk and lots of cresses will do me more good than the distillation of cinquefoil Lochru has prescribed," Angas said, laughing. "Look at that, Marda." She held her arms out and looked down at her abdomen where it seemed to thump and roll as if it were some sort of great sack full of puppies. "A mighty child! He'll probably pop out, fists flying."

Marda smiled at the queen, trying to hide her concern. Keagh had been growing increasingly anxious about the baby's position.

"It lies with its head in her pelvis as it should," he'd confided to Marda, "but its spine lies along the queen's spine so that the little forehead will present instead of the crown of the head. If it turns not in the birth canal, she'll labor in vain, Marda."

"Is there nothing you can do, Keagh?"

He had stared for a long time at a bunch of wrens dusting themselves. "Once, when I was first a student under an old man named Lucan who'd studied in Rome, I saw him use a sort of paddle contraption to grasp the baby's head and turn it. But it was very tricky, he said. If used too soon, it would snap the child's neck and destroy it and if too late, the mother would likely die from the rigors of a prolonged labor. Angas's child is a big one, too, so that turning it would be difficult. I don't know if I have the skill." He shook his head worriedly. "Perhaps it will change position yet, although by now, usually the child has assumed the birth position."

Marda stared at his anxious expression.

"Can't you make such a contraption, Keagh? In case the baby doesn't turn." She thought of gentle Angas struggling in vain to bear her child. Mothers died, Keagh said, when the babe wouldn't turn. Her palms grew sweaty and she shuddered.

He threw her his whimsical, one-eyed grin. But there was more than a hint of worry in it, as well as humor.

"I already have, beloved. When I saw how things were likely to be with her, I drew a sketch of what I'd need and the smith has cast me one in bronze. It looks much like old Lucan's, shaped to a baby's head and like crossed, connected spoons. God willing, I will be able to ease and guide the baby into the right position. But I have never done it, and even Lucan was sweating blood before he had the mother safely delivered."

"You will do it, Keagh," Marda said proudly, snuggling against his chest. "Does Angas know you're worried about her?"

He shook his head and stroked Marda's cheek.

"It seemed cruel to tell her, for then she'd not only have to endure what may be a hard ordeal but worry about it in the bargain. I have just told her that I want her to send for me at the first sign of labor, even if it be in the middle of the night. Lochru, who doesn't think as kindly of me now that I am a Christian, said I was a young fool but I think Angas will do as I asked."

"I will see that she does, Keagh," Marda said firmly.

And indeed, she seldom left Angas's side unless Breeca or Daneen, who had also been pledged to send for Keagh at once should labor begin, were with her.

As she stared at the lovely queen, Marda thought Keagh was quite right not to have burdened her with a worry she could do nothing about. Angas had been pregnant frequently before but had always miscarried early. Despite the difficulty of this pregnancy, she was radiant and delighted with her child's size.

But the entire court seemed to watch with bated breath for the birth of Angas's child. She was much beloved by the people and everyone at Tara knew that Patrick had declared Laeghaire's seed, save for this child in Angas's womb, would never rule at Tara.

Marda sighed softly and returned to her sewing. So much depended upon the safe delivery of this child.

And only Keagh could do it. Her heart filled with a misty tenderness. One more reason, aside from her great love of him, to thank God for saving him from the ocean.

If Angas died, she would have lost a mother.

Marda usually rose before the rest of the queen's court to spend some time in her garden. Although it had suffered some neglect just at the beginning when she and Keagh had gone north to find Patrick, it was flourishing now. Each day she weeded and loosened the earth around the plants, watering it during the few days there was no afternoon shower for the weather had been rainier, stormier this summer than usual. Lucat-mael said it was the gods being unhappy with Patrick's coming.

She loved this early morning hour better than any other of the day. The world seemed to sparkle under a clean, bright sky, and even when the night had been rainy and mists clung to the ground as they did this morning, every leaf and twig, every early wandering insect seemed etched with crystal. The scent of flowers and newly turned earth and grass from Colmagh's scythe intoxicated her senses and the grass beneath her bare feet felt like soft, damp silk.

She stopped and gazed out across her garden to the sweet

swelling hills, partly forest-clad, and the grazing kine, her heart swelling with hope and joy and happiness. Patrick had already begun to convert a goodly share of Tara's residents. Indeed, the people listened to his message and believed as if they'd been starved, suffering, waiting for years for just such a kindly creed to follow. Soon, even Laeghaire would stop resisting. He was her foster father. With all her heart she wanted him to surrender to God's love. She had tried to tell him the delight, the aliveness, the deep and perfect love they all felt since they'd accepted God, but still Laeghaire, under Lucat-mael's thrall, fought against God as if He were a conquering warrior.

Thinking of the king's druid, she knelt down and began to pull tiny sprigs of grass from around her kale plants. She knew that Patrick had high hopes of converting even Lucat-mael.

"The apostle Paul once persecuted the Christians," he said optimistically. But Marda thought Paul could never have been as bitter in his hatred for the Christians as Lucat-mael was. He was Patrick's mortal enemy and no sign of moderation did he show.

Like Lucifer, she thought solemnly.

A shadow fell across her as she knelt beside the kale plants. Startled, for she'd heard no one approach, she looked up to meet Lucat-mael's eyes. It was almost as if her thoughts had summoned him.

She brushed her hands and scrambled to her feet, backing away from him a little and watching him warily.

"I thought I might be able to speak to you alone here, at this hour," he said, almost triumphantly.

Marda stared at him, trying not to let her fear of him show. To be sure, she could scream for help but the garden lay some distance from the nearest building and, indeed, perhaps no one would hear her. He was between her and the settlement, too. Behind her lay the woods. And, should she be foolhardy enough to flee him that way, he'd easily overtake her and she'd be even farther from any aid.

"What do you want of me, Lucat-mael?" she said icily. "You have no claim on me. Even the ardri has stopped insisting I marry you."

He watched her, his eyes hooded, shielded by his heavy brows, as if he deliberately lowered his head to hide them.

"We have gotten off to a bad start, Marda," he said in a more conciliating tone than she'd ever heard him use. "I did wrong not to woo you as that impudent Christian liaig has done. If he had never come to Tara, no doubt you'd have favored my suit." His head came up, then, so that she could see into his eyes. They almost seemed to plead with her.

"Even had I never met Keagh, I would scarcely want to marry a man old enough to be my father," she said, not saying that she loathed him, because of a strange pity she suddenly felt for him. Hard it must be, she thought, to be feared and hated, conciliated and flattered, but never loved. Keagh never sought power, scorned to be deferred to, yet people loved him dearly. He'd only been at Tara for a few months and already he counted his friends in scores.

"Marda, well do you know that I still consider you mine. Our ardri has broken faith by vacillating on his promise to give you to me." He waved his hand as Marda opened her mouth to speak. "Aye, I know what you are going to say—that you won't be 'given.' Though I am a traditional man, though I believe you are but a woman whose wishes needn't be consulted in the affairs of society, including marriage, I understand you feel otherwise. I have said I am willing to woo you. Already, I have begun building a fine house for you. A worthy rival to the ardri's will it be! I give you leave to visit the site and tell my builders anything that would please you. Is that not earnest of my willingness to woo you?"

Marda shook her head and attacked a weed furiously.

"Leave me alone, Lucat-mael," she said softly. "Why don't you go home and do something kind for your poor wife?"

"Gaida? She is nothing to you, Marda; forget her!"

"Even if there were not Keagh, even if I could find it in my heart to care for you, I am a Christian, Lucat-mael. Christians have but one spouse."

"Easily could I rid myself of Gaida, then."

Marda gasped and stiffened.

"I can't even talk to you; you know nothing of right or wrong!"

"The 'right' of your Christian god?" he asked contemptuously. "I curse that sort of 'right!' Right is looking out for one's own interests and serving the ancient gods. Strong and fierce and sure and powerful and *right* they are!"

Marda walked away from him, her heart hammering, pushing past him to return to the grianan, but he grasped her arm and swung her around to face him.

"Take your hand off me," she said evenly, meeting his eyes calmly.

"You'll marry me!" he shouted.

Marda deliberately reached up and released his fingers from her arm. "After what you tried to do to Keagh? I swear to you, I would be tortured to death before that! Leave me alone!"

"I have humiliated myself before you," he breathed fiercely. "I have wanted you as I never wanted a woman before and, because you are Laeghaire's fosterling, I was willing to marry you to have you. I offered you the highest honor a woman of Tara could have, being wife to the king's chief druid. Lowborn little chit! You have challenged me as surely as an enemy hurling insults before a battle. So be it."

He lifted both arms to the sky, his muscles bulging, threw his head back and closed his eyes.

"Dagda, most powerful, mighty Bel, Morrigan, mother goddess, hear me. Give me strength to smite all Christians into the earth so that their very blood nourishes us all!"

His powerful voice seemed to carom across the heavens. In spite of herself, Marda felt the hairs at the back of her neck stir at the hate and fury of Lucat-mael. She turned on her heel and continued toward the grianan.

"I summon today all virtues between me and these evils," she prayed silently, reciting Patrick's lorica, "against every cruel, merciless power which may come against my body and my soul: against incantations of false prophets, against black laws of heatheny . . ."

Lucat-mael was silent as she walked swiftly away, but just before she reached the queen's lodgings, he called out again.

"And Clidna, queen of banshees, aid me in getting Marda into my bed by whatever means."

Patrick had been working diligently ever since his Easter arrival at Tara. He'd instructed all the Gael who were interested in learning about Christianity, healing many of their illnesses that even Keagh hadn't been able to by asking God's help for them. Big MacCarthen had headed a building crew as well and the little church they built on the land Conall had given them neared completion.

Laeghaire watched impotently. Although he himself had given the fine land to his brother as a marriage gift, he would appear niggardly in the eyes of his people were he now to question Conall's right to do with the land as he pleased, but it went hard with him to see the Christian church rising at Tara.

If it bothered Laeghaire, it infuriated Lucat-mael. Daily his incantations and maledictions against the Christians grew more vehement, and he brooded over the great final test between him and Patrick which Laeghaire now countenanced, now withdrew from.

And Patrick's church was to be dedicated on the next to last Sunday of July.

Marda was awakened at dawn of the dedication Sunday by the sound of a woman softly weeping.

She jumped from the pallet in Angas's room where she'd been spending the night for more than a week as the queen's time drew near. Angas was lying on her back, her hands to her mouth in a vain effort to stifle her sobs. Marda ran and fell on her knees at the ardrigan's side.

"My lady, what is wrong?" she cried.

"Ah, dearest child, I'm sorry I awakened you . . ."

"Have your pains begun, lady?"

"Aye, these many hours past. Indeed, shortly after you retired last night." She gasped and dug her hands into the softness of the feather mattress. The veins stood out on her neck as she threw her head back and closed her eyes.

"Oh, Angas, why didn't you let me know?" Marda cried, pityingly. She held the queen's hands in hers until the pain ebbed a little. Angas smiled, brushing her tears away. "It's only become bad the last eight hours or so," she said bravely, "and I thought you should rest while you could."

Marda remembered that Keagh had asked Angas to send for him at the first sign of labor. "You've not sent for Keagh, then, either," she said chidingly. "Never mind, lady, we'll get him now."

She flew to the door and pulled it open, awakening the gilla, Bughd, a saucy twelve-year-old who adored Angas and had slept on the floor outside her room since Marda had taken to sleeping on the pallet.

"Is it time?" he cried, scrambling to his feet and blinking sleepily.

"Aye, Bughd, and long past it, too," Marda said worriedly, glancing back into the room. "Get Keagh at once!"

The boy was off like a flash of lightning and the queen's grianan, awakened by his running, began to stir. Marda ran back to the ardrigan who was having another pain. She had rolled onto her side and gripped the side of the bed until her knuckles bulged white. She whimpered softly. Sweat rolled down her forehead and mingled with the tears on her cheeks.

"Hold on, my lady, Keagh will be here soon."

Marda snatched up a corner of the sheet and gently wiped Angas's face. The pain ebbed.

"It will be better when Keagh comes," Angas said confidently. "He said he'd have potions to ease the pain."

"Yet you sent not for him when it started."

Angas stared at her solemnly. "Marda, Keagh didn't have to tell me I would have a long labor," she said softly, "for, surely, such a great child will not come easily into the world. Therefore all of you who help me will have need of rest before it's over. I had no intention of making you all sit helplessly and watch me suffer until it was needful."

Another pain was growing already. Marda could only hold her hand and watch. Her eyes misted. Poor Angas. She had thought only to be unselfish in not calling for help until she had to. She didn't realize, of course, that Keagh was worried about having to turn the baby.

Daneen and Breeca came into the queen's room, still in their night robes.

"I thought that was it when I heard Bughd running as if the banshee were after him," Daneen cried, watching Angas bite her lip against the pain. It was over, then, and Angas smiled at her.

"There's time for you both to get dressed, Daneen," she said softly. "Marda, too. Have the others prepare more linens and water."

Breeca nodded and went out, Daneen at her heels.

"I'll go change when Keagh gets here, lady," Marda said. "Let me rub your back."

"Oh, aye, I'd like that. The pain seems greater in my back than anywhere."

Marda massaged and kneaded and soothed the queen's back until Keagh came in, his bulging medical bag hanging from his belt. Marda knew he had with him the contraption he'd ordered made. She swallowed hard and prayed silently that she'd be a strong and worthy nurse.

Keagh motioned to her to come outside with him.

"How long, Marda?"

"For hours and hours! Oh, Keagh, I never heard her and she thought to spare us for as long as she could. Will she be all right?"

"I'll have to determine that when I examine her. Get dressed while I'm with her, darling; it will be a long day."

He went in to the queen while Marda found clothing and threw it on, fastening her sandals with shaking fingers. She left her own room and went back to the queen's just as Bughd arrived.

"Where have you been?" she scolded, scarcely able to control her own worried voice. "There'll be much we need done . . ."

"I sent him for Lochru, Marda," Keagh said, looking up from washing his hands. "He *is* her physician, though he's left her in my care; I thought he should be notified."

"Forgive me, Bughd, my concern for the queen makes me brusque," Marda said.

Daneen and Breeca paused from assembling towels and linens on a table they'd brought in.

"Better the old fool stays away," Breeca snorted.

"He will," Bughd said, grinning. "There were naught but women at Lochru's house. They said Lucat-mael and the ardri had ordered a mustering on the parade ground."

"I wondered why my lord hadn't visited me yet this morning," Angas said, her eyes glazed by pain. She clutched her abdomen at the sides. "The pain is growing stronger in the back," she whispered weakly.

Keagh moved toward the ardrigan, patting her shoulder comfortingly, then moving his hands to palpate her abdomen. He threw Marda a worried, puzzled look.

Why are they mustering?

She knew he could read the question in her eyes as clearly as she did in his. Nevertheless, his sure hands moved over Angas's bulging abdomen, feeling the baby's position. Then he covered her gently and mixed a potion in a cup of water.

"Sip this, my lady," he said. "It will be a while yet."

Angas nodded and took the cup.

Keagh took Marda's arm and guided her out of the room, shutting the door softly behind him.

"Marda, you've got to go warn Patrick," he said urgently. "Today is the dedication of the new church and most of the Christians will be there. No hosting should there be this morning! Laeghaire and Lucat-mael are planning another treacherous attack, I know it."

Marda nodded, her throat constricting with fear as she remembered Lucat-mael, his arms raised to the skies, as he invoked the fury and aid of the old gods against the Christians.

"I'm sure you're right, Keagh," she cried, clutching his arm, "but send Daneen or Breeca. I can't leave Angas!"

Breeca came out in time to hear her last words. She folded her arms across her breast and shook her head adamantly.

"Make her go, Keagh. I saw you palpating the ardrigan's belly and well I know what you found out. The baby's spine lies along the mother's, doesn't it?"

Keagh nodded grimly.

"Then an experienced liaig will you need, and not a green girl. Nor will I hear of Marda being subjected to seeing her foster mother in such travail. Go, girl, warn Patrick of this new treachery against him. You but do God's will."

Marda looked from Breeca to Keagh. He smiled pityingly at her and kissed her gently on the lips. "Go, darling. I swear to you, I'll do all in my power to bring her safely through." He took her arms and turned her firmly around, giving her a little push.

Marda took to her heels. They were right, of course. She knew nothing of birthing and Breeca and Keagh were much experienced. Angas needed them.

And, Patrick's little congregation needed her.

Outside, the day was already sizzling hot although it was just past dawn. Over the western horizon monstrous clouds, pale gray like druid mist, hung menacingly. Indeed, once she thought she heard the rumble of far distant thunder. Even the birds were silent as if oppressed by the hot, heavy air.

She moved into the shelter of the building and looked out toward the parade ground from concealment. Bughd was right. Far at the other end, almost to the oak wood, Laeghaire, resplendent in saffron-dyed shirt and trews, his plaid wrapped around him, stood out in front of a body of several hundred men, facing them. They appeared to be readying themselves for a march on the church, which lay to the north behind the Rath na Seanaid where Laeghaire had received Patrick on his coming to Tara.

Swiftly she ran from the shelter of Laeghaire's new dun and behind the huge main rath where she'd been reared and where the court still resided. She could move far more fleetly than the army, and after a furious dash she reached the church and burst through the door just as Patrick, dressed in his best robe, came onto the raised place before the altar, Benen carrying the Sacrament at his side.

"Father Patrick, Laeghaire and Lucat-mael are assembling the host against you. They come this way!" she cried.

The congregation stared at her for one long, strained minute. Then children began to cry and people jumped up in panic.

Patrick raised his arms as if to bless them.

"Peace, my children. Don't panic or you'll be their victims. Here, now, sing the lorica and leave the church by this back way. You must take shelter in the woods."

"You are fleeing, Father Patrick!" MacCarthen yelled incredulously, the great procession cross held out in front of him.

"By my God of judgment, you know better than that," Patrick snapped. "But the women, children and old men must be gotten out of here."

"Oh, hurry, they were already starting toward the church when I left the grianan," Marda cried, taking a child from the arms of an old woman and starting from the church at the rear.

"Smite them, Father Patrick," Benen cried, his wide eyes dark blue in the building's dim interior.

Patrick frowned. "God will protect you," he kept saying as he hurried folks along to safety. Patrick pushed the little boy toward Marda, who took his hand and drew him along with her.

Together, they clambered into the woods behind the banqueting hall from where they could see down to the cleared space in front of the little timber church. Marda put Benen down and pushed the child farther back where the women took charge of him. She stationed herself in the shelter of a big tree. The host had reached the edge of the clearing and had surely seen them climb into the woods, but Patrick and the men stood between them and the army as they took up their defiant post in front of the church.

Laeghaire's chariot, flanked by those of Lucat-mael and Lochru, rolled in front of the marching men. Patrick watched them come. Lucat-mael's dark eyes roved along the edge of the woods, his lips curled in a cynical smile. When he caught sight of Marda, he frowned.

"Why come you, thus armed, to my church?" Patrick thundered.

Laeghaire didn't answer but urged his chariot driver onward with a poke to his ribs. Off to the west, the dark clouds seemed to be massing and Marda distinctly heard the rumble of thunder.

By now she could clearly see the men marching behind the row of nine chariots which contained the company commanders as well as the ardri and his druids. They seemed to question each other as they marched and, curiously, they slowed, failing to keep pace with the steadily moving chariots. Laeghaire, hearing the murmur that swept the ranks, looked back in annoyance.

"You said we were but training, ardri!" came a voice from the ranks.

"Who said that?" yelled Lucat-mael furiously.

But there were many cries of protest, now that the host understood their true purpose.

"We march not against this just man!" "Leave the Christians in peace on their day of dedication!" and, occasionally, a shout of "Kill the Christians, by Dagda."

The host came to a halt and Laeghaire's charioteer turned his vehicle so that the ardri faced the army, his back to Patrick. A tall soldier stood out from the rank, resting his long shield on the ground beside him with one hand and his spear on the other side of him with the other.

"Laeghaire, I trust you have brought us here to do honor to Patrick on his special day," he drawled, "and unseemly it is that we are armed."

Lucat-mael turned and hissed furiously.

"Attack the Christians, destroy them!"

Overhead, a crack of lightning rent the heavens. Marda jumped nervously and she was not the only one. Benen crept to her and twined her skirt in his hand. "Patrick will smite them in God's name, Marda," he said comfortingly.

"Nay, sweetheart, you have been listening to those silly tellers of tales," she murmured.

"We will not kill unarmed men, some of them aged," cried another man. "Unworthy of an ardri of Tara is such a shameful act."

"He speaks wisdom, oh Laeghaire, son of Niall. Your father would cringe in shame to see you!"

"You dare to lecture me?" Laeghaire cried. "Kill them, I say!"

Another bolt of lightning struck a tree to Laeghaire's right and rent it to the ground. The cracking sound and the burning in the heavy air caused even Lucat-mael to cry out in superstitious awe.

"Wipe them out or, by the Dagda, they will destroy us all," the chief druid cried and some of the soldiers, eyes glazed with fear, surged forward, spears upraised, as if to comply. Marda, her heart hammering with fear, knelt and drew Benen against her, prayers on her lips.

But an angry buzzing swept through the rows of soldiers and as many of them who tried to obey Lucat-mael, that many and more refused, turning on them who would attack the Christians. Patrick stood, the sudden, driving rain pouring down on his white head, his crosier aloft as if it were a banner.

"See, by the Dagda, he curses and destroys you," Lucat-mael screamed, grabbing the reins from his driver and beating his horses with them so he could roll right over the old man. The horses, terrified by the thunderous storm, reared and screamed, upsetting the chariot and the men in it.

Marda held Benen tightly against herself and pushed with all her strength against the great oak tree as if she could gather courage from it. Never had she seen such a storm. Trees fell, crushing men and horses, while battle-axes and spears drank deeply. Men screamed and fell, milling around in the rapidly muddying ground, while behind her, sheltered by the woods, yet afraid the lightning would fell the trees on them, women and children wailed.

And through it all Patrick stood, his crosier aloft, as if an invisible, impregnable wall stood around him. His eyes were tightly closed and his lips moved in prayer.

"He curses you," cried Mantais, the king's druid.

Marda stared down at him. "You fool," she cried, "your own wicked deceit curses you! Patrick but prays for our safety!"

Behind the ardri and the druids, the carnage grew. Soon men were literally climbing atop bodies to fight. After an endless time, the storm seemed to abate and the last of them fell.

Only Patrick and his people on the church porch, Laeghaire, Lucat-mael, Lochru, and Mantais had survived the bloody and stormy battle!

Slowly, the Christians began making their way down to the church. They were drenched, crying silently, gazing with awestruck eyes at the terrible battlefield. Only the cries of the dying broke the sudden stillness as the storm rolled off to the east across the sea.

Suddenly, grabbing a battle-ax from the hand of a dead soldier, Lucat-mael let out a horrible cry and ran frantically toward Patrick.

"In the name of God, stay your hand, oh wizard," cried MacCarthen, stepping out and bringing the procession cross down on Lucat-mael's arm, sending the ax flying harmlessly through the air. "How dare you strike at holy Patrick! How dare you try to kill his innocent ones!"

"You call *me* wizard," Lucat-mael shrieked. Marda could see stark terror in his face. He pointed a shaking hand at Patrick. "With my own eyes, I saw him call down lightning and thunder from his god to strike the ardri's host dead!"

Laeghaire backed away from Patrick, his face ashen. Slowly he turned and surveyed the ruin of his army. "They are all dead, their heads food for the great queen, the Morrigan," he said, his voice thick with dread. "You maledicted them so they fell on each other in madness and committed mayhem on each other!"

"Not I, oh son of Niall. *You* caused this!" Patrick said stoutly.

Laeghaire sagged against his chariot.

"I know not how you did this, oh Patrick, but I acknowledge you the stronger man."

"Never!" Lucat-mael yelled wildly. "Tricks and spells he has, it is true. I have underestimated him! But then, I have disdained to use my best magic on him. Beware, Adzehead!"

Marda released Benen who ran to Patrick as she stepped forward, joining the men. Her hair and clothes streamed water and the sun came out. The smell of fresh blood gagged her. She resolutely kept her eyes away from the slaughter.

"A fine day's work, my lord Laeghaire," she cried scornfully, her eyes streaming too, "to commemorate the day your wife suffers to bring forth your child!"

Laeghaire looked at her dazedly.

"Angas is in labor?" he cried, stunned.

"Aye, and suffering greatly, too. Since early last night."

MacCarthen looked up at the blazing sun's position.

"It's late afternoon now," he remarked.

Marda gasped. It couldn't be! All day long the battle had raged while they stood and watched, and it seemed but an hour.

"Why didn't you tell me?" Laeghaire cried, face contorted.

"Would you have listened? You think of nothing these days but doing Lucat-mael's evil bidding."

Lochru stirred and started toward the queen's grianan. "I will go to the queen," he said, casting fearful glances at Laeghaire.

"No need," Marda said scornfully. "Keagh is with her."

"He dares attend my patient?" cried the aged little druid.

Marda fixed him with an icy stare. "Aye, and fortunate for my lady that he does for, even if you could help her, you were nowhere to be found! Keagh says she may die. The babe lies with its back along her spine. . . ."

"If that be so, she will surely die," said Lochru dolefully.

Laeghaire cried out in agony and jumped into his chariot, beating the horses and guiding them toward the grianan.

"Come, Marda," Patrick said, taking her arm gently. "We will carry what's needful to Angas, for if Lochru is right, she will need the rites of the church."

"She will not die, Patrick," Marda said fiercely. "Keagh will save her, you'll see!" Together they followed Laeghaire's muddy tracks while the others began the bitter, hard task of burying the dead. There would be few duns at Tara this night without mothers' and widows' tears, Marda thought sorrowfully.

"I pray you are right, Marda, for by my God of judgment, I fear Laeghaire will kill him if she is dead."

But, when they finally reached the queen's room, she was lying against fresh linens, wan but smiling, her eyes clear. In her arms was a baby, big and fair with a shock of startling red hair. "A boy," Angas cried weakly. Laeghaire knelt beside her, tears streaming down his face, making tracks in the mud, yearning to touch his wife and son, yet too filthy to dare. Keagh slumped against the wall, exhaustion evident in every line of his body, yet smiling in triumph. Behind him, Breeca and Daneen and two gillas worked together to clean up the mess of childbirth. Marda saw Keagh's bloodied, double-spoonlike contraption lying on a pile of rumpled towels. Her own face split in a happy smile and she fell on her knees at Angas's other side, touching the little boy's hair reverently.

"You are well, then, my lady?" she said, laughing in nervous relief.

"Aye," said Angas serenely. "Thanks to my wonderful new liaig." She glanced at Laeghaire with a fond smile. "I'll never have another," she added as if daring him to disagree, Lochru having been his court physician before Keagh's coming.

Laeghaire nodded. He looked at Keagh gratefully.

"Lochru said if the child's spine lay along hers, she would surely die," he said brokenly. "You have my gratitude for as long as I live. You may ask of me what you will and if it is in my power, I will grant it."

Keagh gazed at Marda, his dark eyes caressing.

"There is only one thing I want of you, oh ardri," he said.

Marda, meeting his gaze, walked solemnly toward him. She stood beside him, holding his hand, and together they turned to stare silently at the ardri.

Laeghaire colored and squirmed as if he'd stumbled upon an anthill.

"Ask instead your weight in gold, liaig," he cried.

"But what I want is permission to marry Marda! All the gold in your kingdom would not be worth so much."

Laeghaire stared at his sandals, cracking the knuckles of his big hands.

"Nothing else on earth would so raise my chief druid's fury," he muttered. "You ask too much, Keagh. I *have* lifted the order that Marda is to be considered his betrothed until she is seventeen. . . ."

"You equivocate, Laeghaire," Angas said faintly. "Why do you fear him so—he has no power except what you let him have! Don't you yet realize that? And but for Keagh, I . . . your fine son . . . we would be dead!"

Keagh and Marda stood silent, watching the king. His face was a study of conflict. At last he clenched his fists into balls and looked up at them.

"I know what I would like to do," he said. "With all my heart, I'd say yes to your marrying. But none of you—nay, not even you, dearest Angas—understands why I resist Patrick. All my life I have believed in our ancient ways, that is true. And Lucat-mael has far more power than you credit him with—power given to him by virtue of his position in our society, power given by the gods Patrick despises.

"But even if I didn't believe that, as ardri of Eire I am the representative of all our kings, back through the ages. I cannot destroy our culture! Those who have gone before would rise up from their graves in protest."

"With all *my* heart, I believe you have no choice, oh Laeghaire," Keagh said quietly, putting his arm shelteringly about Marda's shoulder. "Patrick's God is not just some powerful brother to the mythical gods of history; He *is* all of them! Has it not occurred to you that long ago, in the very beginning, God revealed himself to all men, all over the world. Too many of our ancient tales resemble Patrick's. And he says others, too, in far lands have three gods in one, a mother of all mankind. . . . Oh Laeghaire, we too had this God of love long ago, perhaps, but evil men have corrupted the stories—"

"But Patrick's tales are pure, free of such corruption," the ardri sneered.

"Patrick's God, too, may have been misinterpreted by well-meaning people," Keagh conceded, "but the message that men are to love one another, help one another and, in so doing, serve God, that is not corrupted!"

Breeca came and took the baby out of Angas's arms.

"Enough!" she snapped. "My lady is exhausted in a way you men can know not of. Get ye out of here and let her rest."

Keagh nodded. "She's right. Angas, I'll be here first thing in the morning to attend you. And Breeca, if she needs me during the night, send the lad for me."

Laeghaire leaned over and kissed his son's tiny forehead. The baby made a little grimace as the red-gold beard brushed his face. The king's eyes were full of love for the little boy. He turned and kissed Angas.

"Sleep well, my queen. When I come in the morning, I hope you will be much rested and stronger."

"I will be better if you treat my liaig and my dear foster daughter well, oh Laeghaire," she said sternly. "Give them permission to wed."

Laeghaire sighed deeply.

"That, I just can't do. But Patrick has proved his god has much power by the events that have happened since he's been here. I will therefore grant him the courtesy of a trial of power. He and Lucat-mael will contend. For once and all, let us have proof if his god can vanquish the old ones. Tomorrow I will order Lucat-mael to devise such a test."

He lifted his hand as Keagh opened his mouth to speak.

"And he whose god or gods win shall have the girl."

CHAPTER 8

The court was in an uproar over Laeghaire's decree.

As the awful piles of dead from the great battle were buried, Lucat-mael's treachery repelled many. Ever a cunning, powerful speaker, though, he managed to convince others that the awful carnage was Patrick's fault, not his. Patrick had called upon his god to send the storm. Patrick had called down the magic fog so that the druid's men fell upon each other, thinking they were the foe. Patrick had come to destroy the Irish and fill the island with a society of men who despised women, and so, necessarily, practiced all sorts of abominations. As the days wore on toward Brom Trogan, the harvest festival that always occurred on August first, Marda realized that Lucat-mael was using any foul means to gain support.

Tara buzzed with gossip. It was true that Lucat-mael had acted shamefully, always setting snares for the Christians, men said, but was it right for Patrick to maledict their kern? To be sure, no one could blame him for meeting treachery with a malediction; that had ever been the way of the world. But, yet, wasn't that in contradiction to what he'd been teaching his followers?

Marda and the other Christians tried to counteract Lucat-mael's lies but the people of Tara were deeply afraid of the druid. They watched him covertly, holding their children close to their sides. After all, there was talk that the ritual sacrifices might be reinstated if things did not go well with the ardri and the druids and no one wanted Lucat-mael to remember that they opposed him.

Word that Laeghaire had decreed a great test between Lucat-mael, as representative of the old gods, and Patrick, as representative of his one, swept through Tara's lis. Aye, the citizens said, that is good. A final testing to prove, once and for all, whom to follow.

Each morning the ardri, Patrick, and Lucat-mael met in the ardri's private chamber, trying to agree on a proper test. They'd emerge at noon, Patrick smiling, the ardri and his druid scowling.

"God will be with us," Patrick said confidently to the Christians who gathered to hear of the morning's arguments.

"Have you devised a test, Father Patrick?" MacCarthen asked one morning near the end of July.

"I'm agreeable to almost anything they want to do," Patrick said, drawing Benen onto his lap. "God did not free me from captivity, send me into my long odyssey of learning, and bring me safely back to Ireland to have me fail Him. I am but the instrument of His will, dearest children. It is Lucat-mael who objects. The ardri suggested we throw my gospels and Lucat-mael's books into the Boyne and then draw them out. Whichever one escapes getting wet, his would be the winning credo."

Keagh laughed. "Sounds like an exercise in futility to me."

Patrick smiled gently. "If that silly test had been used, God would have kept my gospel dry," he said serenely. "But Lucat-mael would not agree to it."

"Why? Couldn't he think of a way to cheat?" Breeca said cynically.

"He says I worship a God of water and so He would favor me!" He laughed. "Because I baptize with water. He is right, though my God of judgment is the God of all things."

"Do you think there will ever be an agreement?" Marda asked.

"Aye, child, it is God's will," the old priest said. His eyes took on a faraway look as he stroked Benen's fair hair. "It is a contest between good and evil now," he added softly. "Between God the creator, the builder, the healer, and—those dark forces who follow the fallen angel. It may not be pleasant, but God will prevail, have no fear. He has promised us, He will be with us always!"

Marda thought of Keagh's observation that perhaps God had revealed himself to all men, to the Gael as well as to the Jew, long, long ago. And that men had interpreted Him to suit themselves. The druids, ancient and brilliant, had craved power and so had made stories of God to favor themselves.

And somehow, along the way, some of them had served the fallen angel, not God. She shivered in spite of herself. She wished with all her heart that she had Patrick's confidence, but Lucat-mael could and certainly would have all the aid that dark forces could give him.

She and Keagh discussed the coming test as they left Angas's chamber the last evening of July. Angas and the baby were thriving, although the queen was regaining her strength slowly and Keagh insisted that she stay in bed most of the time.

They walked hand in hand in the twilight, content, for the moment, just to be alone together.

"They've been closed up in Laeghaire's chamber all day," Keagh said. "Lucat-mael keeps insisting the test must be on Brom Trogan, tomorrow, when the gods are listening."

Marda laughed ironically. "He no doubt thinks that will give him an advantage."

"It's all so silly. One of the gillas who took food and drink to them says Lucat-mael even tried to poison Patrick's cup, but the old man must have suspected something; he evidently knocked it over and had the gilla pour him fresh wine. The druid is frightened, Marda; in his heart he knows that in a real test, God would prevail."

"Then, why doesn't he just capitulate? Leave the Christians in peace?"

"Because then he would not be the virtual king of Ireland any longer. And he wouldn't have you, beloved."

Marda frowned and leaned back against a tree, gazing thoughtfully at the stream flowing at her feet.

"What if, by some foul trick, he manages to win whatever contest they devise, Keagh? You know anything he agrees to will be heavily weighted in his favor. If Patrick is defeated, Ireland will crawl back into darkness and ignorance. Patrick's school for *all* the children will never be started—"

"And we, my Marda, will have to run away at once," he said softly, so that she knew he'd been thinking about it. He drew her into his arms, kissing her with quick, fierce passion. She clung to him, her heart bittersweet with longing.

"Aye, Keagh, so we must," she answered, kissing him again and again at the thought of Lucat-mael's winning. "And for Patrick, too, I fear, for Lucat-mael will never rest until he talks the ardri into destroying him and the other Christians."

"No, Marda, I don't think even Lucat-mael will do that. After all, Angas is a Christian now and Patrick baptized little Lugaid, the baby, last Sunday. He can hardly destroy the king's wife and child."

She shook her head sorrowfully.

"If Lucat-mael wins and Patrick is killed, perhaps they will no longer be Christians. Perhaps no one in Ireland will dare!"

But Keagh was never one to be discouraged for long. He lifted her chin and smiled down at her. "We are talking like doubters, my darling. We must have faith! I—I have felt the hand of God about me all summer. When Laeghaire challenged me, making that sarcastic remark about Patrick's tales being all true, I started thinking a lot about—all of this. Maybe Patrick and the Holy Father in Rome don't have all the answers, but they're a very, very great deal closer to it than Lucat-mael! And I would give my life for God, Marda. That's all I know."

"I love you, Keagh," she cried.

He smiled and bent to take her lips again. A sweet, quiet, yet powerful feeling of joy flowed through Marda. Keagh was right. She too felt God's presence with them. When they were together like this, it was as if God smiled and blessed their happiness. As if they stood at the beginning of a long journey they would take together. What could possibly come between them?

Suddenly they heard someone running headlong down the path from the settlement. They turned together to see Benen, his tunic flapping furiously about his legs, blue eyes wide, coming toward them. He ran into Keagh's arms and was swept up.

"Slow down, boy, what's the hurry?" he said, laughing.

"Patrick said . . . Patrick said . . . you and Marda are to come . . . come to the Rath na Seanaid. Everyone . . . is summoned."

Keagh turned to Marda. His dark eyes were alert.

"It's come, beloved; the test is ready."

Only the very old, young, or sick were absent from the Rath na Seanaid.

Laeghaire sat in his great thronelike chair, Lucat-mael standing beside him, a malevolent smile on his face. The other druids of the ardri's council sat in their usual places in a semicircle facing the ardri. Patrick stood with his back to them, facing the king and Lucat-mael so that he seemed almost like a man on trial.

Marda and Keagh made their way to the front of the hall to stand beside Breeca and Colmagh. When Patrick saw them, he smiled and nodded. But Marda thought his eyes seemed troubled.

Almost as if he'd been waiting for their appearance, Lucat-mael then stepped forward.

"As you all know, tomorrow is Brom Trogan," he said, and instantly there was complete silence in the vast hall. "Since mid-July, we have been passing through Lugnasa. The great god Lug established August first, the day his foster mother died, as a great festival and so it is fitting that tomorrow we have a final test between the ancient ways and Christianity."

Marda looked from Lucat-mael to Patrick. The old priest, too, seemed to be hanging on Lucat-mael's words.

"We have spent enough time dickering over a fair test," the druid continued, his forehead creasing. Laeghaire opened his mouth as if to speak but the druid ignored him. "Tomorrow, at break of day, will the test be," he barked.

"You have not yet told me where and what it will be, oh Lucat-mael," Patrick called out.

The druid smiled down at the old man maliciously.

"You said it mattered not what test I chose, old man," he said with a curl of his lip. "You said your god would answer any challenge."

Patrick nodded, not taking his eyes off the druid. Marda felt her mouth grow dry. She took Keagh's hand. It was feverishly warm and he watched the druid as intently as did Patrick. *What made him smile so gleefully?*

Laeghaire cleared his throat.

"He is right, oh Patrick," he said almost apologetically. "You were agreeable to putting your books and Lucat-mael's into the Boyne, to submitting them to fire as well."

"But your druid claimed that I worshipped water because I baptized your son with water, and that I worshipped a god of fire because I was not killed for lighting the Paschal fire on Beltane eve," Patrick drawled.

A slight titter traveled through the hall, but as Lucat-mael glared at the crowd they fell into an uneasy silence. Marda looked from the druid's taut face to Patrick's gentle, unlined and serene visage. Couldn't they see the difference between them? With Patrick was all goodness, gentleness and peace; with Lucat-mael, fear and hate.

"Ready do you find me, ardri, to submit to any contest of faith you want," Patrick said. "But these two weeks have we discussed what this test will be and haven't reached any test acceptable to Lucat-mael. Now, without telling me what it is to be, he calls the entire kingdom here to reveal it. A courtesy would I consider it had I been told in advance."

Lucat-mael laughed mirthlessly.

"Your god would protect you, whatever we chose," he said mockingly.

Patrick merely bowed his head.

Lucat-mael strutted up and down, even passing in front of the ardri in his arrogance. He met Marda's eyes and she found she couldn't tear her gaze away from his.

"You, maiden, have scorned the house I ordered built for you," he cried. "And so I have had it finished for another purpose! It will be the site of the final test."

Keagh put his arm around her shoulders and, with a great effort, Marda pulled her eyes from the druid's face and looked at the young liaig. Her heart had begun to beat furiously in her breast as a great dread of Lucat-mael's test began to grow.

"Look at me, girl," the druid shouted. "Did you not wonder why work continued on the house although you swore you'd never live in it?"

Marda stared at him wordlessly. The druid's eyes shone fanatically.

"The half of the house built in the early summer was of good, dry, seasoned wood," he continued without waiting for her to answer—and indeed she could not have if her life had depended upon it. She knew—she *knew* that somehow the test was a great sham. He had manipulated them all to announce it and he held the entire assembly in the palm of his hand. She looked wildly around the hall. His soldiers were everywhere. "The half built these last two weeks is of newly cut wood," he continued imperiously as Laeghaire stared at his hands.

"Tomorrow, at daybreak," he continued, "I will enter the half made of dried wood, wrapped in Adzehead's cloak. The door will be locked from outside. At the same time Benen, Patrick's gilla, will enter the side constructed of green wood, wrapped in my tunic. The door on his side, too, will be locked from the outside. The house will be set afire. . . ." Here the entire assembly erupted in excited whispers but Lucat-mael, grinning evilly, simply spoke above it. "He who escapes unharmed will be the servant of the more powerful gods!"

"No!" Marda screamed.

Lucat-mael smiled maliciously.

"What's the matter, girl? I thought this god of yours would protect his followers from all evil," he mocked.

Patrick lurched forward. Keagh released Marda to go to the old man's aid, for he looked as if he would faint.

"I—I accept the test, save only using the boy!" Patrick said loudly. "The contest is between us, oh Lucat-mael; let the peril be on us, too."

"Your god picks and chooses whom he will aid, then, oh holy man," the druid mocked gleefully. "*You*, he protects; your gilla he will leave at the mercy of the flames!"

"God will protect Benen as His representative as readily as me," Patrick roared. "But, druid, 'tis criminal to frighten a child!"

"Let me take Benen's place," Keagh said, his arm around the old man.

Lucat-mael stared at him malevolently.

"You don't know how much I'd like to do that, oh liaig," he said with a sneer. "But I want you alive to realize you have lost. You and Patrick will die soon enough!"

Marda ran to Laeghaire and threw herself at his feet.

"Foster father, you cannot allow this," she cried. "A dishonor entirely it is! Oh, Laeghaire, why don't *you* speak? Why do you let this evil man make of your name a disgraceful sound?"

Lucat-mael grabbed her wrist and jerked her up beside him. Keagh started forward to intervene but the druid brought his hand down and, as if they'd been watching for the signal, the soldiers seized him. Throughout the hall, others of the royal guards secured MacCarthen, Odran and the other able-bodied Christian men.

"Take them all to the hostage mound," Lucat-mael shouted over the uproar. "Lock them up securely and double the guard. Tomorrow, by Dagda, Ireland will be rid of this Christian plague."

Patrick shouted for attention.

"If you lock them up, you must lock me too!"

Lucat-mael stared at him contemptuously.

"You will be watched, old man. Don't try to take the boy and run away, for it will do you no good—and will be construed as an acknowledgment of defeat."

Patrick lifted his head proudly. He put his hand on Benen's bright head and the little boy wrapped his arms around the old man's leg.

"We won't run away," Patrick said.

"Nay," Benen echoed, "we won't run away. God will protect me as well as He would Patrick." He looked up at the old man, his eyes shining. "I am not afraid, Father Patrick."

They dragged Keagh and the others away then. Marda, tears running down her cheeks, pulled her arm violently away from Lucat-mael's grasp, rubbing the place where he'd touched her as if it were unclean.

"You won't intervene, oh Laeghaire?" she cried.

The ardri wouldn't look at her.

Patrick sent word throughout the settlement that he and Benen would spend the night in the church, keeping a prayer vigil, and invited them all to spend it with them.

Daneen offered to stay with Angas, who hadn't been told of the test.

Dark was falling as Marda and Breeca made their way from the queen's grianan to the church.

"Are you all right, little one?" the old woman asked.

Marda shook her head.

"Nay, Breeca, I'm not all right," she said sadly. "I know Father Patrick says we are in God's hands and everything will be all right, but I'm deathly afraid. That precious child will die in agony. And then Keagh, Patrick, the others. And I will be at that evil druid's mercy."

"I wish I'd maledicted that weasel—before I became a Christian," Breeca cried. "Ah, he was ever a self-serving wretch! Laeghaire is not an evil man. Indeed, unanimous was the vote of the tuath to make him ardri when Nathi was killed. But he listens to every vile lie Lucat-mael utters. By trickery, the druid has enslaved him."

Marda felt tears rolling down her cheeks and she paused to wipe them away. Breeca took her into her arms, murmuring soothingly.

"I always thought Laeghaire was basically just and good, too, Breeca," Marda said bitterly; "now I don't know. Keagh saved Angas's life and Patrick has brought nothing but blessing to his kingdom. Yet, he sacrifices them both willingly, not to mention my happiness, for fear of Lucat-mael. Indeed, he even banished you, poor wight. Why cannot he see that the old ways he's so fond of are evil?"

"Patrick says God will protect Benen," the old woman said, patting Marda's shoulder as she released her and they resumed walking toward the church.

"Even if He does, Lucat-mael will still be alive, I know it! He would never have devised such a horrible test unless he knew he'd have a way to escape. And then it will just go on as it has, Lucat-mael leading Laeghaire around by the nose, Ireland sinking farther and farther into pagan hate!"

"But he'll not be the winner, Marda. It won't be over."

Marda passed a shaking hand over her eyes. "He'll find a way, Breeca. Oh, I'm so tired. I wonder if Keagh's all right. Maybe . . . maybe I ought to give up, tell the druid I'll marry him if he'll only leave Keagh and Patrick and the others in peace."

"Don't be a fool, girl," Breeca snapped. Her old eyes glinted as they stepped into the circle of light from the church windows. "Do you honestly think you could trust Lucat-mael to keep his word? On that or anything else?"

Marda sighed.

"No, I guess he wouldn't." She raised her eyes to the crucifix that hung over the altar as they paused in the church doorway. Already people were kneeling in prayer and, on all the paths, others headed toward the little church to join Patrick in his vigil. Marda felt her eyes drawn and held by the suffering Christ. Even

He had not been spared from evil. Resolutely she marched down the aisle.

And if God would not spare His own son, what right had she to demand He spare the Irish Christians? Or herself?

Yet, as Patrick came in from the rear door she felt a sort of peace descend on her.

"Oh, God," she prayed, "forgive my rebellious and wayward heart and comfort my fears. Cast your loving protection over the child, Benen, and deliver us all from evil . . ."

Breeca, too, knelt in prayer. From the corner of her eye she watched Marda's lovely, troubled face. The pain in her hip, grinding as if the miller had put her old bones between his stones, flared, hot and dogged. Her shoulders sagged with every one of her nearly fourscore years. She frowned and tried to concentrate on Patrick's words as he led them in prayer. The words of his lorica, his charm against evil, comforted her. Then Patrick stood up and spoke to them about God's loving care and how He surely had everything in hand.

"He will not leave us orphans," the old man said gently. "Fear not the druid's enchantments, for God will take care of us."

Breeca thought about that. It was not that she didn't believe in God—Patrick had explained that God had been looking out for her all those lonely years in the little hut in the woods.

But it was Marda who had brought her the food and blankets that had kept her alive.

And while she knew God had delivered Keagh from the sea, it was by the hand of the old fisherman He did it. He, not God had put the knife in Keagh's hand.

Maybe, when God's will prevailed, it was because He used humans to do things for Him!

She put her head down on her hands and thought about that for a long time. Patrick had stopped speaking and was kneeling in prayer again. She remembered how Keagh had fixed her torn lip and how Angas had welcomed her into the grianan and the way little Benen loved to climb into her lap for a story. Marda, she had loved with all her heart since the child had come to her secretly in the forest, bearing the means of life. And now these dear others, too, were precious to her.

Perhaps she could help God to take care of them.

She thought of Marda's remark that Lucat-mael would never have devised such a plan unless he knew he could escape unharmed. He'd been powerfully occupied with finishing his house these last two weeks. Indeed, men worked all day and at night the hounds of Tara seemed restless, sniffing men abroad. She remembered a trick box she'd had as a young druidess. It was composed of two compartments, each with a door. There was a brightly colored box you put into one compartment and, by trickery, you could convince your audience that you'd moved it to the other side by magic. In fact, when you opened the door of the second compartment, the audience *saw* the other box.

But it was only a false door you released with a spring!

As Patrick's lorica sounded around her, Breeca realized there had to be some way Lucat-mael intended escaping from the burning house.

She murmured something to Marda about being too old for an all-night vigil. The girl patted her arm gently and whispered that she'd see her in the morning. Breeca slipped out of the pew and left the church.

The night was clear and star-bright. Every house at Tara was dark. All the Christians were at the church and the druids, by the sound of things, at the king's rath. She heard men singing and a woman's high-pitched laugh.

Breeca smiled cynically. Already they celebrated their victory. "Revel well, oh Lucat-mael," she said complacently. "God's helper, Breeca, will confound you!"

She slipped cautiously into the shadows as she descended the hill to the site of Lucat-mael's new house. Perhaps the druid would have set a guard.

But there was no one near the house. Moving quietly, keeping to the shadows, Breeca walked all around the perimeter of the building. It was, as Lucat-mael said, constructed half of well-aged oak and half of new pine redolent of pitch. She smiled and shook her head.

"If he expects the new side not to burn, he's mistaken," she muttered to herself, "for it's full of pitch which will feed it."

But maybe that was exactly what he had in mind. The house was as big and grand as Laeghaire's new li, half sunk into the ground so that one had to go down a ramp to enter either of the two doors. There was nothing unusual about that; all Irish houses were so constructed to protect them from the summer's heat and the winter's cold. Nor that there were no windows in either side. The two doors, one in the green-wood side and one in the dried-wood side, were the ony significant difference. She tried the door in the dried-wood side and found it unlocked. Within, the star-light revealed only the empty room. She shut the door softly and started to the side Lucat-mael would be locked into, but sud-denly she heard someone coming down the cobbled street. Swiftly she darted behind a bush and peered out.

Lucat-mael, dragging something heavy behind him, was turn-ing off toward the house. As he passed Breeca, she saw that what he pulled behind him was the newly disinterred body of old Darni the weaver, who'd died and been buried two days since. She bit her lips to prevent an exclamation of surprise. What on earth did Lucat-mael want with the old man's body?

He opened the door to the newly constructed green side of the house and pulled the old man's body through after him. Breeca stayed quiet, trying to see into the house but the door stood open to block her view. In a few minutes, however, Lucat-mael came out alone, smiling in triumph, and walked briskly up the hill toward the king's rath where the sounds of revelry still rolled out across the night.

When she was quite sure he was gone, she slipped out of her hiding place and went into the door of the green side. She shut the door quickly behind her and pulled her flint, a bit of tinder and a stub of candle from the sewing bag on her belt. She struck a light in the little pan and lit the candle, lifting it to survey the room carefully.

There was no sign of the body. Only the solid partition that separated the two rooms of the big li. She blinked.

Then, obviously, there was a hiding place here somewhere, she thought. She knelt on the wood floor, peering for some sign and, as she'd surmised she would, she saw where Lucat-mael had dragged the body across the threshold and into the big room. Following the track, she realized it disappeared at a spot midway on the back wall.

She felt all along the newly installed wooden paneling and, sure enough, her gnarled old fingers found a knothole that came out, and underneath it a catch that obviously operated a hidden door. She pressed it down and instantly a section of paneling swung outward, into a small tunnel, perhaps three feet across, dug into the earth near the bottom of the half-submerged room. In it lay the corpse.

She sat back on her heels, studying the tunnel.

"So that's what he planned," she said. "After they'd put him into the house and locked the door, he'd just open the trapdoor, pull the corpse within and make his escape. When the fire died down, he'd emerge from the safety of the tunnel and claim he'd been miraculously saved.

"No you won't, Lucat-mael," she whispered to herself. "God has chosen me to confound you!" She replaced the knothole carefully.

She crawled into the tunnel, pushing the dead body to the side, shuddering in spite of herself as she touched the poor thing. She held her candle in one hand and shut the door behind her with the other. The candle flame wavered in a heavy draft. She began crawling toward the night air.

"If I know him, he'll have a tunnel into the other side, too, just in case someone should insist he take the dried side instead," she muttered dryly. And, sure enough, there was a branch to the left as she crawled. She went into it and, after a while, found the door. There was no way to open it from this side.

Pondering, she made her way out of the tunnel, whose mouth was well hidden under a trapdoor strewn with leaves and dead wood. She went back into the house, this time into the dried-wood side where Benen would be and found the "key" to opening the hidden door.

She would have to tell Benen. She would have to let the child know how to escape and be there in the tunnel to help him against Lucat-mael. There was no other way.

She went back to the queen's grianan to clean herself and change her clothes, for she was filthy from dragging her old body through the tunnels. When she'd made herself clean, she went back to the church. Benen, his blue eyes owly as he fought to stay awake, knelt beside Patrick, determined to keep the vigil with the adults.

Breeca settled down to pray.

"Thank You, dear God, that You led me to the tunnel," she said inside herself as she'd learned from Patrick to do. She smiled. It was so. He was truly there and would help those who served Him. Breeca knew that she was sometimes confused lately, doubtless because of her great age. She prayed that the confusion wouldn't overtake her this day when Benen's and all the others' fates depended upon her. Weary from her own exertions, she leaned her head back against the church wall and dozed. She would wake when the morning came as she had for almost eighty years. And then she would take Benen in hand and explain about Lucat-mael's treachery.

Suddenly Niall of the Nine Hostages was there in the little church.

"Noble the deed you do this day, Breeca," he said, "for I would grieve to have my kinsman Laeghaire guilty of the blood of innocents."

Breeca jerked upright, surprised to see Niall back from the grave, but it was only Patrick, shaking her gently.

"It is time, Breeca," he said calmly. "Have you been praying for the triumph of God?"

She blinked in the faint morning light.

"I have been . . . praying, oh Father Patrick. Indeed I have," she cried. "Where is Benen?"

The old priest nodded toward his acolyte who smiled and came forward to embrace Breeca.

"One story, Breeca," he said, nestling his little face against hers. "I have been a very good boy. Tell me a story while we walk to Lucat-mael's house."

Breeca lifted the child in her arms. Although he was really too heavy for her, no one protested. He was a great favorite of all the Christians, but old Breeca was perhaps the child's favorite next to Patrick.

"A grand story will I tell you, oh Benen," she said, stepping out briskly so as to distance herself and the boy from the others. "Once upon a time, there was an evil druid who built a strange and devious house. . . ."

CHAPTER 9

All through the long night, Marda knelt in the little church, praying with all the fervor of her heart that Benen would be safe.

Around her the little church was filled with other Christians although they had lost most of their able-bodied men when Lucat-mael had so cravenly attacked on the dedication morning, for there had been many of their number in the ardri's army. By their death they had protected Patrick and the others, and the old priest said they were martyrs of God as surely as Saint Peter had been.

They couldn't expect that sort of miracle again, for the test involved only Benen and Lucat-mael. She'd hoped vaguely that somehow Keagh and the Christian men might be freed, but they were outnumbered many times for Lucat-mael had been gathering allies from throughout Ireland by the looks of the great numbers of strange kern at Tara.

Yet, through the long night as she knelt with her friends to pray, Marda's heart swelled with love for all of them. Patrick had come to Tara on May first, only three months ago, and already he had a churchful of sincere Christians—not an easy task when you considered the well-known contentiousness of the Gael. And the many long centuries of paganism in their heritage.

Breeca and a couple of the younger women whose babies began to fret for their cribs had gone off early in the night but the old woman, newly washed and changed, had returned long before dawn and dozed now, her head resting against the church wall. Marda smiled tenderly at her, noticing that despite the fact she was better fed and clothed now, her tired old face seemed etched by pain. Although Breeca didn't complain much, she was finding it increasingly difficult to breathe and her back and hip hurt abominably from rheumatics. She had been working entirely too hard, first walking all over Ireland in the quest to find

Patrick, then helping with the preparations for the new baby, and finally striving at Keagh's side all through Angas's travail. She shouldn't have even attempted the vigil. The old woman adored Benen, though, and Marda knew she must have felt weary and ill indeed, even to have taken off for two hours or so of rest.

An hour before dawn Marda, too, returned to the queen's grianan to make sure all was well with Angas and the baby. She peeked into the queen's chamber where Angas slept peacefully. In the nursery next to it Daneen and the baby, Lugaid, were also quietly slumbering. Marda gazed down at the little one fondly. He was the first newborn infant baptized at Tara. He snuffled softly in his sleep, lifting his little bottom up from the bed and hunching his legs in under him as he lay on his stomach. His downy head caught red glints from the rushlight. Gazing at him, suddenly Marda felt a warm, profound peace descend on her troubled spirit.

Lugaid represented the birth of the Christian faith in Ireland. Deep in her soul, Marda knew it was true and strong—like the house built on a rock that Patrick told them of, the very simile Our Lord Himself used. Forever, Ireland would be Christian. Lucat-mael and those like him would become part of the misty folklore, like the good and bad fairies and the luchorpan, the fairy shoemaker who must give anyone who is fleet enough to catch him his cauldron of gold. Keagh said the Irish were changing, growing up, understanding that while they were created beings, they'd not been formed by some crazy committee of gods.

She shut the door of the nursery and went into her own small room which normally she shared with Daneen. Soon it would be morning, and all over Tara the druids and the other unconverted ones would awaken and go to Lucat-mael's house for the great testing. She felt sure they'd bring Keagh, too, and the other Christians they'd arrested.

They would expect to find a bunch of cowed and frightened people, she thought wryly.

Well, despite her hard-won serenity, she *was* a little frightened. They all knew Lucat-mael would use any trick, any evil power he had to defeat the Christians. But, with God's kind help, she'd not let him see her wan and terrified. Deliberately she poured water from the pitcher by the door into the basin and washed herself, dropping her rumpled clothes on the floor and donning her best, the soft green gown she'd worn that first night Keagh had been at Tara. He had remembered it and mentioned it to her at the beginning when they were first starting to fall in love. She donned her gold neck torc and, loosening her braids, brushed her hair briskly, rebraided it and looped it in great wheels at the sides of her head. If they did bring the captives to view the test, Keagh would see her and perhaps take heart because she was dressed as if for a celebration.

She left the grianan and went back to the church, no longer needing a light to guide her. Far off, somewhere beyond the eastern sea, faint, pearly light was starting, enough to see the path. When she entered the church, Patrick was shaking old Breeca's shoulder gently. The old woman yawned and awakened. She threw Marda a quick smile, then picked up little Benen who was clamoring for a story. Marda started forward; the child was much too heavy for the old woman. Then she checked herself. Breeca and Benen needed each other during these final moments before the gruesome test.

Patrick lifted his crosier and, in the absence of MacCarthen, one of the younger lads lifted the processional cross. At a nod from Patrick, the Christians all fell into processional order and began marching slowly toward the druid's new house, singing Patrick's lorica softly.

> ". . . I bind myself today to the virtue of heaven
> light of sun,
> brightness of moon,
> splendor of fire . . ."

Marda thought of Lucat-mael's claim that Patrick worshipped a god of fire and one of water. He didn't yet understand that Patrick's God was creator of all things. She remembered the wonder of the deer coming to shield them all as they made their destined way to Tara. Benen had kissed the fawn's nose. Aye, God would protect him . . . and so all of them, this day.

But she wished there'd been some way without all the bloodshed and sorrow that had preceded this day.

Breeca kept whispering softly in Benen's ear. The little boy listened to her, his big blue eyes fastened intently on the horizon as if he saw the story she told him acted out there. Every so often he nodded as if in answer to her queries.

From every street strange kern came, marching toward the druid's house. Druids with their wives and children came too, laughing as if this were an ordinary Brom Trogan when a king and queen of the corn would be chosen and peddlers would sell fairings and sweets from wooden counters carried here on their backs or on carts. Indeed, there were a few peddlers among the crowd. The Christians, though, stood together, still singing, their faces composed and confident.

"Remember, my children, God is with us," Patrick cried as a large party of soldiers conducted their captive men, Keagh and MacCarthen at their head, to join their women and children. They were all shackled. Marda's heart lurched as she saw that Keagh's wrists were bloodied from his efforts to pull his hands through the rings around his wrists. She brushed past a tall guard to embrace him and smile encouragement to the others. Keagh's eyes caressed her and he smiled.

"You are beautiful as the morning, my Marda, and proud of you I am that you come not in rags and ashes."

"I would not give the druid the satisfaction," she said spiritedly. "Fear not, Keagh, it's going to be all right. God is with us this day."

"He'd better be," said the tall soldier beside them, "else the little lad will be fried!"

"A malediction on you," cried Colmagh furiously, pulling at his chains.

The soldier only laughed.

The druids of the king's council came with him in splendid procession, Lucat-mael, Lochru, and Mantais preceding the ardri. Accompanying them were more soldiers and they wore little except their shields and helmets. Their hair was lime-washed, pulled into peaks around their faces, as if they marched to battle. The ardri himself was handsome in his plaid trews and saffron shirt, his golden neck torc no brighter than his hair. Yet, his face was pale. Two gillas, carrying his great ceremonial chair between them, placed it on the cobbles above the druid's house, where the ardri could view the proceedings. Laeghaire sat down without preamble and gripped the arms of the chair.

Lucat-mael's eyes glittered balefully as his gaze swept the gathering of Christians. Marda lifted her head pridefully, her hand resting on Keagh's arm.

The druid frowned.

Benen had come to stand beside Marda and Keagh. She wondered that Breeca had let him go, so earnestly had she been holding him. Lucat-mael glared down at the little boy.

"Catch the brat," he snapped.

"You've no need to 'catch' him," Keagh said scornfully. "He'll not run from the likes of you."

The little boy pulled a contemptuous face, such a close imitation of the expression on Keagh's that the spectators laughed despite the tension in the misty air. Benen, always delighted to have an appreciative audience, put his hands on his hips and swaggered past Lucat-mael.

"Are you prepared, then, oh Laeghaire?" cried the druid, with a grand air of finally, belatedly giving the ardri leave to speak.

But Laeghaire didn't take advantage of it. He merely gripped the arms of his chair more tightly and nodded.

"It is not too late, ardri, to call this shameful thing off," Marda cried. "Cowardly will you seem in the tales of the bards, to have subjected a child to this test."

The druid's lip curled.

"Fearful she is, oh Laeghaire, that I will beat her soundly for having aligned herself against us when this is over."

Keagh made a choked sound.

"Never will you lay a hand on her!"

Lucat-mael laughed.

"You will not stop me, for you will have been crucified like your eunuch god!"

"Nay," cried Benen, "for I will not burn; God has already sent—"

"Benen!" cried Breeca from the rear of the crowd. "Soil not your tongue arguing with the wicked druid!"

Benen nodded and was silent.

Marda knelt and held her arms out to him. He ran to her and hugged her warmly.

"Don't worry, Marda, it's all right, truly it is!" he said, then turned and ran to Patrick.

The old man picked him up and anointed him with holy chrism.

"God will protect you, my child," he said confidently.

"Aye, Father Patrick, I know that," was the happy reply. The little boy hugged Patrick tightly around the neck, kissing the bearded cheek. When Patrick released him, Colmagh, Keagh, many of the others, too, reached to embrace him, their chains rattling.

"Enough," said Lucat-mael fiercely.

He beckoned Lochru and Mantais to come forward, Lochru bearing the tinderbox, Mantais the unlit torch. Lucat-mael ceremoniously struck the flint and lighted the tinder. Mantais thrust the torch into the flickering flame and it flared up brightly. There was an almost involuntary moan from the Christians, then they began reciting the Psalm which Patrick had taught them about the Lord as a shepherd.

Marda stood beside Keagh, blinking tears of pride.

"Come, boy," Lucat-mael said, clipping his words.

Benen walked to him, still jauntily, and stood quietly as Lucat-mael took his tunic off and put it on the little boy. It dragged about his small, sandaled feet.

Patrick took his cloak off and handed it to the druid. Marda's eyes swam so that she seemed to be staring at the dramatic scene through a crystal bowl full of water. The homely old woolen cloak had sheltered Patrick through many a long night as he slept on the floor, a stone or log for his pillow. Lucat-mael held it away from his immaculate white undertunic disdainfully. He didn't put it on as he walked toward the new side of the house, motioning Benen to enter the other side. The little boy started to run but stumbled on the long tunic. Laughing, his cheeks pitted with dimples, he caught it up and walked more sedately toward the door. Keagh muttered ominously beside her. He strained against the chains in vain.

"Peace, Keagh," Benen called merrily. "God has it all in hand!"

Incredibly, the Christians all seemed to believe him too. They joined hands, smiling, and began singing. Colmagh was shouting encouragement to the little boy, but as Benen disappeared through the heavy door and had it barred upon him, his old voice cracked. Even Patrick's shoulders seemed to sag a bit then.

Marda looked around for Breeca but the old woman was no longer near the back of the crowd as she had been. No doubt she hadn't been able to bear the sight of that bright little head disappearing into the druid's house.

Lucat-mael, his manner arrogant, strode into the right-hand side and turned to face them, Patrick's cloak still over his arm. He gave the sign for the door to be shut and barred.

Then Mantais, grinning evilly, turned and held the torch aloft. "For you, great Lug. On your holy day. And when Lucat-mael has triumphed, we go by chariot to Mag Slecht to sacrifice a firstborn bull to Cromm Cruach. All these deluded Christians, who will by then have come to their senses, are welcome!"

And, with a great, keening howl he started running around the house, where gillas had been piling dried hay, lighting it and the thatched roof from his torch.

The hay, of course, flared with a great *whoosh*. Despite the high-hearted confidence of the Christians, Marda felt them all gasp at the awful sound.

She couldn't stand it! She lurched forward, determined to force Laeghaire to call a halt, get Benen out before it was too late, but the soldiers held her.

"Stop it, oh Laeghaire," she cried and she realized Keagh, too, was shouting at the ardri.

"Courage, my children," Patrick called, and for one panicky moment Marda was unreasonably angry with him. Then, shamed, she realized he could no more have prevented this terrible thing than she and Keagh could have. "Sing with me," he commanded and his voice, strong and true, began singing the lorica where they'd left off:

> ". . . Christ to protect me today
> against every poison,
>   Against burning, against drowning,
>   against deathwound . . ."

Marda realized MacCarthen's bass and Keagh's sweet tenor had joined Patrick. Others quickly joined in too. The flames leaped into the heavens, scorching the leaves on the trees that surrounded the house. The early morning mist, moist and heavy, bore the smoke downward so that she could scarcely see the ardri now, where he sat above them. He was still as a statue, staring at the burning house, for now the entire building flamed, the green side as well as the dried. Indeed, pockets of pine pitch exploded in the new walls. The burning was like a great rushing, roaring beast. Marda shuddered and lifted her own voice in the hymn for protection. She thought of little Benen within that awful conflagration and it took all her strength of will not to scream out in terror for him. She clung as to a lifeline to the thought of all the wonders God had already wrought for them. The heat of the fire was overwhelming. Everyone fell back. But at least, as it warmed the air, the smoke began to roll away and upward.

Then the screaming began.

"It isn't working! The door's stuck! Oh, Bel, Lug, Cromm Cruach—Ah-h-h . . ."

The voice was still recognizable as Lucat-mael's.

"Let him out!" Marda cried. "Oh, it's too horrible, even for him."

But Laeghaire himself motioned her to silence. She stared wildly at the flames. Benen's side was burning far more fiercely than Lucat-mael's. Yet, he uttered no sound. She looked at the ardri, who was watching the burning building as avidly as the others. His knuckles were white from gripping the arms of his chair and his glorious hair and beard reflected the firelight as though they too were burning. His household and the other druids watched the house, their eyes hot and frightened. They stood, frozen in place, and occasionally glanced at each other questioningly as if to ask how it was that Lucat-mael was keening like a captured banshee.

"Let me through. Let me through, I say," came a querulous voice from behind the ardri's chair and the soldiers gave way to reveal a tiny, frail woman with an air of past beauty. It was Gaida, Lucat-mael's cetmuinter, his first wife. She hung weakly on the arm of her maidservant, her large blue eyes widening still further, an expression of disbelief on her wan face.

"It *is* his voice," she cried. "It is! Lucat-mael is burning!" To Marda's horror, although she wasn't greatly surprised, the poor woman's face moved and formed itself into an unpracticed smile. *How awful. Even his wife rejoices.*

The screaming seemed to go on and on. Yet, there was no

sound from Benen. Marda couldn't stand it. She clapped her hands to her ears, trying to shut out the terrible keening. He could not survive, that was certain. And so, at least, the druids hadn't won the test. She stared at Lochru and Mantais. They'd long since dropped the tinderbox and torch and stood silent, their backs to the crowd, staring at the conflagration and listening to the screams.

At last the roof fell in.

Then, at least, the screaming stopped.

Marda looked up at the sky. From the position of the sun, she realized the greater part of the morning was gone. Then black smoke poured out from under the collapsed roof. For a while the fire burned more brightly still; then at last it began to die down. The spectators pressed forward anxiously, peering to see through the smoke. There seemed to be no sign of either Lucat-mael or Benen.

"Lucat-mael is dead," Gaida cried, unable to hide her joy. Then, as if aware that her reaction was not what would be expected of a wife, she shut her mouth and turned aside in embarrassment. "The flame-retardant potion he meant to pour on Patrick's cloak did not save him," she remarked quietly to her maid.

"Aye, he is surely dead," Patrick said, replying to her first remark. Marda didn't think he'd heard the latter.

"Then Benen must be, too," cried MacCarthen sadly.

"Nay, MacCarthen, he is not," Patrick snapped. "He is a child of the light; he lives!"

Marda stared at the old man. His hands were clasped together and he stared ecstatically up beyond the smoking, sullenly burning ruins, up beyond the trees even, to the deep blue August sky.

He meant, no doubt, that Benen lived on in heaven, she thought heartbrokenly. She felt tears running down her cheeks and when she looked at Keagh, he too was weeping unashamedly. The tears made white furrows on the smoke-darkened cheeks. She put her head down against his chest. She was freed from marrying Lucat-mael but Benen stood not among the blackened ruins of Lucat-mael's house.

"Release my people, oh ardri," Patrick demanded. "You yourself heard your druid's death cries."

Laeghaire stared wildly at Patrick. His eyes were glazed with mortal fear. Marda could see his naked thoughts. If Lucat-mael was dead, then he'd obviously overestimated the old gods. He motioned for the guards to unlock the Christians' fetters.

"Unlock their chains," he croaked, his voice sounding as if it hadn't been used in days.

The command seemed to stir Lochru and Mantais. Lochru ran toward the ardri's chair.

"Lucat-mael is dead, my lord, and so I am now your druid of rank. I forbid you to release them! The test is not yet complete. If Lucat-mael died in the flames, then so did the Christian child."

But Laeghaire leaned forward in his chair. His eyes were wild.

"Unlock them at once! Do you want their god to strike you too?"

The soldiers moved quickly to comply, as if the very notion of offending the Christian god further frightened them. As Keagh's chains fell away he drew Marda into his arms. They stood thus, together, watching as the flames continued to flicker weakly.

No one made any move to leave. There was nothing they could do until the flames burned out. Even the Christians were silent now. Indeed, there was no sound except the dying fire. Even the birds seemed to have deserted Tara, frightened away, perhaps, by the heat and noise. Poor Gaida leaned on her servingwoman, staring at the fire, trying to keep her expression seemly.

Marda shook her head. How could anything possibly survive in there? Benen was very small, but there seemed no darkened heap that could be him. The crowd moved ever closer as the cooling ruins allowed it.

"Look!" "By the saints, look there!" one man after another cried, pointing.

The rear wall of either side had collapsed, the dirt falling in.

Benen's side appeared to be empty but a charred, shrunken heap wrapped in Patrick's *unburned* cloak lay near the rear wall of Lucat-mael's side.

"Lucat-mael, the house, they are ashes! Yet, the holy wizard's cloak burned not!" cried Mantais.

MacCarthen leaned forward over the smoldering ruins and whipped Patrick's cloak up and away from what had been Lucat-mael. It must have been hot, for he dropped it on the ground and shook his hand to free it from the ashes.

But it wasn't burned.

Marda remembered Gaida's remark to her servingwoman. Had Lucat-mael drenched the cloak with some flame-retardant substance? The Christians regarded it as a miracle. They were talking excitedly and making the sign of the cross on their bodies.

"Father Patrick, here I am!"

Benen's voice.

They whirled around in time to see Benen struggling, kicking and coughing, up from the pile of collapsed dirt at the rear of the green side. He was so covered with dirt and ash that only his great blue eyes and wide, happy smile identified him.

"Benen!" Marda screamed, running toward him, heedless of the hot ashes.

Behind them, Tara was in an uproar. Laeghaire shouted unintelligibly. But Benen didn't wait for Marda's embrace. He grabbed her hand tightly and began running toward the bushes at the rear of the house. Keagh, Patrick and Colmagh followed. The others, caught up in the general delirium, milled around the ardri and his remaining druids as MacCarthen boomed out extravagant praises to God.

"Wait, child, the ardri will want to talk to you," Patrick called, hurrying to catch the little boy. "They are clamoring for me to baptize them, even in the ruins . . ."

"We've got to help Breeca," Benen cried. He scrambled into the bushes, and after a moment the others followed him. No one paid any attention to them; they were crying out their contrition to Patrick's God. "Hurry, Father Patrick, the tunnel seemed to collapse as I pushed my way back into the house just now."

"Tunnel?" Keagh said in bewilderment.

Benen was down on his little knees, scratching wildly at the earth. There was a deep depression there.

"So that's it," Keagh said, understanding at last. Gently he lifted Benen out of the way, handing him to Marda, and began tearing furiously at the softened dirt with his hands.

"Hurry, Keagh, oh hurry," Benen was crying. "She was in the tunnel to help me. She told me the wicked druid had made tunnels so he could escape, whichever side he took. But he didn't tell *me!* Breeca said God sent her to tell me. She was almost out when it fell."

Keagh dug rapidly, like a dog after an animal in its burrow. Marda put Benen down and knelt to help him as did Colmagh and Patrick. Soon they uncovered the old woman's thin feet in their worn sandals. They tore desperately at the loose dirt and within a few minutes had her pulled free of it.

"Pray God it is soon enough!" Keagh said, rolling the frail old woman over. She was covered with dirt, and blood oozed slowly at her forehead. She wasn't breathing.

Keagh wiped his hands on his tunic and began clearing dirt out of Breeca's mouth. He put his mouth to hers and blew, then pumped furiously at her chest. Marda slumped back on her heels, drawing Benen protectively into her arms. He stared at Breeca sadly.

"Is she killed, Keagh?" he said softly, his voice catching.

Keagh didn't answer, just laid his ear against the old woman's heart, his face worried. Suddenly he grinned.

"She's alive!" He began working her arms vigorously, pulling her upright. "Breathe, Breeca," he commanded urgently. "Breathe!"

"Breathe, Breeca," Benen echoed him. "Oh, it worked, Breeca. The latch was under the knothole as you said. And I jammed a stone in the door so I could go back through when the fire had died down. You know; you helped me. I did just what you said. Breathe, Breeca. For the love of God."

The old woman's eyelids fluttered as if she obeyed Benen's command. She opened her eyes slowly and smiled at Benen's smoke-blackened face.

"Ye . . . ye . . . look like an imp of the dark angel . . . instead of Breeca's . . . Breeca's little saint," she choked. She coughed violently and Keagh held her up. His face was worried, though.

"Don't try to talk yet, Breeca," he said.

She silenced him with a long, pitying look.

"Talk . . . talk I must . . . if I will . . . Haven't long. Thank you for sewing my lip, boy. Make the lass happy. Where . . . where is Father Patrick? Must talk to him."

Patrick moved up beside her and took her hand. His old face, too, was wet with tears.

"You wish to make your confession, Breeca?" he asked gently.

She nodded weakly.

The old priest motioned for the others to leave them alone but Breeca lifted her hand and laid it on his sleeve.

"Don't make them leave, Father," she gasped. "I . . . I . . . would look at them all as long . . . long as I can. Where's that old fool, Colmagh?" She smiled faintly when she saw his head appear behind Marda's. "Tell Angas . . . Daneen . . . all . . . all Christians . . . I love . . . I love them." She shut her eyes and coughed weakly. Marda bit her lip to keep from crying out. Breeca was slipping away from them.

But she opened her eyes again and looked directly into Marda's.

"My darlin' girl . . . long, happy life . . . with Keagh. Patrick . . . I . . . old Breeca . . . but God's helper . . ."

"You discovered the tunnels, Breeca?" Patrick inquired, trying to help her.

She nodded.

"Lucat-mael . . . had body . . . old weaver. . . . He meant to get into tunnel . . . shove body in to burn. When everyone thought *he* was burned with Benen, he'd come back . . . like resurrected Jesus . . . like my blessed Jesus!" She frowned darkly, coughing violently. "No! Breeca God's instru . . . instr . . ."

"God's instrument, Breeca?" Patrick prompted. She nodded and was silent again, struggling to gather strength. She clutched at Patrick's hand. "Lead me . . . lead me not into temptation," she cried out, then she began to sob weakly. "I . . . I was tempted. Forgive me, Father, for I have sinned. Not only did I save Benen . . . I . . . I . . . for one bad moment, I was a druid again. I used the weaver's . . . body to . . . jam door . . . Lucat-mael's side!"

Marda put her hand to her mouth in order to prevent herself from crying out. The old woman clung to Patrick's hand, her eyes never leaving his face. Gratefully, Marda saw that his expression didn't change much.

"Breeca . . . *Christian*," came the choking cry. "Christian! Not druid. I . . . I saved Benen. I . . . God's hands. Like Marda . . . when . . . she brought food . . . God forgive?"

Patrick was crying too. He took his crucifix from around his neck and held it for Breeca to kiss.

"Tell Him you love Him, my poor Breeca," he said compassionately. "He alone will judge you and surely, you will be with Him soon."

Breeca kissed the crucifix and then a great, rolling rattle sounded deep in her chest. She slumped back against Keagh's arm. Then, even the rattle stopped.

Benen cried out once, then he buried his little face in Marda's neck. He clung to her, sobbing softly, as Patrick said the prayers of absolution.

At last Keagh got to his feet, the old woman in his arms, and carried her back toward the milling crowd. Patrick and the others walked solemnly behind, little Benen staring sadly at the old woman's long braid as it swung in the dust.

They tried to get the crowd's attention, but delirium reigned. When MacCarthen saw the little boy in Marda's arms, he snatched him from her, wiped at the dirt on the child's face and held him aloft so they could see him.

"Behold!" he cried. "Benen lives and is well, though the house burned to ashes around him. And Patrick's cloak, too, survived the fire. Lucat-mael is only charred bones. So does God smite His enemies."

He pointed steadily at the ardri.

"You have demanded proof, oh Laeghaire." He held Benen out so that Laeghaire could only stare in wonder. "Is *this* sufficient proof?"

Laeghaire had been standing in front of his chair, unable to tear his eyes away from Lucat-mael's bones. Now he looked painfully from Patrick's face to the little boy. He merely glanced at Breeca as if the death of one aged woman didn't matter or have any significance to him. He slumped back into his chair.

"With my own eyes I have seen, and so I can no longer deny that your god is more powerful than all those Lucat-mael served. With my own will, I submit to him!" He passed a hand across his eyes. When he looked up, there was naked fear in them. "Tell your god not to punish me, oh Patrick, for I but did what I thought it right I should do. Now, I submit."

"He will not smite you, oh Laeghaire," Patrick said kindly. "You have been misled by your druid. Let me tell you . . ."

"Even at the risk of being punished, I cannot hide behind the dead," Laeghaire cried in anguish. "I chose wrong. I was cruel to Marda and Keagh—indeed, to that old woman. Has God smitten her because she was a druid? Never mind. You may establish your church here in peace, henceforth. I know when I have been bested!"

"He thinks what happened was a miracle of God," Marda began, but Keagh silenced her with a smile.

"Perhaps it was, beloved," he murmured.

Slowly the Christians fell into step, making their mournful way back to the queen's grianan with the pathetic burden Keagh carried. Wordlessly MacCarthen took her from Keagh, his look saying that *he* was Patrick's strong man, after all.

Marda walked behind him, Keagh holding her right hand, Benen her left. They would need to wash Breeca's body, prepare her to lie in the little church. All of Tara would come to pay her homage. She would miss Breeca. Always there would be a void in her heart that no other would fill. Slowly she realized what Breeca had done for all of them. Not only had she saved Benen, she'd freed her, Marda, so that she could marry Keagh.

And, more important than either of those things, she'd prepared the fields so that the seed of faith could be sowed and nurtured at Tara. As the ardri went, so would all the rest of Ireland. The Christian faith had found a home where it would be nourished for eternity.

Behind her, Patrick walked, saying prayers for Breeca's soul. What she had done had been a terrible thing for a Christian, yet hadn't Patrick told them many times one was allowed to take a life to protect others? If there was no other way? If Breeca had not barricaded the door, even now she and Keagh, Colmagh and MacCarthen and Patrick might be dying on crosses, for she knew in her heart she'd have demanded that death with Keagh rather than marry Lucat-mael.

As they approached the new li, Daneen burst through the door of the queen's grianan, her eyes wild.

She caught sight of Laeghaire and ran toward him.

"My lady has fainted, oh Laeghaire," she screamed.

Keagh released Marda's hand and bounded forward, reaching Daneen as quickly as Laeghaire.

"Fainted? Where is she?"

"In there, on the floor. I . . . I can't arouse her so I came for help. I only left her for a moment to get her something to eat . . ."

Keagh swept past her, Laeghaire and Marda at his heels.

"She's not out of the woods yet," he muttered worriedly.

They burst through her chamber door together. Angas had apparently tried to reach the nursery door when she collapsed.

CHAPTER 10

Marda cried out in alarm as she came through the door and saw Angas lying there. The ardrigan's pretty, pink coloring had returned after the baby's birth as she rested and gained strength, but now her face was colorless again. She lay like a lifeless thing, on her back, her head turned to the side.

Laeghaire pushed past Keagh and would have lifted her but Keagh put a hand on his arm.

"Wait, my lord, let me examine her for broken bones first," he commanded. He knelt beside her, first listening for a heartbeat, his face exhibiting concern, but as he straightened up he smiled encouragingly. He moved her limbs carefully, checking them for breaks, nodding in satisfaction, but when he grasped her chin gently to turn her head, a large bruise and slight cut on her forehead came into view.

"Oh, my poor ardrigan," Daneen cried, "I only left her for a moment; why did she get up? The baby's not crying or anything."

Keagh and Laeghaire lifted her gently and carried her back to her couch. As they put her down and covered her, she moaned softly and her eyelids flickered.

"Daneen? Daneen?" she cried anxiously. "Help me!"

Keagh sighed with relief.

"At least she remembers who attended her . . ."

Angas's eyes opened wide and she winced, putting a hand to her head as her gaze fell on Laeghaire, hovering anxiously above her.

"Angas, you were not to get up unless someone was with you," he scolded, stroking the fair cheek. "You are still not strong, my love . . ."

"You promised me you would not, my lady," cried Daneen, her pretty face creased with unaccustomed worry.

Angas looked from one to the other of them in bewilderment. "Why are you all looking at me like that?" she said, frowning, her fingers at her temple. Keagh took her hand away gently and put a towel dampened from her water bowl against the bruise. He held up his left hand, four fingers extended.

"How many fingers do you see, my lady?" he asked.

"Four," she said obediently. "Oh, Keagh, why are you asking me such a silly question?"

"You must have fallen and injured your head, my lady," he said kindly; "I just want to be sure there is no injury to your brain."

She gasped and struggled upright. Her pretty face twisted in horror.

"Now I remember—I didn't fall. Lochru and Mantais!" She tried to scramble from the bed but Keagh pushed her back gently.

"Let me go, Keagh! They took the baby!"

"What?"

Laeghaire crossed the queen's chamber in two giant strides and tore aside the curtain in the doorway to the baby's room. His big body shook and color drained from his face. He went in and came back immediately, holding the blanket Lugaid had been wrapped in.

"She's right—Lugaid's gone!"

"They said—oh, no, they said Cromm Cruach should have a—a better gift than a young bull!" Angas screamed as memory flooded back.

"Take care of her," Keagh shouted to Daneen, jumping up and racing for the outer door. "My lord Laeghaire, give orders for chariots. Quickly!" He turned briefly at the doorway. "I swear to you, my lady, we'll catch them."

Marda ran after him. Outside, gillas were bringing up horses and chariots, quickly fastening harnesses. Below them, from the direction of Lucat-mael's house, smoke still curled lazily against the bright August sky. Word of Lochru and Mantais stealing the ardri's son as a sacrifice to Cromm Cruach spread through the settlement and many of the citizens who'd been finally heading homeward came racing to Laeghaire's new li with offers of help.

The great stone that represented Cromm Cruach stood on Mag Slecht, the Plain of Protestations, some thirty miles northwest of Tara. Fortunately one of the king's high roads, Slige Asail, stretched almost to the site. It was paved with stone, wide enough for two chariots to pass, and always well maintained. Marda ran and grabbed Keagh's hand as he climbed into the first chariot, taking the reins from the charioteer.

"I'm coming, Keagh."

He frowned, sweat running down his smudged face. "No, Marda—"

"If the baby is hurt, Keagh, you may need me!"

He smiled grimly and grabbed at her hand, pulling her into the chariot beside him. "You're a determined little thing. Hold on, then."

He snapped the whip over the horses' heads as the men of Tara also took to chariots. Marda gasped and hung on to the front of the chariot for her life as the two mighty horses bounded forward. Keagh's muscles bulged as he leaned toward the horses, giving them their head, yet alert to guide and control them. She glanced back. Laeghaire and his charioteer were right behind them, Patrick and Odran next. Then she turned her face to the wind, her eyes fastened on the high road for signs of Lochru and Mantais's passing.

"There, at the side of the paved part," she cried when they'd covered a mile. Laeghaire's chariot was about level with them now. Keagh followed her pointing finger and nodded. There were wheel marks where a chariot had left the road briefly as if the chariot driver was in a hurry and hadn't properly controlled it.

"Pray God they don't kill the poor baby before they even get there," Keagh snapped. "Go—go—go!" he shouted to the horses, snapping the whip across their backs. The powerful beasts strained forward as if they understood this mad ride was as important as a battle charge for which they'd been trained.

Onward, always northwest, they rolled, talking little for the merciless wind beat their words to the back of their throats. Marda's braids were whipped free, the golden balls that held them gone. She clung to the chariot with all her strength, for so furiously did Keagh drive the horses that she felt as if she too would be whipped away as her hair ornaments had been.

Yet, though they'd outdistanced the other chariots with their heavier burdens, there was only an occasional wheel mark at the side of the road to mark the druids' passage, and once a fresh welter of broken stone where a chariot had recently grazed a bridge curbing. Marda felt as if every bone and joint in her body had been shaken in a great sack. How could the poor tiny baby stand it?

Late in the afternoon they caught a glint of metal far off in the distance. They strained forward, squinting against the sun which seemed to burn furiously in the western sky, even as dark clouds presaging rain rolled toward them.

"Aye, it's them!" Keagh shouted and turned to motion to the chariots behind that he'd sighted them. "Come on, go, go, go, good fellows," he shouted at the horses. They were so lathered now that great flecks of foam flew back into Marda and Keagh's faces but they valiantly surged forward yet harder.

He was right. It was Mantais's own great chariot, pulled by two enormous black horses. Lochru was clinging to the front of the chariot with both hands, a bundle—presumably the baby—lashed across his back. Mantais, big and blond and powerful, glanced back at them, his blue eyes burning malevolently. He shifted the reins to his left hand and, with his right, reached into his pouch and withdrew something. He threw his arm out behind him as Colmagh did when he broadcast seed in the spring.

"Can you see if the baby's all right?" Marda shouted above the wind.

Keagh smiled grimly. "I can hear him howling!" he said.

Marda strained her ears. "Aye," she agreed. At least he was still alive and capable of voicing vigorous protest.

"They want him as a sacrifice, Marda," he yelled. "He's Laeghaire's firstborn to Angas. Powerful magic."

Just then a great black cloud seemed to billow up from the road. The horses whinnied and jerked nervously.

"What is it?" Marda cried, coughing.

Keagh was struggling to keep the horses under control. "Some rotten, druid trick," he shouted. "Easy, there, easy, good beasts."

But he was having a hard time calming the horses. They wheeled and reared, almost upsetting the chariot. They could hear excited shouts from those coming behind.

"They've loosed the druid fog on us," cried a voice. "Cursed enchantments!"

Indeed, it seemed as if they had. For several minutes no one could see his hand before his face. Then Keagh got out and took the horses' bridles, standing reassuringly between them, and led them forward.

"It's better up here," he shouted above the clamor. "Lead your horses out of it."

He jumped back into the chariot and urged the beasts forward again. The druids were out of sight. Keagh muttered furiously.

They bounded ahead. Shortly they could hear chariot wheels and the cries of the child ahead, but those behind hadn't gotten themselves out of the dark fog yet.

"There, approaching the wood," Keagh cried exultantly. He snapped the whip again but, in truth, the horses seemed to have no need of it. They responded to Keagh's shouted encouragement as readily as to the whip. They were covered with white foam. Poor, gallant beasts, Marda thought distractedly.

Suddenly the chariot lurched sickeningly, throwing Marda and Keagh violently against the back where they slammed, then flew to the ground, Keagh still holding tight to the reins.

"The wheel! Lost the wheel," Keagh roared.

He scrambled up, half running, half dragged behind the rampaging horses.

"Whoa, whoa, whoa. Good lads. Whoa."

Marda staggered to her feet, every part of her body screaming protest, but she didn't think she was seriously hurt, thank God.

"Hold them, Keagh," she cried encouragingly.

He managed to stop them at the side of the road where the chariot fell off out of the way. Quickly he unhitched them and jumped astride one great, heaving body. He twisted his hands in the horse's mane, clutching his legs around the heaving belly.

"Follow if you can, Marda," he shouted and was gone off down the high road.

Marda finally managed to get up on the big horse. As she turned him toward the high road, she saw that the other chariots had begun to emerge from the dark fog. Soon she was nearly abreast of Keagh, her body slick with sweat, hers and the horse's. Keagh didn't look at her, just bent over the horse's neck. She, too, held her head low, making less wind resistance for the lathered beast, but she stole a quick glance ahead. The druid chariot was just turning from the high road onto the bohereen—the little road—that led to the dread Mag Slecht. Almost as if nature itself lay in dread, the dark clouds rolled more furiously above them and a low peal of thunder shook the very earth. Wind rose suddenly, bearing spatters of rain.

And from the Plain of Protestations, suddenly a hideous, terrifying screaming arose. The horse reared in fright, and as Marda held tightly to the mane she felt her own hair prickle along her scalp at the awful sound.

She passed Keagh as they rounded the turn. She was staying on the horse's back only by holding the mane, now; her legs could no longer clutch the horse's belly. She had never been so frightened in her life. They would kill the baby before she and Keagh could reach him.

And all around her lay the terrible Mag Slecht.

From her childhood, she had hated it and had gone to the holy day sacrifices only under the most vigorous protest. There were dark, enchanted trees ringing the idols of stone—Cromm Cruach, the great one, stood towering above the tallest druid offering sacrifice and twelve lesser stones. They were carved with awful faces, like fierce animals in torment, and when the wind rose the horrible keening grew louder. Little sun ever touched the place and woodbine curled everywhere, hiding God only knew what horrors.

The druids' chariot screeched to a halt and the horses slumped in their tracks, a dread sacrifice to the great idol.

Marda urged her horse forward; she could hear Keagh just at her horse's heels. She glanced quickly at the awful stones. One great stone and twelve lesser ones. Wildly, incongruously, she thought of Keagh's remark that perhaps God had revealed Himself to all men and that man himself had corrupted the revelation. Some of the Christian priests claimed that the early missionaries had even reached Ireland after Christ's death. Could these terrible idols be an obscene parody of Christ and His apostles?

She hauled at the horse's mane, slowing it, and slid off his back, her legs trembling so violently that only the grace of God kept her erect. Lochru was just staggering weakly from the chariot, but Mantais, his great, long ceremonial knife in his hand, was striding toward him as though he would kill the child on Lochru's back.

"No!" she screamed, running, running, arms outstretched.

But Mantais had been only cutting the bindings that bound little Lugaid to Lochru's back. The poor baby was screaming, a sound only slightly less powerful than the mystical howling that filled Mag Slecht with terror. The knife parted the infant's swaddlings and Mantais snatched him, naked as he'd come from Angas's womb, and held him aloft triumphantly.

Marda fell full length on the ground, sobbing furiously, just as Keagh's horse slid to a stop. She jumped up, gagging at the smell of ancient blood and fear and fetid earth that filled the awful place.

"Cromm Cruach has been greatly offended by the Christian god; his thirst must be assuaged," Mantais cried wildly. He turned with the baby, pinning him with one hand to the great, dreadful stone. Thunder rumbled above and lightning began to flash as the sun dropped lower. The rain came all at once as if someone had broken a dam in the heavens. Marda, her breath all but spent, lurched forward as Mantais drew back the great knife. Lochru stepped up in front of her but she struck furiously at his face, feeling a sharp, primitive joy as she felt his blood rush over her hand. She had split his lip. He staggered back, crying out in fury. She snatched at the screaming baby, pulling, tearing him from Mantais's big hand even as she bunched herself into a ball, protecting him, her back to the druid.

He slashed furiously, meaning to hit the baby, but she had him; the knife struck the idol, hitting sparks into the storm and grazing Marda's interjecting shoulder.

Keagh pushed her out of the way and she stumbled against Lochru, the baby held safely in her arms. He was screaming so loudly she couldn't hear Keagh's furious words, but she turned as he kicked the knife from Mantais's hand and then started pummeling the big druid unmercifully. Small he was, her Keagh, the druid a full head taller and much wider too, but Keagh had him back against the idol; he tried in vain to protect himself from the physician's fury. Lochru whimpered at her feet. She ran back away from him as Patrick's chariot, followed closely by

Laeghaire's, thundered up to the idol. The rain lashed at everyone and the day grew steadily darker as the sun fell nearer the horizon, somewhere behind the storm clouds.

"Back, Keagh, by my God of judgment, I command you," Patrick shouted. Odran sawed at the reins but the horses were still sliding in the mud. One of them hit the screaming Lochru, lifting him up bodily where he bounced against the horse's back, then the chariot.

By the time he hit the ground, his screaming had stopped.

"Stop, Keagh," Patrick repeated as he jumped to the ground. Marda stared at him with her mouth gaping as she cuddled the baby, trying to quiet him. No one would ever have known that the old man had watched through a long night without sleep, prayed through the ordeal of fire, then ridden on a journey that would have killed most men younger than himself by ten years. "You cannot be guilty of the blood of this evil man, Keagh," he thundered. "God will judge him!"

Keagh dropped his hands, staring at the druid's ruined face. Mantais cringed away from him and from Patrick, whose face looked like God's judgment day.

Patrick ignored the beaten and bloody druid now. His fiery eyes traveled up the height of the great idol and he gasped. He lifted his hand and made the sign of the cross. "An abomination," he said, horrified. "God, creator of all goodness, strengthen my arms," he called out. His voice sounded like the thunder, drowning out the awful keening of the wind. Suddenly he appeared as tall as Cromm Cruach. His fury was awesome. *"Christ* is our sacrifice!" he shouted, charging the great statue like an avenging angel.

Laeghaire had arrived and alighted from his chariot. Cursing with anger, he charged Mantais, kicking Lochru's body out of his way. The druid put his hands up to shelter himself, falling backward behind the great idol.

"I had to, oh Laeghaire, to save us all from the Christian god!" he cried, "Have mercy . . ."

But a great wrenching, grinding roar, like the day of judgment, froze them all. Marda looked up uncomprehending. Even the baby stopped wailing temporarily, astonished by this new sound.

Cromm Cruach was falling!

Patrick, God's messenger to the Gael, had toppled it.

Mantais looked up in terrified disbelief and his throat-tearing scream was abruptly terminated as the great stone fell on him and broke apart.

No one moved. Almost all the chariots had arrived now and men and horses slumped dully, staring at the dread drama in the fading light. Rain streamed over them, plastering hair and beards to their faces, and their eyes lit fearsomely in the flashes of lightning. Marda held the baby close, too awestricken to do more than kiss the little head comfortingly. Lugaid quieted to a soft, weary mewling.

"My God, he has toppled a stone that fifty men must have erected!" MacCarthen cried, falling to his knees in the mud. "My God," he repeated reverently. The others followed suit, the non-Christians glancing fearfully at the Christians, emulating their signing the cross on themselves.

His blood lust slaked by the miraculous toppling of the stone, Laeghaire stared at the little priest wordlessly, his eyes rolling in his head with awe. Patrick seemed unaware of the furor he was causing. His head thrown back, his eyes lifted to heaven, he ran amok, toppling the lesser stones, any one of which was the size of two chariots, his words of prayer booming across the plain.

"My God of judgment, Thou knowest that I have come softly into Ireland," he cried. "I listened for Your voice and it seemed to me best to lead Your people gently. But never did I dream of such evil. The blood of victims is a stench in Your nostrils and mine. I am Your mighty hand, oh God!"

And with that, he toppled the last idol.

The storm raged on around them for another moment, then rolled off toward the eastern sea as if it had been sent for the purpose of witnessing Patrick's triumph. Indeed, the evening lightened a little as a wan moon glowed behind the drifting clouds. The men of Tara, thirty strong, shook themselves as if awakening from a dream. They began to talk wonderingly among themselves and the weary horses stood exhausted, heads hanging.

"Why do you sit here idle?" Patrick said. "Someone walk the horses else they'll never return to Tara but die of their exertions for God. Keagh, see to Marda; there's blood on her shoulder."

Marda stared wonderingly at him as Keagh came to kiss her gently, then bind her wound, saying it was only a scratch, by the grace of God. Patrick seemed to have shrunk, become again only a tired, simple elderly priest. He started to slump forward, and with a great cry MacCarthen caught him up in his arms as if he'd been a little child.

"Rest, Father Patrick, rest now," the big priest crooned.

Patrick shook his head and struggled free of his strong man's grasp. He did, however, sit down on a chariot floor.

"We have to find shelter for the night. There was a bohereen to the left a mile or so back on the road to Tara. A village lies at the end of it, no doubt. Send someone to take word to Angas that her baby is safe."

Laeghaire shook himself and came forward then, falling on his knees. He was a proud man, ardri of Ireland since his youth, and it wasn't easy for him to thank the old man. He stumbled over some inadequate words, then finally just lowered his head against the old man's foot.

"Whatever your god asks of me, henceforth will I do, oh Patrick," he said humbly.

Keagh took the baby from Marda and checked to be sure he was not hurt. The little fellow now slept in exhaustion, his chubby cheeks shaking with his deep, sobbing breaths. The night was coming on. Slowly the little company turned the chariots around and walked the horses back to the high road. In a little while they found the tiny village, where the inhabitants exclaimed in awe at having a visit from the ardri.

"Are you rested, Father Patrick?" MacCarthen's big voice came back to Marda where she walked beside the chariot, the baby in her arms.

"Aye, though never have I been so weary. A good day's work, ridding Ireland once and for all of such bloody enchantments. Druid enchantments!"

Marda gazed lovingly up at Keagh who was smiling down at her in the moonlight.

"There is one druid enchantment I would not be freed of," she said, smiling at him.

"Your enchantment is greater, far, than any druid's, beloved," he murmured, reaching out to touch her hair. "Why don't you get into the chariot?"

Marda shook her head. "Tomorrow, I'll have to. But for now, both the baby and I need a rest from the jolting."

The villagers were helping them anyhow, climbing aboard the chariots, taking the horses in charge and the weary people into their homes. They'd even found a wet nurse for the baby, and her husband had set off through the night to tell Angas that all was well.

When the baby's needs were met, they all sat around a fire pit filled outside, for none of the houses were big enough for them all, and ate hastily gathered bread, fruit and ale. Keagh's arm held Marda tenderly, mindful of her injured shoulder.

"I saw the damage you inflicted on Lochru's mouth, sweetheart," Keagh said mischievously. "Like the great queen Maeve you were, vengeful in battle."

Marda laughed uneasily, ashamed of her un-Christian fury.

" 'Twas not the behavior Patrick counsels," she said ruefully.

Keagh nodded soberly. "Nor was mine, Marda. The murdering rage was on me. Pray God, we've seen the end of such evil in Ireland."

Marda stared at the fire for a long time. "We must guard our own hearts, lest it return," she said quietly.

Angas rested against the heaped cushions of her couch, her soft brown hair falling in lovely profusion like a gleaming curtain around her. A dark blue bruise still marred her smooth forehead where Mantais had struck her with the handle of his knife . . . she had remembered, but even the headache was growing less persistent, she assured her visitors. Certainly she looked glowing and happy, her face flushed with excitement as she laughed and talked.

Laeghaire sat on the little stool beside her bed, resting his big shoulders against the wall, his little son cradled expertly in one arm while he held his wife's hand with his free hand. She gazed up at her husband and baby tenderly, then lifted their joined hands to plant a kiss on the back of his.

Marda and Keagh, sitting together on floor cushions, exchanged amused glances. Fierce Laeghaire had become greatly subdued since the events of Brom Trogan. The hand that cupped the baby's little feet was eloquent in its tender stroking. Although Laeghaire had many children to his previous wives, Angas was the darling of his maturity and her son seemed to have a special place in his heart.

Perhaps it was because he'd come so close to losing them both that he cherished them so, Marda thought contentedly. She savored Keagh's supporting shoulder as he put his arm around her. How well she knew that feeling! Through all this long summer she had fought endlessly for her love, and that one dreadful night she thought she'd lost him forever, too. It was wonderful, now, having the ardri's blessing and knowing that their troubles were all behind them. Indeed, Angas had summoned her physician and foster daughter this morning especially to discuss their marriage plans with their ardri and ardrigan.

Laeghaire glanced at Angas and, though his manner was solemn, his sea-colored eyes glinted with merriment.

"Now that we have discussed the excellent health, beauty, and lustiness of our son, and the coming baptism day of the ardri, I think we should get down to the business of discussing Keagh and Marda's hopes for marriage, my love."

Keagh sat up straight, releasing Marda who also leaned forward attentively. There'd been so much to do, getting poor Breeca decently buried, and she'd helped Keagh with the many minor injuries that were results of the mad chariot race to Mag Slecht. They had pledged to Patrick that they'd not pressure Laeghaire to move up their wedding day, although she was sure her father wouldn't have minded had he been fortunate enough to have met Keagh. Still, the wishes of one's elders, especially their dying wishes, had to be obeyed, Patrick said, or where would society be?

"Happy I am that you've sent for us, my lord," Keagh said, his demeanor showing that he was mindful of the solemnity of the occasion. "We've been talking, setting the day. Since Marda will be seventeen on November fourth, Sunday, this year, we'd like to be married on her birthday. . . ."

Laeghaire frowned, to Keagh's bewilderment.

"Not so fast, son," he said sternly. "Just because you're the golden lad around Tara these days doesn't give you the right to fly in the face of custom."

Laeghaire released Angas's hand and captured Lugaid's to prevent the little boy from tangling his tiny hand in the great fiery beard.

Keagh stared at him in confusion.

"I realize, oh Laeghaire, that our marriage contract wasn't ratified during Lugnasa, the week before Brom Trogan, as is the custom," he said reasonably, "but, then, neither was any other couple's, what with the test at Lucat-mael's house and the baby being kidnapped."

Marda glanced at Keagh. She could see that he was keeping his temper with difficulty. She threw Angas a beseeching look but the ardrigan was leaning forward, taking her baby from Laeghaire's arms as if deliberately avoiding Marda's eyes. Her hair swung across her face, shielding it from their view.

"That is very true," Laeghaire replied. "Unfortunate it is, too, for now, all that is to do. I can see no recourse but to wait until next Lugnasa."

"It isn't fair," Marda cried out impulsively. She took Keagh's hand and his grip was fierce, almost painful.

"Never will I do that, oh Laeghaire," Keagh said briskly. "Marda is right. Unfair, entirely, does that seem to me. Marda and I have dealt with you honorably. We have heeded her dead father's command although we know he would approve of her marriage to one who loves her and will honor her all her days. We have recognized your rights over her as her foster father. A sorry way do you deal with us!"

Laeghaire developed a sudden fit of coughing. He bent over, struggling to overcome it, wiping his eyes and finally mastering it. He straightened up and stared at them balefully. The baby, startled by his sire's outburst, jumped and stared wide-eyed at the big bearded man. Angas leaned over him, her face still shielded. The baby grabbed a handful of her shimmering hair and she cried out in laughing pain.

Laeghaire folded his arms across his chest, scowling at them, his lips twitching in anger. Marda thought Keagh had gone too far. After all, Laeghaire was the ardri of Ireland.

But, oh, how could he treat them so?

"You argue persuasively, liaig," he said. "All right, you may marry on Marda's seventeenth birthday as you've been planning. If you're sure that's what you wish."

Keagh smiled broadly and pulled Marda into his arms.

"Aye, I wish that more than anything on earth," he said. "I know it will be hard to build a home and a place for myself here at Tara with a wife; it would be impossible without her!"

"I'm glad you brought up the matter of building a home. That takes substance, oh Keagh. And you'll need kine, goods to make a home. You seem singularly poor to me."

"That is true, oh Laeghaire, but Marda says she cares not for riches."

"Yet, she knows that you must have the bride price."

Keagh stared at him, crestfallen.

"The bride price?" he stammered.

"Aye! Well known it is that in all other nations on the face of the earth, the woman's father or foster father pays the bride price. But Ireland's beautiful women are worth ten times, and more, that of any others. And so our bridegrooms have always considered themselves honored to pay the bride price!"

"I haven't even thought of that," Keagh cried, frowning.

"Well, it's high time you do, then! Marda has great, great worth to my wife and me. Not only do we love her dearly, she is diligent and skilled in all things. No maiden at Tara can spin strong yarn to match hers, nor weave it into as fanciful coverlets. Her embroidery work is worthy of the queen of heaven's grianan! Besides all that, only Colmagh can get the yield from the soil that Marda does. Now, what do you offer for her?"

Keagh stared at the ardri in dismay.

"My lord knows that I have never charged a fee for my services to the people of Tara but have contented myself serving the ardri's household for only my place here. Nor have I any riches from my father, for he has many other children. Besides the robes I wear on my back, I possess only my medical books and medicines which could have no value to you and the loss of which would diminish *my* value as your liaig. Beyond that, I own only my coffer of cedar which was my parents' gift to me when I completed my medical studies."

Laeghaire stared at a spot above Keagh's head. His foot swung rhythmically.

"I have no use for a cedar coffer," he said contemptuously. "The maiden is surely worth a good piece of farm land, a fine timber house, a yoke of oxen, a milk cow, four pigs, and a flock of—"

"You say you love me, oh Laeghaire," Marda cried angrily. "A fine way of showing it you have!"

Angas bent studiously over her baby. She seemed distressed; her shoulders were shaking.

"Nevertheless, a bride price must be paid; it is the custom," Laeghaire said imperturbably.

"The ingratitude of you is equalled only by your pig-headedness," Keagh exploded, scrambling to his feet, pulling Marda up beside him. "By the cloak of Patrick, Laeghaire, though you are a stubborn man, not swaying with the wind, as befits the ardri of Ireland, I thought better of you. Your wife and baby's life! That is the bride price!" He drew Marda into his arms. "I would gladly give you all the gold in Ireland for her, but surely your loved ones' lives are worth more."

He broke off at a strange sound from Angas. It was a sort of choking snort, inelegant entirely, followed by a great, exuberant burst of laughter. The queen swept back her hair. Her face was rose-pink from holding back her laughter and her dark eyes danced with glee. Laeghaire looked at her and he, too, burst into loud guffaws.

Angas reached both hands toward Marda, tears of laughter rolling down her cheeks.

"The bride price, my darling, the land, the timber house, the kine—all—all—*we* will pay it. With full and grateful hearts. But to you, our beloved physician."

Keagh stared at her wonderingly. His handsome face eased into a shamed smile.

"They've been but teasing us, beloved," he murmured.

"Aye, so we have, physician," Laeghaire said, jumping up and pumping Keagh's hand as if he would take it off. "Go to Patrick, then, tell him to prepare for the first Christian wedding at Tara."

Marda looked at Keagh, her heart in her eyes. Happy tears were springing to his eyes. He was gazing at her with love so deep that she wanted to die of joy. He opened his arms, then, and she embraced him, her arms wound tightly around his slender body. He kissed her hair, her cheeks and her eyelids. Then he laughed, a great, joyful, wonderful sound entirely.

To Marda, it was the sweetest sound in Ireland.